Leave of Absence

Leave of Absence

Stephen Leon

ACKNOWLEDGEMENTS

I would like to thank the beta readers who helped me see Leave of Absence *through from beginning to end. They are: Mary Ann Donnaruma; Beth Henriques; Robin Osborne, Paul Rapp, Nicole Robertson; and Laura Clark Stedman. Their critiques and insights helped me to shape the novel in both subtle and more substantial ways, and also to reconsider certain details, as when a character said or did something that didn't seem quite like them.*

Most of all, I would like to thank them for their encouragement and enthusiasm for the project. There is nothing quite like hearing from a beta reader who is anxious for more to keep that creative fire burning.

This is a work of fiction. Names, characters, places, and incidents are the product of the author's imagination or are used fictitiously. Certain locales in the book are based on real places, but otherwise, any resemblance to actual persons, living or dead, or events, or incidents is entirely coincidental.

Chapter 1

West Hartford, Connecticut, March 1985

Marion Maloney's copy of *The Unbearable Lightness of Being* sat closed on the bar beside her glass of white wine, the bookmark sticking out between pages 34 and 35. She always brought a book with her when she went out to the Kettle & Cork in West Hartford, the one restaurant in the area where she felt comfortable alone. And she was reasonably certain that Creepy Man had no idea she frequented the place.

Usually she ordered two glasses of wine and an appetizer as she lingered over her book for a couple of hours. On this evening, Milan Kundera would have been perfectly good company. But then the Man with the Dreamy Blue Eyes strolled in. He had taken a stool two seats away from her and ordered a Maker's Mark with a splash and a twist of lemon. He sipped his drink slowly, nonchalantly, for about 10 minutes before turning his head toward her and remarking in a smooth, husky voice, "I'm Rick. I've heard of that book. Is it good?"

Marion took in his boyishly handsome face and neatly styled blond hair before speaking. "Well, yes, so far, anyway. I'm only 35 pages in. It's beautifully written. Kind of existential, I guess. Oh, sorry, I'm Marion. What authors do you like?"

"Well, I just finished *The Hotel New Hampshire*. I'm a big John Irving fan."

Soon Marion had invited Rick to the closer seat, and they were comparing notes on *The World According to Garp*, and then Tom Wolfe, Virginia Woolf, Joyce, Hemingway, Faulkner, and so on. He was at least as well-read as the next college English major, only sexier. Marion went on for a couple of minutes about how much she loved Faulkner and also female Southern writers like Eudora Welty and Flannery O'Connor.

"Hmmm," thought Rick out loud. "Good group."

"Here's a little quiz for you," she said playfully, smiling at him. "Can you name the female Southern writer who really set the table for that gang, in terms of narrative style and themes?"

"Um ... Early 20th century? Maybe late 19th century? You wouldn't be talking about Kate Chopin, would you?"

"Wow, you're good!" Marion exclaimed.

"We read her in Comparative American Lit," Rick said. "One of my favorites, actually. I majored in English at Wesleyan. If I remember correctly, *The Awakening* was not well received by critics at the time."

"She was feminist before anyone in America even called it that," he continued. "Men were threatened by her sexuality and her desire to free herself from society's constraints."

"I hear there were some male readers who were actually pleased," Marion added, "when she walked into the Gulf of Mexico at the end of the book, and kept walking until she disappeared and drowned. That was brave!"

"OK, so what was the last book you read before Kundera?" Rick asked.

"Hmmm," Marion thought for a few seconds. "Oh, yeah, isn't that funny. Another book in which the female protagonist appears to commit suicide. I must have an attraction to tragic women!"

"Which book?"

"*Lady Oracle* by Margaret Atwood."

"Canadian author, right? I've heard of her, but I don't know that book."

"It's about a woman, a writer, whose life brings her trouble whether she's screwing up or succeeding. So she fakes her own death and moves to Italy! I love it!" Marion laughed and smacked her hand down on Rick's knee, quickly apologizing for breaking the plane of their polite, arm's-length literary discussion.

"Oh, that's OK," Rick deadpanned, "Maybe I like being slapped."

"Well then," she replied, "just tell me where you like it, and I'll see ... Haha, just kidding."

Marion's second wine was running low as Rick drained the last of his first Bourbon. The clock was ticking on their discussion, which was becoming an increasingly suggestive game of pickup chicken as they both considered their next moves. Rick, who was 29, sized up Marion and decided she was probably a little older (she was in fact 34) and probably a gym goer. He found her thick chestnut hair, lightly freckled face and full lips attractive; and as best he could tell, she also appeared to have a shapely figure under her baggy sweater and wool slacks.

For her part, Marion had already concluded that she was interested in her new acquaintance, and was trying to gauge Rick's interest before saying anything too forward. Divorced three years, and living in semi-isolation as a prep-school teacher for the last year and a half, Marion had begun to miss both companionship and sex in a way she never thought she would after the pain of her tumultuous marriage and divorce had driven her to a period of contented isolation. Unsure how to proceed with Rick, she finally spoke.

"And who let this handsome man out all alone this evening? Isn't there someone waiting for you at home?"

"Oh, I'm currently unattached," he replied. "You?"

"Same," she said. "Are you up for another?"

As their drinks were poured, Rick said, "And on the subject of identity, didn't Jean Valjean change his several times to escape his past?"

"Yes!" Marion laughed again, and slapped Rick's knee again. "And Javert kept finding him! I teach *Les Miserables* to my kids."

"Wait a minute—you have kids?"

"No kids. Students. I teach high school English."

"You teach English! Good for you. As I said, I majored in English at Wesleyan. I wanted to get a master's, but I got sidetracked. Maybe I still will. My dream is to teach at a university and write books."

"So you're not teaching, and you're not back in the master's program, and you're not writing books."

"Right."

"So where are you working, Mister Still Sidetracked?"

Marion, now feeling a little buzz, giggled at the silly nickname she had invented for him, then composed herself. "Well?"

"Banking. Society for Savings. I started as a summer teller, but they kept promoting me. Now I'm a fund manager. Don't laugh."

"Hey, why would I laugh? I don't have an advanced degree either. I'm not publishing poetry, which is my dream. And I'm teaching high school English. To overprivileged boys who wouldn't understand *Of Mice and Men* if Lennie walked up and smacked them on the knee." And with that, she smacked Rick on the knee for a third time.

Rick's response was to place his right hand gently upon her left thigh. As soon as he was sure that was OK, he began to drag his fingers along her slacks in deliberate back-and-forth motions, with such expert pacing that his gentle stroking took her neurons by surprise and sent an unexpected jolt through her body. Embarrassed as she shifted slightly in her chair, and preferring not to get too drunk by consuming the entire third glass, she blurted out, "Well then. This is interesting."

She smiled, and Rick just smiled back. After a long pause, Marion said, softly, "Would you like to come to my place?"

They left the bar to find their cars parked side-by-side in the lot; hers a Mazda 626, his a Honda Accord. "Look at that," she laughed. "Our cars were attracted before we were."

"I sure hope they're not touching each other," he said.

"You're gonna laugh when you see where I live," she said. "A little house in the woods. I teach at Avon Old Farms School. It's not that far from here. You should follow me, but if we get separated for some reason, take 44 over Avon Mountain, turn left on Old Farms Road, and hang a right onto Scoville Road. But I won't lose you. I hope not anyway."

"You live on the campus?"

"Yeah, but not exactly. I live in Brooks House on Scoville across from the main entrance. There are only a couple of single female teachers here. Last year I joined the faculty late in the year, after another teacher left suddenly, and lived off-campus. This year they gave me Brooks House, I think to give me some privacy from the herd. But enough talking. Let's go."

Marion, surprised at her sudden eagerness, was tempted to drive faster, but she didn't want to get pulled over by a cop. And she didn't want to lose Rick. But the Honda followed the Mazda without a hitch.

"See? You wouldn't even know this little building was here," said Marion as they got out of their cars. She unlocked the front door and led him into the sitting room, where she offered him a glass of wine.

"Sure," he said.

"White or red?"

"Whatever you're drinking. Actually, I prefer red, if you have it."

Marion found a bottle of pinot noir, and with a skill she had perfected during many years of waiting tables, quickly dispatched the cork.

"That was good," said Rick, smiling. "Such dexterity!"

"Well, I hope I can keep up with you!" she smiled back, the memory of his touch at the bar still stirring an involuntary sensation inside.

They made more small talk about books, and each drank several sips of wine, until the anticipation became too much for Marion to bear. She took his hand and led him into her bedroom, where she quickly kicked off her shoes and let her pants fall to the floor. As she pulled her sweater over her head, it became momentarily stuck.

"Allow me," Rick said, gently freeing it from her shoulders. He flung the sweater into a corner, then traced his fingers down the back of her head and neck, over her white cotton tee, down to the small of her back.

"Your hands should be illegal," she whispered as she worked his belt buckle. Soon they were naked on the bed, exploring, breathing ever heavier. Rick noticed the breeze coming in the window. Earlier, Marion had opened it about two inches because she thought the room was getting stuffy.

"Do you want me to close that?" he asked, motioning to the window. "It's not bothering me," he said. "It's a nice night for late March. I just wanted to make sure--"

"That they wouldn't hear my moans?" She smiled at him.

"What about mine?" he smiled back. "Depending on what you have in store for me, of course--"

"Oh, nothing much," she cut in. "Just a nice, slow ride to paradise—if you're up for it. Ha, I guess you are up for it—I can see that."

Marion giggled. "And don't worry, no one will hear us out here," she assured him, then covered his mouth with hers for a long kiss before they got down to business.

"I'm just warning you, I'm like a ticking time bomb tonight, thanks to those hands of yours."

A couple of positions gave way to Marion's favorite--her on top. She enjoyed the control, and also the look on men's faces when they saw the full glory of her most prized attributes hovering over them. As their mutual need intensified, she arched her back, grasped his thighs, and began to moan.

Careful," Rick said, breathing heavily himself. "The squirrels might hear."

Marion's moans finally subsided but did not stop. Now Rick was moaning more loudly until he reached his climax, which propelled her to a second one. At the height of their ecstasy, it almost sounded to each of them as if there were more voices joining the symphony than just theirs. The intense pleasure of the moment was so great that they each let that thought slip out of their minds.

They lay back on the bed, smiling and spent. Marion placed her head on his chest near the crook of his right arm. His fingers teased her hair playfully. She ran one hand slowly down the unoccupied side of his chest.

This time they both heard it. A loud thud, as if someone or something had crashed into the back of the house, followed by rustling sounds coming from the woods behind it. Rick ran to the window and peered out, but saw nothing in the darkness. He closed and latched the window, and got dressed. "I'll be back," he said. "I just want to take a look."

"It's probably deer," Marion said. "Lots of 'em around here."

While he was outside, she wrote on a scrap of notebook paper: *Marion Maloney, (203) 404-1844.*

Rick came back in a few minutes later, this time with news from the animal kingdom. "I definitely saw something moving from somewhere behind the house on a diagonal out toward the road. But I didn't see it cross the road."

"Running? Leaping like a deer?"

"Nah ... didn't seem like a deer ... You have bears around here?"

"Bears? I suppose we could. But I haven't seen one."

Marion had put on her panties and tee. She stood up, walked to Rick, put her arms around his waist, and gave him a tight squeeze. "Thank you for coming over tonight. I do get lonely out here."

"You OK?"

"Yeah, I'll be fine."

"I mean, do you feel safe out here?"

"Oh sure, as long as I don't forget to lock up!"

"I probably should go."

"I know. We both work in the morning."

Marion pressed the scrap of paper into Rick's hand. "Call me if you'd like to get together again," she whispered, almost as if someone else were listening in. "You don't have to say anything now. If you feel like company, surprise me with a call."

Rick smiled and gave her a long, sensual parting kiss. "I had fun," he said. "You were awesome."

"You were beyond awesome," she said. "Good night."

As Rick left, he weighed the pros and cons of telling her what he saw. He didn't want to frighten her without knowing himself what it meant.

But he was pretty sure of one thing: The figure he saw running away was a man.

Chapter 2

Avon Old Farms School, March 1985

Sam Field held a sheet of paper in front of him as he strolled around the perimeter of the classroom, sizing up several rows of junior boys in jackets and ties seated at their wooden desks. Nearly two years into teaching history at Avon, he felt much more at ease than he had back in September 1983, when he worried that he would be eaten alive by a bunch of rich spoiled brats who didn't need him to get through high school any more than they needed lessons in how to act privileged.

What Sam understood better than he had then was that these boys were not all the same, that most of them had major insecurities bubbling under the veneer of privileged overconfidence, and that while they didn't need him per se, they not only enjoyed him as a teacher and a sometime sparring partner, they also secretly admired him and craved his approval.

"The war was winding down," he said finally, lowering the paper to his side. "Can you name any important events that happened in 1945 in the European theater?"

"I don't know, Mr. Field," deadpanned Reese Gilmartin. "Is that when *Oliver Twist* opened in London?"

Sam half-frowned at his perpetually wisecracking student, but couldn't bring himself to chastise him—after all, Reese and Sam had become something like friends after almost two years of Reese serving as Sam's equipment manager on his soccer and baseball teams.

"And here I thought I'd have a quieter year with Banks and Hennessey out of my history class," Sam smirked. "But you seem to have filled that void rather nicely."

"Maybe you'll get them back—I hear they might get kicked out of their other history class," said Reese. "By the way, is that a cheat sheet in your hand? I may have to report you to Mr. Dickleman."

"Ha ha. I think of it as a handy list of references. In case you say something that's close enough to one of these examples to not be completely wrong."

Pete Staley, sitting at Reese's left, turned to him and said, "Nice try, Reese, but I don't think the London theaters were open in 1945. What with air-raid sirens going off and all that rubble."

"Nineteen-forty-five ... Is that when we dropped the bomb on Hiroshima?" asked Nico Arpante, sitting to Reese's right.

"With his paper clenched in one hand, Sam rested both fists on his hips, and shot Nico an "Are you kidding me?" look. He was about to speak when Charlie Morton blurted out, "That's the Pacific theater, stupid. As in Asia."

"As in Japs," offered Reese.

"Reese," Sam reprimanded. "That's not a cool word to use. To many Japanese people, it's considered disparaging."

"Disparaging?" Reese replied. "What's that? I haven't even cracked open my SAT study guide yet."

"Aren't you a junior? You should be taking the SAT this spring. Do you even know the test dates?"

"I'll find out, and I'll make sure to register by the afternoon of deadline day. Then I'll start memorizing those big useless words."

"Disparaging," Sam continued, "as in derogatory. As in offensive."

Charlie Morton spoke up again. "The term 'Japs' was used a lot in anti-Japanese propaganda, especially during the war era."

"Very good, Charlie," said Sam. "And that was the 1940s. Now it's 1985. And the Japanese and the American governments have much better relations."

"And there's a Benihana down the road in Farmington," added Reese.

Nico, pissed off at being scolded for naming an event on the wrong side of the world, waved his hand frantically.

"Yes, Nico?"

"Wasn't that when all the fascists committed suicide because they had lost the war?"

"Well, not all of them. Hitler and others committed suicide. Mussolini was captured and hanged by his own countrymen."

"So about a week after Hitler's death, the Germans made their unconditional surrender to the Allied forces, which had also been liberating the concentration camps. And yes, over in the Pacific, the United States dropped the atomic bomb on Japan."

"Two bombs," corrected Charlie.

"Yes, of course," said Sam. "Hiroshima and Nagasaki."

"Mr. Field, do you think the second one was necessary to make the Japanese surrender?" asked Charlie.

Sam smiled at Charlie, who had been his top student all year. "No one will ever know for sure," offered Sam. "But a lot of people think one bomb was enough and that the second one, as one of my professors put it, was 'gratuitous slaughter.' "

"Mr. Field, can you please save some of these big show-offy words until I've done my SAT study prep?" asked Reese.

"In fact," Sam continued, ignoring another chance to spar with Reese, "that professor wrote a book arguing that Japan may have been ready to surrender before Hiroshima, and that the bomb was not so much to convince the Japanese they would lose, as to show the Soviet Union—an ally then, but with clear designs on European dominance—who was boss. And maybe to warn them not to try to develop their own nuclear weapons."

"Well," Reese said, "that worked like a charm."

"As for Europe," Sam continued, "the end of the war also meant the end of the Holocaust."

"If you believe the Holocaust actually happened," piped up Lindy Bauer, a peculiar boy who sat in the back, wore coke-bottle glasses, and looked more like an encyclopedia salesman than a prep-school student.

"Oh, and why would you think the Holocaust never happened?" asked Sam. "It's well-documented. And questioning or downplaying it is very offensive to the families of all those who suffered."

"My father doesn't believe it," replied Lindy. "And neither does Arthur Butz."

"Arthur Butz?"

"He's a Northwestern University professor who published a book in 1976 called *The Hoax of the Twentieth Century*. My father—"

"Wait a minute," Sam interjected. I haven't heard of this guy. And I somehow don't think they'd allow him to teach history at a prominent university like Northwestern after publishing views like that."

"He doesn't teach history. He teaches electrical engineering. And he's tenured. My father—"

"OK, OK, your father thinks this Butz guy is on to something the rest of the world hasn't figured out? Well, I suggest you keep an open mind."

"You too," Mr. Field. "The truth is not always what it seems."

The bell rang, sparing Sam an argument he didn't really want to have.

Out in the quad after class, Sam noted that the weather had not improved much since he had left breakfast at the refectory to teach his two morning classes. It was a little after 11 now, and the skies were still gray, the air still chilly and damp. Sam wore a parka over his tweed sport coat, and he was still shivering. He crossed the quad toward his apartment, stopping on the way to chat with his friend and fellow teacher Joe Grisman; Juan Ortega, the Cuban head varsity soccer coach who always seemed to have new dirt on students, teachers, and/or headmaster George Dickleman; and Marion Maloney, an English teacher in her first full year at the school.

Juan was asking Marion how her English classes were going. "You have Banks and Hennessey under control yet?"

Marion smiled. "They're not so bad. When they act up, I make them recite one of the poems they're supposed to have memorized. That works for a little while."

Sam laughed. "I had them last year. Nonstop goofiness. I finally printed up some pop quizzes to keep in my briefcase and pull out when they wouldn't shut up."

"And now you have Reese Gilmartin," said Joe. "It never ends. That's why I like teaching freshman math. They haven't figured out what they can get away with yet. Juan teaches mostly seniors—how do you keep them in line? They seem like they're afraid of you."

"I'm not giving out my trade secrets," replied Juan, laughing a hearty laugh. "Now Marion, do you get out much? I'm an old guy with a wife and kid. But the young bachelors here, they sneak off into town some nights to have a few beers. You guys should invite her. I think you'll have a good time. I've chaperoned a couple of dances with Marion—she's funnier than the rest of you put together."

"Sure, I don't see why not," Sam said, smiling at Marion. They already had established a pleasant friendship, and he didn't want Juan to push the conversation to something more suggestive, as he often did, so he quickly added, "Gotta go, see you all soon enough!"

Sam let himself into his apartment, set down his briefcase on the coffee table, took off his parka, and was about to sit down when he heard a knock on the door. Opening it about an arm's length, he was surprised to see who was standing there.

"Marion!" he said. "Long time no see! To what do I owe this surprise visit? Would you like to come in?"

There was only one other single female teacher at Avon (Nathalie Frelet, the French teacher) before George hired Marion the previous spring to replace Ted Barker, who had been caught drinking pitchers of beer on Route 44 with a naïve freshman boy who may not have realized what Ted had in mind. When another teacher saw them and reported it to Henry Hitchcock, the dean of faculty, Ted was whisked away from campus so quickly that no one saw him leave in the wee hours of morning. Marion, in her mid-30s, lived off-campus for the remainder of that year; the school renewed her contract and gave her Brooks House for the current year.

Unlike Nathalie, who had made no secret of her sexual interest in Sam, Marion did not flirt with him. Although Sam never gave much thought to dating women who were significantly older than him (Marion was about eight years his senior), he had noticed that he did find her sexy. But he enjoyed the platonic relationship they had formed, based on common interests and a playful sense of humor that came naturally to her and seemed to rub off on him in small doses (he had never considered himself a funny person). They also seemed to share an intuition about people's complex and sometimes contradictory personality traits. And Marion saw in Sam a sensitivity to women that was hard to come by on the male-dominated grounds of Avon—which was why she had paid him this visit.

They sat down at his kitchen table; Sam offered tea or water, but Marion replied, "That's OK, I'll get right to the point. I need to share this with someone before I go crazy. And I'm not sure who else on this campus I can trust."

"Sure," he said. "Go ahead."

"I'm being stalked and harassed."

"You're what?"

"Yes, that's right—stalked and harassed." She hesitated.

"It started in the fall with little things I thought I could overlook. Ever since Christmas break, it's gotten worse."

"Oh my god, Marion, that's terrible. You mean right here on campus? Is it another teacher?"

"Yeah, but I can't say who, not yet. Too dangerous."

"No hint?"

"No—" Marion broke off and laughed, having just had a funny thought, even though the topic was serious. "I'm sorry, it might be like in those spy films, where if I tell you, I'll have to kill you."

She laughed again, then ran a flat hand across her face to try and wipe away her silliness.

"I do call him Creepy Man, if that helps."

"No, that doesn't help, but okay then," Sam replied. "I'd rather you not kill me. Is he threatening you?"

"Not threatening—not yet, anyway. He'll just catch me alone in the quad, or outside my classroom, and make a remark that looks innocent to anyone passing by, but is anything but innocent!"

"You mean like innuendo?"

"It started as innuendo! You should hear it now!"

"At first," Marion continued, "it was like, *We should get together.* Or *You must be lonely.*"

"Then: *Aren't you missing it?* And *Don't you need a man yet?*"

"Sometimes he'd comment on my appearance in a sexual way. *Your boobs look so hot in that tight sweater.*"

"Next he started referring more directly to himself and what he could do for me."

"Do for you—like *that* kind of 'do for you' "?

"Yes, that kind. *You should see what I can do to please you.*"

"*I'm saving it all for you, baby.*"

"In the light of day, right here in the middle of campus?"

Marion tilted her head and thought for a second. "You know, he's like those drug dealers in Washington Square. He walks past nonchalantly, and suddenly his mouth opens a crack, and out comes another offer. Such delightful surprises!"

"Has he tried calling you? We all have each other's phone numbers, right?"

"Actually, no. But in the last week or so, he's started slipping notes under my door, and his tone has gotten even more disgusting. *Say the word and I'll come give you some hot lovin' that'll make you scream.* Or, *Once you've had my hammer in you, your pussy will never settle for less.*

"And the most recent note—" Here Marion lifted her index finger and pointed it toward the back of her throat. "Wasn't actually a note. It was a picture. Ugh. What possesses a man to do that?"

"I don't suppose you mean a picture of his face, or even the rippling muscles on his chest."

"Nope."

"Don't know—I've never done it," Sam replied.

"Ugh. It looked gross. Like, really big and scary looking, like a big scaly snake or something. But it was clearly attached to the rest of him."

"Um ... Well, you were married, at least. Surely you've seen a few of these before. Was it—"

"Of course I have. And it was bigger and scarier than any I have seen. But what worries me more is that he is now coming to Brooks House—too close for comfort."

"Don't you think you should report this?"

"I can't. Not yet. I have to think about it more. And now I have to get to another class. Can we grab coffee in town, or maybe lunch on Saturday?"

"Sure, let me know. Hey, I'm sorry to hear all this. You shouldn't have to put up with it. I wish I knew who it was."

"Yeah, well, that might get us both fired." She laughed. "Or killed."

Marion stood up and stifled a tear. Sam offered a hug, and she accepted.

"Thank you. I just don't know what to do."

After her class, Marion walked over to Brooks House. No new notes (or pictures), but there was an envelope in the mail slot:

Internal Revenue Service
William R. Cotter Federal Building
135 High St., Hartford CT 06103

Hmm, she thought, carrying the envelope over to her answering machine, which disappointed her yet again: no new message from Rick.

She opened the letter.

March 29, 1985

Dear Ms. Maloney,

We have reviewed your petition seeking relief, under the federal injured spouse rule, from tax liabilities incurred by Miller Maloney Sloane Investment Partners. Because you are listed as a partner on the company's articles of incorporation, and because you, by your own admission, occasionally provided services to the partnership, we reject your argument that you were a mere silent partner who was deceived by your ex-husband about the company's financial condition. We thereby uphold our previous demand that you either pay the partnership's liabilities in full or enter into a payment plan. These liabilities are detailed on page 2 of this letter and include unpaid taxes, interest, and penalties.

"Goddamn," she cried out loud, then fell on her bed and began sobbing. "And why should I have to pay in full, anyway? They're coming after me because he has no money. Like I have any money to speak of! I have a job. I bet he doesn't even have a job yet. What an absolute dickhead. He can just go fuck himself. God fucking damn him."

Chapter 3

Nathalie Frelet let out her last French class of the day and surveyed the quad from the doorway. It was late March, but it seemed like the daylight was dying more rapidly than it should have been. Or maybe it was the dark gray clouds that were massing over the endless suburbs and picturesque small towns that stretched out across Connecticut to the west. She wrapped her shawl more tightly around the skirt-and-blouse ensemble she had worn to look sophisticated and perhaps catch Sam's attention. Her legs were bare down to the anklets she wore under her black suede chunky-heeled boots. Whatever the visual effect, it did nothing to ward off the chill.

Nathalie knew that Sam Field and Joe Grisman would be a few minutes late to newspaper club due to their sports commitments. The printing workshop was housed in an otherwise unused backroom off of the refectory; that way they didn't have to move the vintage-model printing press or drawers full of type between each meeting. The goal was to produce two issues of the newspaper before the end of the semester. Student editors would assign, collect and edit stories; Sam and Joe, as faculty advisors with college-newspaper experience (Sam had edited the *Daily Princetonian* his senior year), would oversee them, offering guidance and final edits. Then Mr. Grim would run it off the press.

Volunteer advisor Max Grimsby, who wore vintage three-piece suits (well, actually, just the pants and the vest, over a white button-down shirt and bowtie), and puffed on cigars, had supplied the printing hardware from some long-ago gig at a prominent area newspaper (some days, Max claimed it was the *Boston Globe* or *Hartford Courant*; inside word said it was the *Torrington Register*), and taught the students how to set type, which they actually found fascinating. "You know why they call the space between the lines 'leading'? Max would growl in his tobacco-coated baritone. "Because this separator is nothing but a piece of lead!" At that he'd cackle fiendishly, and replace the lead in its case. The students called him Mr. Grim, and he seemed happy with that.

Nathalie stopped at the press-room door and peered inside. There was Max, setting up type cases and composing sticks on long wooden tables that looked at least as old as the type. Several students had just arrived and were hanging their sport jackets on pegs. Nathalie hesitated; she wasn't sure the students had accepted her as a worthy advisor yet. She also wasn't sure if Sam and Joe accepted her yet. Max liked her, but it was obvious why.

Now in her second year teaching at Avon, she was more at ease on the level of the classroom, where there was no doubt she knew what she was doing, and the students were grateful that she was patient with them as they tried to learn the nuances of French pronunciation. And she was happy to teach both beginning and advanced classes.

Outside the classroom, she was less sure of herself. At newspaper club, she wanted to impress Joe and especially Sam; she had mentioned to them that she had written a few stories that were published in her native France, but she was vague enough about them that the men weren't sure if she meant fiction or nonfiction, and what outlet published them.

Earlier in the year, after listening to George bellow "Behave, behave, behave" at the students as they filed into the refectory, and observing that the school seemed like a factory producing dutiful servants of corporate America who would know how to navigate the country club but wouldn't know how to appreciate art or poetry, she wrote an essay satirizing the way the school operated. She titled it "Bee-hive, bee-hive, bee-hive," and showed it to Sam and Joe. They never published it (the newspaper was meant to be written by students), and although Sam thought he should provide her some feedback, he never got around to it.

Nathalie once reached out to the English teacher Marion Maloney when she heard that Marion wrote poetry; they met once to discuss starting a poetry club for the boys, but never got it off the ground.

As the air outside the newsroom began to turn colder, Nathalie finally stepped inside and slowly unwrapped herself from her shawl and hung it from one of the pegs. She felt a shiver go through her; maybe it was the chill from outside, or an involuntary reaction to the fact that Sam would be walking through the door any minute.

"Hello Max," she said cheerfully. "Hello students."

"Good afternoon, Miss Frelet," Max boomed, taking in Nathalie's toned bare legs. If her carefully chosen ensemble didn't impress him, it was mainly because he wasn't looking at it. One glance, and he had already resigned himself to the fact that she wasn't showing any cleavage on this day, so his eyes remained fixated on her legs. The museum-bound typesetting tools and antiquated printing knowledge weren't the only things about Max that were old school. And while he didn't mind having Nathalie around, it had nothing to do with any ability she might demonstrate to help out the boys with the newspaper.

Headmaster George Dickleman had hired Nathalie as a French teacher for the 1983-84 school year; he renewed her contract for 1984-85. George, widely known for his many affairs with Avon students' mothers, had not appeared to ever come on to Nathalie, who was, like Sam, single and in her mid-20s. There were plenty of rumors around campus, however, that she had slept with George's son Tom, who also was in his second year at the school, teaching history and coaching various levels of football and basketball, and varsity golf.

Nathalie had spent her youth in France, and now lived in the West Hartford apartment she had taken while finishing her degree at the University of Hartford. She had been a quiet presence on campus her first year, seldom eating any meal besides lunch with the students and other faculty, and driving home after classes. She was rumored to have a boyfriend somewhere in Hartford, but that relationship apparently had ended, and suddenly she was more visible at Avon. She spent more time on campus, and volunteered with student activities that her contract had not required her to, like helping edit the school newspaper along with Sam and Joe.

And she began going out to the local bars, mostly with a crowd that included Tom Dickleman, Mark Lehrer, and Terry McSweeney, an affable black Canadian man in his late 20s who coached thirds hockey with Sam. One night the four of them were having beers in Tom's apartment, and when the other men left and Nathalie didn't, the rumors began. But whatever Nathalie had going with Tom, she had her eyes on a different prize, because after a couple of months working with the school newspaper, she knew whom she really wanted to sleep with.

Nathalie was sitting with several students, looking over a list of proposed stories for the April issue, when Sam and Joe walked in together. She looked up and smiled, trying not to look too eager to see Sam. Joe and Sam talked over each other saying "hello" to Max, Nathalie, and the students, maintaining a casual vibe that did not betray any feeling on Sam's part.

Nathalie held up the story list and spoke to the two young men. "You know better than I, but my input was that they should try to find another story or two in the realm of arts and music," she said.

She passed the story list to Sam, trying and failing to find a way to position the paper so their hands would brush together.

"Let's see," Sam said. "AOF hockey celebrates championship season." "Baseball and lacrosse updates (most recent info at press time)." "Dean Hitchcock retires, plans move to Virginia to be with his family"—at which Joe Grisman muttered in a low voice, "plans move to Arizona desert to be with his lizard family."

Sam squelched a chuckle and continued. "Joe Kraft retires, plans move to Maine to live by his beloved ocean."

Sam could sense another wisecrack coming from Joe, who wanted to make a gay joke but knew Sam would frown at him—and probably Nathalie too. "I wonder," said Sam, "will he need an extra moving van just to fit all that nautical crap he has in his house? Or is he leaving a maritime museum as a gift to the school?"

Back to the list. "Date set for college fair." "Date set for annual ice cream social." "Date set for the father-and-son pheasant shoot."

And finally, a single word: "Leach."

"Leach?" asked Sam. "What's that?"

"Brian Leach," replied Trip Westbrook, the senior student editor. "He's new this year. He's a junior and he's already breaking hockey records. I hear he's a baseball phenom, too."

"Oh, yeah, I've heard of him," Sam replied. "Check the spelling. I don't think this is how he spells his last name. Always check the spelling. Even if the name is John Smith. Because it could be J-O-N and S-M-Y-T-H-E."

"Interview the kid," Joe added. "And talk to the senior hockey captain. And don't forget Coach Gardner."

"But as to Nathalie's point," Sam interjected, "she's right. Where are the stories about the arts? Talk to Mr. Chadwick about the spring play. What is it going to be? Are there any staging or casting issues? Is he recruiting any girls from Miss Porter's or Ethel Walker? And music? Anyone make the All-State Music Festival?"

Nathalie was both thrilled and terrified that Sam was responding to her suggestion, and positively at that. She shot him a loaded glance, and Joe noticed.

Later, as Joe and Sam walked around the building to the main entrance of the refectory, Joe suddenly blurted out to his friend, "When you gonna fuck Nathalie and get it over with?"

"What?" Sam responded, stopping in his tracks to look Joe square in the face. "Are you out of your mind?"

"No," Joe laughed. "I'm not out of my mind. But you might be. You don't have any game right now, from what I can see. I don't either, but Nathalie isn't checking me out. What, are you holding out for that Walker's girl who's at college now? And I haven't seen Katie around here lately. This chick is hot, and she's French, and she wants you."

"Wait, wait, wait. First off, 'hot' is in the eye of the beholder. She's okay. Nice enough body, I guess. Second, how do you know she wants me?"

"Because I have eyes. And ears. And she's offering herself to you. On a platter. With Hollandaise sauce."

They had begun walking again, but they both turned their faces to the other. Joe was smirking at his own joke, and Sam was rolling his eyes.

"What does that mean, anyway, she's French?" Sam asked. "Does that make her more desirable somehow? A better tongue kisser? If she gets me off, am I going to see fireworks erupting over the Eiffel Tower?"

"I don't know," said Joe, his voice rising up playfully on "know." "The French girls, they know things. And France is not like here. No one teaches them that sex is bad. Especially not their movies."

After dinner, Sam lingered for a few minutes to chat with Joe, Nathalie, and a few other faculty. Then he slipped away from the group and headed back to his apartment.

Joe had gotten him thinking about women. He was right, he hadn't seen his ex-girlfriend Katie Trimble in a while. He had visited her in Boston in the fall, they had seen each other in Northampton over Thanksgiving, and she had come out to Avon for a weekend in December, in spite of her concern that students and faculty would eye her curiously as if she were a zoo animal. The locals were better behaved than that, and Sam and Katie had fun driving around, going out to dinner and beers, and mostly, screwing in his apartment. Sexually, they never tired of each other. But neither one of them had broached the subject of giving a real relationship one last try. And when Sam was feeling lonely, he worried that she would fall into a serious relationship in Boston, where the pool of potential partners was infinite compared to Avon.

Then there was Maggie Duchesne, his forbidden crush from the previous school year, when she was a senior at Ethel Walker. Maggie was best friends with Annie Green, who was dating a junior on Sam's hall named Warren Cochran. Sam and Maggie had gotten to know each other, then fallen into a couple of intense make-out sessions, which they both agreed were wrong, but allowed to happen anyway. The day after Maggie graduated, they had one more long, sensual kiss goodbye amid vague promises to get together sometime.

Sam secretly yearned for Maggie to come back and surprise him one day with a knock on the door and a renewal of the smoldering lust of their previous kisses—and perhaps more, now that they didn't have to hide anything. But Maggie was hours away at Georgetown University. Sam had looked at train schedules, but even though they had kept their promises to write each other or talk on the phone once in a while, neither of them had revisited the idea of getting together. And with Maggie immersed in the fast-paced life of a college fresh-man in a big city, Sam could feel the connection slipping away.

In the midst of his reverie about Maggie, at first Sam didn't notice the gentle series of knocks on his door. "Who could that be?" he thought. He had made no plans to go out. Maybe Steve Morrow needed to borrow a few bucks. Maggie would have been the answer to his prayer, but this was not possible.

He opened his door, and Nathalie was standing there, a pleading look in her eyes as they silently took each other in. When she finally spoke, her voice came out as a breathy and desperate whisper.

"When are you going to give in and just take me?" she demanded.

Sam was startled by the forward question. "Take you? He responded. "I don't know--"

"Oh, you," she shook her head as she entered the apartment and slid past him. "Don't act so innocent. You know very well what I mean. I've been coming on to you for months now. Can't you tell by the way I look at you?"

"I'm not sure I know what you mean," pleaded Sam. He had considered what Joe said without deciding whether he was right or not. Clearly Joe was right. And Sam had not pre-pared for this moment. He needed a strategy for backing away and giving himself time to think about it.

Nathalie, frustrated that Sam was being so aloof, said, "Or maybe you're still fucking the teenagers."

Sam took a deep breath and spoke in bursts of barely con-cealed anger. "I have *not* been having sex with teenagers!" He paused for another deep breath. "Not this year, not last year. Where did you get information like that?"

"Oh come on. Now you're just playing dumb. Everyone saw that girl coming out of your apartment last year. Several times I heard."

"Oh really?" Sam said. "And who told you that? Tom Dickleman?"

Now Nathalie was angry that Sam was pushing back with innuendo about her own not-so-secret sex life. "You were banging that brunette bitch from Walker's. Everybody knew."

"Her name is Maggie Duchesne, and she's a very nice young woman, and I never had sex with her. Case closed." He was furious at the boldness of her accusations. "As for you, is this how you seduce all the guys?"

Frustrated that her attempt to lure Sam had turned so awkward, Nathalie turned and walked toward the window, rubbing her eyes and stifling a sob before turning and walking back toward him. "I'm sorry, Sam. I let my passion and temper get the better of me."

They were standing about three feet apart. Nathalie looked down for a moment, then back up at Sam's face, her eyes pleading once again. Sam thought her face was very pretty, but now she was scrunching it up like she was about to burst into tears. *Why do they always do this with me?* He thought.

While he had always found Nathalie attractive, he had never considered her his type. So he surprised himself when he allowed her to come closer and throw her arms around his neck.

"You are not like the other men here," she whispered. "I bet you are an amazing lover."

Sam's feelings, and senses, were starting to blur as Nathalie took control of the encounter. *Maybe French women do know things*, he thought.

"Well, what do you think?" she said, raising her lips close to his. "Then again, maybe the trick is not to think. You Americans can be so funny about sex, like there are all these conditions you have to put on it in order to enjoy it."

"Oh, no," Sam laughed nervously. "I like sex. I just don't want to jump into something that might get someone hurt."

"See? You're thinking too much. Just let me show you how good I can make you feel. I bet I can do things to you the Walker's bitch has never even heard of."

Annoyed again, Sam lifted Nathalie's wrists off his neck, and held them in front of her with a couple feet between them. "Whatever else you want to say to try to get me into bed, please leave Maggie out of it. I don't know what your sources think they saw, but I never had sex with her. And she's a very nice girl."

"Ah, yes, girl. Maybe it's time you had a woman."

As she came closer again, there was no hiding that Sam was aroused in spite of himself. Nathalie smiled as she pressed herself against him.

"I am not looking for a relationship," Sam said as Nathalie pulled him even closer and practically melted into him.

"I'm not here for a relationship," Nathalie countered.

Sam could feel her breath hot against his face. The sweet scent of her perfume wafted into his nostrils. As she gently pressed her moist lips into his and offered, at first, just the tip of her tongue, he felt desire overcome him.

He turned to his door and locked the deadbolt.

Chapter 4

April 1985

"Watch the cap," said Sam Field. "It almost always has something to do with the cap."

Sam, Joe Grisman, and Reese Gilmartin sat at one end of the Avon bench on a crisp, sunny Saturday morning in early April, with about a half-dozen substitute players scattered across the bench or standing nearby to watch Avon take on Kent School in a thirds baseball game. It was the top of the first, and Beavers ace Carlton Beaumont, a sophomore and a lefty, was on the mound.

Beaumont struck out the first Kent batter he faced, and the second one grounded to Keith Rizzo at shortstop, who threw to first baseman Chaz Gleason for the out. With no one on base, there was little to watch for, but Sam, Joe, and Reese studied the mannerisms of the Kent third base coach to get an idea what he tended to do and say when there was nothing to deliver an actual sign for.

"Come on batter," he barked, offering up a predictable sampling of chatter. "Let's go, Mikey. Give it a ride."

Mikey didn't exactly give it a ride, but he dribbled a slow roller down the third base line, too slow for Charlie Morton to make a play. Now there was a runner on base, and the Avon sign-stealing trio went to work. "He does tug the brim of his cap a lot," whispered Joe. "Keep your eye on that—it might be the 'hot' indicator."

"And he claps a lot," added Sam. "Too much for my taste."

"And he just scratched his ass," said Reese, grinning, "but maybe that wasn't supposed to be a sign."

"Although," he continued, "I heard of one coach who picked his nose to call a pickoff attempt." Sam and Joe both turned to make skeptical faces at the chubby, wisecracking junior who was fulfilling his spring sports requirement as equipment manager.

"OK, maybe I made that up," Reese admitted.

At the thirds level, most pitchers were too young and unsophisticated to have more than one or two pitches—most just threw the ball as hard as they could and hoped for the best. So there was no point in trying to steal signs from the catcher. Now and then the coaches would call for a sacrifice bunt, but rarely did they try anything as fancy as hit-and-run. Basic base stealing was common, however, and most runners got away with it unless the other team was able to steal the sign. And if you had a lefty on the mound like Beaumont, it was easier to pick off a runner at first because you could turn and throw at the last second and not be called for a balk.

Beaumont's first pitch was a ball, and the coach didn't do much before the pitch. But as Beaumont went into his set, the coach tugged the brim of his cap twice and then clapped twice. Mikey broke for second, but the pitch was fouled off.

"OK, we might have it," said Sam. "Leave the chatter to me so Carlton doesn't get confused."

"Go get 'em, Carlton," Sam boomed at the volume necessary to make sure his pitcher could pick out his voice from the others. "Hum it in there. Let's go, Louisiana. Show him your lightning."

Beaumont was from Louisiana, and his teammates and coaches had nicknamed him "Louisiana Lightning" after New York Yankees pitcher Ron Guidry. "Hum it in there, Lightning."

As Beaumont got set to offer his third pitch, the Kent third base coach touched his wrists a couple of times and clapped a lot. But he did not touch his cap. So Sam did not use the word "Bayou," which was the signal for a quick, sneaky pickoff attempt.

The pitch was in the dirt for ball two. Mikey, with a tiny lead, did not run.

Finally, the coaches set the show in motion. The Kent coach tugged his cap twice and clapped twice. Sam responded.

"Hum it in there, Louisiana. For the Bayou."

Beaumont went into his windup. Mikey started for second base. Carlton turned, stepped toward first, and whipped the ball to Chaz Gleason, trapping Mikey in a classic rundown. Mikey trotted slowly toward second, and Chaz started toward him, pumping his arm. Mikey made a dash for second. Keith Rizzo took the throw and tagged him out. The Avon players erupted in whoops of delight.

When Carlton picked off another would-be base stealer in the top of the third, the Kent coaches changed their indicator sign. But it didn't fool Avon for long, and the Winged Beavers coasted to a 5-2 win.

After the high fives and handshakes, the players collected their gear and made their way back to campus. Joe excused himself to drive to Danbury to spend the afternoon with his parents. "Beers tonight?" Joe asked Sam, who nodded.

Reese collected the bats, balls, catcher's gear, and other stray items and shoved them into a large duffel, which he dropped on the ground behind Sam's Mercury Capri while Sam unlocked it and opened the hatchback. For a minute or so, the two of them just stood there, apparently content to pause for a moment and take in the lovely spring weather.

"Well," Sam said finally, "I guess the only thing standing between us and lunch is you leaning over, lifting up the equipment bag, and tossing it into the hatch."

"Funny you should say that," Reese responded. "I was just contemplating how nice it would be to have a forklift for this job. Or a coach who wasn't so tired from keeping a scorecard and stealing signs that he might just do it himself."

"Ah, well, I wouldn't want to have to tell George that you weren't getting the full benefit of your physical fitness assignment, now would I?"

"Well, you could always tell Mr. Dickleman to go ... Oh, never mind."

"Shall I drop you off near the refectory?"

"Are you coming in too?" asked Reese.

"Not today—hot lunch date!"

"Um ... let's see ... I haven't seen you hanging out with any Walker's girls this year. Too bad Maggie graduated ... Have you been sneaking off to Miss Porter's instead?

"No, Reese, I have a lunch date with another faculty member. Miss Maloney."

Reese looked at Sam and smiled. "I can't figure you out, Mr. Field. At first you went for the underage ones. Now you're going after a woman who's old enough to be my mother."

"And how old is your mother, Reese?"

"Eighty-five if she's a day. Or maybe 45. Somewhere in there."

"Well, let's just say she's got some years on Miss Maloney. I won't say how old she is—it's not polite to talk about a woman's age—in fact, I apologize for asking your mom's."

"Besides," Sam continued, "this is a platonic date, not a romantic one."

"There you go again, Mr. Field. 'Platonic'—I don't know that word. I've heard of 'gin and tonic'—speaking of which, there goes Mr. Dickleman into the refectory now."

"And I'll be late if I don't get going, so ..."

Sam pulled up to Brooks House and was getting out to ring the bell when Marion stepped out, smiling broadly, as if she had just won the lottery.

"What, did Creepy Man leave you another lovely photo?"

"Not today," Marion said, "but did I tell you about the note about wanting to hump me like a horse?"

"Eww," said Sam. It seems like he's getting more and more gross.

"Funny you mention that," Marion said. "When he's on the quad whispering in my ear, he's actually a little more polite about it."

"Not," she added, "that there's anything polite about badgering a woman to give you sex against your wishes."

"Although ..." she continued, pausing to think. "He actually hasn't been whispering to me on the quad lately."

"You have a spot in mind for lunch?" Sam asked.

"Yeah, a place I know in West Hartford," she replied.

They took their seats across from each other at a four-top; once they had chosen, the server collected the other two place settings.

Marion, dressed in brown suede boots, jeans, and a red-and-gold merino wool sweater, was beaming. The sunlight streaking in from the windows danced off the colors in her sweater and the reddish undertones of her chestnut hair.

"Well, you look happy!" Sam said, smiling. "You going to tell me why, or would you have to kill me?"

"Ha, no, not over Rick," she said.

"Rick?"

The cat was out of the bag, and Marion was getting very comfortable with Sam's friendship, so she decided to just tell him.

"Rick called."

"Hmm," Sam said. "I'm guessing there's a little back-story?"

"About a week and a half ago, I was having a couple of glasses of wine by myself at—" she hesitated.

"At—where? Someplace top secret? If you think I might be a government spy," Sam said, "You could always just say 'at a bar' or 'at a restaurant.'"

"Oh, I guess I can trust you," she smiled. "I've already told you more than I've told anyone else. I was at the Kettle & Cork in West Hartford, not too far from this place. I go there occasionally just to get away, relax, and read. I'm fairly certain

Creepy Man doesn't know I go there. If he starts turning up now, I will have you killed! If he doesn't kill me first."

The server stopped at their table to hand them menus. "Something to drink?"

"A glass of the pinot grigio," said Marion.

"Same," said Sam.

"I'd still like to know who Creepy Man is, but I suppose—"

"Stop right there," she said, holding up her open right hand. "I'm going to have to come up with a name for you—maybe the Question Man. Or the Too Many Questions Man. I'll work on it."

"So you were at the Kettle & Cork ..."

"Oh yeah. And in walked this very handsome man. I called him The Man With the Dreamy Blue Eyes," she said, her own green eyes sparkling.

"Anyway, he sat two barstools away from me. And he noticed my book, but he didn't say anything at first. His mother must have taught him not to come charging after any woman who strikes his fancy. She must have known he was going to be a major babe magnet!"

Marion laughed at herself at the silly sound of those words.

"He talked to you about his mother?"

"Ha, no, I just made that up. He was polite." She laughed again. "Until I tricked him into being a little less polite."

"OK, so this guy Rick—does he have a last name? Or did you not get the last name?"

Marion frowned at Sam, then burst out laughing. "Yeah, I got it. Larson."

With an O-N or an E-N?"

"Not sure ... He did look Swedish."

The server returned. Sam flipped through the menu quickly, looking for something to order without having to agonize over it. Marion did the same.

"I can come back—"

"No, that's OK," Marion said. "Broccoli cheddar quiche with a side salad."

"Dressing?"

"Oil and vinegar."

"And I'll have the turkey club," Sam said. "Wheat toast."

Sam turned back to Marion. "OK, so Polite Rick is sitting two barstools away. And you're sitting there reading *Pet Sematary*."

"No!" Marion exclaimed. "I don't read much horror ... I may be living it though," she added, laughing nervously.

"I was reading *The Unbearable Lightness of Being*. And he knew the book. And he finally said something about it. Next thing you know, I invited him to sit next to me, and we started talking about books—everything from Virginia Wolff to John Irving to Kate Chopin to Margaret Atwood. We ordered more wine, and drank it, and had a great time talking—and before I knew it, I was pawing him and inviting him back to my place!"

"Wow," Sam exclaimed. "You're fast! I think I'm a little jealous!" Once again, Sam noticed that he did find Marion sexy, and it occurred to him that if she ever came on to him like that, he probably wouldn't resist.

Marion lowered her head and looked Sam in the eyes. "I'm not usually like this. I don't know what came over me. It's been so long."

The server came over, sliding their plates in front of them, trying not to interrupt their conversation.

"You've been divorced how long?"

"Officially, a year. But sexless for at least four years. That night with Rick was explosive—like the 4th of July. And now I'm seeing him again—tonight!"

"And what does he do? English professor? Rock star? Unemployed?"

Marion smiled. "Oh for three. He actually does want to be an English professor and writer. But before he could get back to Wesleyan for an advanced degree, a summer job turned into a series of promotions, and he can't seem to get out!"

"Hmm ... where?"

"Society for Savings."

"Oh, the bank. Around here?"

"Right around here in Hartford, I think. You from here?"

"Nah, Northampton, Mass. My parents still live there. What about you—you have family? Parents? Siblings?"

"Dad moved to Florida after Mom died. They were getting older when they had me. I have a brother who lives in Providence. He's 10 years older than me. We're not enemies, but we're not close."

"What about your love life?" Marion continued. "All I know is what I see, and hear, and occasionally sense. You're a bit of a puzzle to me."

Sam looked across at her and smiled, absently wondering how much thought Marion had given to his love life. "More like a fizzle than a puzzle. No fireworks in my bedroom at the moment. Nothing to see here! Or to hear or to sense—whatever you meant by that."

Marion smiled at him. "Well," she said, "I have seen one woman, heard about another, and sensed a third. You want me to lay it all out for you?"

"Well, the only one you could have seen was Katie, my ex-girlfriend. She visited in December. Yeah, the temperature in my bedroom does go up when she's around. But we're not—"

"You guys looked like a divorced couple trying to decide if it was worth another try. But let's go back to last year. Rumor had it—"

"Oh Jesus, no, I was not sleeping with that girl from Walker's. We were ... good friends."

"Touchy!" Marion's eyes sparkled. "But I'm most interested in the one I can sense this year. Do you know who I mean?"

"No fucking idea," Sam blurted out, though he knew by process of elimination whom she meant.

"Oh, I just thought maybe you were brushing up on your French, you know, conjugating some verbs—"

"Christ," he muttered, then took a deep sigh and collected himself. "OK, sorry, I refuse to be mad at you. I really like you." Sam paused and looked across at her, careful to make sure they were both locked on each other's eyes. "You and I, we support each other, right?"

Sam extended his arm across the table. Marion reached out and clasped his hand. "I would like that."

"I'm almost embarrassed to say this," Sam said meekly. "I finally gave in to her the other night. She's been working this from so many angles. Glances on the campus, in the refectory, in the printing club. Suggestive little movements. And when she confronted me in my room, she went from the purring little coquette to the badass sex goddess insisting I needed a real woman to give me a working over."

"Wow! And how was the working over? Like fine French cuisine? Or more like the storming of the Bastille?"

Sam looked up at her, chewing a bite of his sandwich. After a long pause, he smiled and said, "She was good. It was fun. I told her I didn't want a relationship. She said she wasn't there for a relationship. But I know she'll be back. And I don't trust her."

"But what about you?" Sam continued. "My problems are minor compared to yours. I'm happy you're having fun with Polite Rick the Banker Man—"

They both laughed at how Sam was starting to imitate Marion's habit of giving everybody nicknames.

"But I'm worried about Creepy Man, and what he might do."

"Yeah, I'm worried too. And I still don't know what to do about it. There's only a month or so left in the school year—hopefully I can stick it out that long!"

"Do you think you'll be back next year?"

Marion finished her last bite of quiche, and looked up at Sam, as both of her eyes began to water. She brushed the tears aside with her fists.

"This is a lot to put up with," she said finally. "And I still have other problems involving my ex that I have to deal with. And I don't want to teach English here forever. I want to publish poetry. Hell, I'd be happy to have more time just to write poetry. Maybe do pop-up poetry slams for teenagers at festivals and farmers markets."

As Marion talked, it occurred to Sam that while he was enjoying his stint teaching at Avon, his own dream of becoming a writer was being deferred.

"But," she continued, "I would miss my kids. I really like them, even if they are privileged. Underneath the veneer, they're just kids stumbling around trying to figure it all out. And I love when something in the literature I'm teaching actually moves them. Once we got into *Les Miserables*, some of them really became engrossed in it."

"And I would miss a few of the faculty. Especially Juan and Kevin. And now you. After talking to you a couple of times these past few days, I already feel like you're my best friend."

In the parking lot, Sam and Marion gave each other a long hug before climbing into his Capri.

Back in his apartment, Sam graded some papers before opting to take a late-afternoon nap prior to a Saturday night out with the other bachelors. As he lay there in an almost trancelike state, an unexpected sensation came over him. He somehow knew he was in a dream, but it felt very real. Motion beneath his body as he slept. The sound of steel wheels rolling.

And visible from a nearby window, pale yellow stalks of wheat swaying in the summer breeze. There was no doubt in his unconscious mind that he was on a train rumbling across the prairie.

Chapter 5

April 1985

Simsbury, Connecticut

"Good evening laddies, good to see ya," boomed Kieran over the din of O'Laughlin's as four Avon Old Farms bachelors stepped through the door. "How's she cuttin'?"

"How's she cuttin'?" Sam muttered, perplexed.

"Irish slang," said Steve Morrow with a wry smile. "Don't worry, it's not a question to be answered. I think he's just doing that for your benefit."

After numerous visits to O'Laughlin's over two years, Sam was well-known for doubting that the bartender was an authentic Irishman. "He's from Iowa," Sam would say, in what had become a recurring and borderline ponderous inside joke.

In one corner of the bar, a band played Irish songs. The Avon men looked around for an empty table, and spotted one in the opposite corner that was abandoned except for several pint glasses and puddles of beer.

Kieran whistled and called out to one of the two young woman who were waiting the tables that night. "Maeve, could you clear and wipe down 12 when you get a moment?"

"Maeve?" Sam repeated. "Oh jeez. They can't be serious."

While Maeve worked on their table, Sam drifted over toward the bar. He waited until Kieran came up.

"Can I get you something, laddie? Maeve will be back to your table shortly to take orders."

"Oh, I'll wait then," said Sam. "Sounds like St. Patrick's Day in here. Oh, well, wasn't that a few weeks ago?"

"We like to keep the spirit going," said Kieran with a wink.

"And keep the tips flowing," said Sam, pointing to a shelf behind the bar where a pitcher sat, stuffed with bills. "Looks like you'll be able to afford a spring trip to the old country," Sam remarked, pausing for effect. "Or to Des Moines—whatever strikes your fancy."

"I've been to Des Moines," said Kieran. "Didn't really feel at home there—not enough green hills." With that, he winked over toward Steve Morrow, who had started listening in and was now shaking his head at Sam's ongoing denial of Kieran's Irishness.

Sam sat down just as Maeve came over to take their orders. "Will you be having a pint of Guinness as per usual?" she said, smiling at Steve.

"Sure as I'm sittin' here," Steve replied, at which point Kevin added, "Same for me. And then we'll have a toast to all us Irishmen."

"I'll have a Guinness too," said Joe, "that is, if you're allowed to serve it to a French Jew."

"And in honor of all the Americans in the room—" here Sam paused to think. "What's that new one from Boston?"

Maeve thought for a second, then said "Oh, do you mean Samuel Adams? I'll check. I think we just got some in. Might just be in bottles though, if that's OK."

"Well, if it only comes in bottles, I'd still like you to pour it into a pint glass!"

"Won't fill to the top," Maeve said, "but that's no skin off my back."

The men settled in and discussed their usual topics: the students' bad habits, the prospects for spring sports, and the prospects for their own sex lives, a conversation that typically turned toward the more interesting sex lives of the married faculty and, especially, George Dickleman, who showed no signs of slowing down in his pursuit of students' mothers.

"How does he *do* it," asked a perplexed-looking Joe Grisman. "And how does he find them?"

"Neither one of those questions requires knowledge of rocket science," said Kevin, smiling. "How does he do it? He knows what he's doing. And how does he find them? Well, as you have seen, the mothers do bring their sons here for interviews and tours."

"But don't the fathers come too?" asked an equally perplexed Sam Field.

"Well—" Steve looked at Kevin, who nodded for Steve to continue. "For one thing, the fathers don't come as often. Some of these families are still products of the old patriarchies. Dad's jetting off to a board meeting somewhere. Mom has more time. And George always encourages the boys to stay on campus for a night to see how the students live. George has that 'secret' apartment we told you about last year."

"So if the father's not here, that's when George scores?" asked Joe.

"And sometimes even if the father is here," said Kevin. "You'd be surprised. Or they set something up for another time."

Sam shook his head. "I just don't get how they work it—"

"They speak in code." Steve said. "And sometimes, believe it or not, they pass notes."

"And George is pretty sharp," Kevin added. "Three out of four men are just oblivious."

"It's basically a survival skill for him," said Steve. "I'm sure you've seen his—"

"And that's the end of this conversation," Kevin said in a whisper, before turning toward some new visitors who had entered the bar."

"Well hello Tom," he said warmly. "And Terry, and Mark, and Nathalie, good to see you out. All you Avon teachers know each other, right? And I believe this tall fellow over here is Dave—Dave Williams? Or do they still call you Tiger?"

"Either is fine," he replied in a friendly if gruff voice.

"Now Tiger," Kevin continued, "played football and golf here with Tom until they graduated in … '77? Sorry, for those of you who don't know all the names, there's Sam Field, and Steve Morrow, and Joe Grisman, and Tom Dickleman, and Terry McSweeney, and Mark Lehrer. And Nathalie Frelet. And I'm Kevin Doolan."

"And while I sort of remember Cody here, I'm afraid I can't place the lady at all."

"Oh, sorry," said Tom. "This is Cody Savard. Another almost townie whose parents live just over the mountain in West Hartford. Our parents went to Yale together, and we did a lot of stuff with their family. Cody went to Choate, then Yale, like me and our dads. Lives in Stratford now and writes for the *Bridgeport Post*. But he still golfs and drinks with us when he's in town—especially since he can afford to lose his money to us on skins."

"And the young lady?" Kevin asked, blue eyes twinkling.

"This is Marcie Merrifield, my best friend from the University of Hartford," introduced Nathalie. "She lives in my building in West Hartford."

While Marcie was not outwardly brash or forward, she somehow emanated a soft glow that heightened everyone's awareness that she was in the room. And she caught Kevin's attention without half-trying.

Kevin Doolan, with his ruggedly handsome freckled face, twinkly eyes, and shock of brown schoolboy locks dominating one side of his forehead, always caught the interest of women in his presence. And when surrounded by fresh new female faces, there always seemed to be one who drew out his native sparkle. But if it was easy to spot the initial attraction, it was harder to trace what became of it; sometimes the woman would turn up later on his arm (or slipping out of his apartment), while other times you never saw her again.

A few of the men in the Dickleman party, notably Tom's town friends, lowered their eyes perceptibly as they took in Kevin's introductory flirt with Marcie, who was smiling at him.

"Well then," said Tiger, "why don't we grab these seats over here before someone else butts in."

The tables were just a few yards apart—but Tiger and Tom were clearly staking out territory, especially when Tom noticed Nathalie making eyes at Sam, who read the whole scene and turned away to say something to Joe. Kevin, who had stood up to make the introductions, sat back down.

Sam turned to Kevin, and spoke in a hushed voice. "Why 'Tiger'?"

Kevin scratched his head, then turned toward Sam and smiled. "I'll give you three choices. One, ask the ladies. He is a big, tall strapping specimen of mammal, after all." Kevin chuckled at his own description.

"Two, ask the opposing players he's hunted down and shredded on the football field."

"Three ... Nah ... could it be this simple? There is an NHL player named Dave Williams. Dave 'Tiger' Williams, they call him. Best years with Toronto in the late 70s. Plays with L.A. Kings now, I think. Good enough to play in the NHL, but not great. Knows his way around the penalty box."

"And sometimes that's all people need, an existing nickname to borrow from. It doesn't matter how well it fits, though in this case, I'd say we have a pretty close match."

"Is Tiger—this one, Tom's friend—a mean, ornery dude?" Sam asked. "I'm not sure I trust his ..." Sam struggled to locate the word he was looking for.

"Disposition?" Kevin offered.

"Something like that," Sam said.

"I'll put it to you this way," Kevin said. "And then I'll leave it alone. I've been drinking with Tom and these Avon guys, a number of times in various combos, including sometimes with Tiger. Let's just say that while I sometimes find Tom to be a little full of himself—the apple hasn't fallen too far from the tree, if you catch my drift—I like him better when Tiger isn't around."

Avon, Connecticut

A couple of miles away in Avon, Rick picked up Marion in his Honda Accord, handing her a bouquet of flowers at the door to Brooks House, enjoying the kiss and squeeze he got for his effort, then helping her prepare them for a vase, and finally holding the door for her as she climbed into his car.

The couple smiled at each other as they took in how nice they both looked on this warm spring evening. Rick wore a French navy blazer, red tie, white shirt and pleated khakis, while Marion wore a smart-looking, deep-gray skirt-and-jacket set over a white ruffled blouse, with sheer stockings and black boots with three-inch heels. Marion, thinking ahead to evening's end, had offered to drive, but Rick had insisted; it was "date night."

Marion was curious to see Rick's place, and that still wasn't out of the question. For now they both enjoyed the drive into Hartford on I-84, through the green, rolling hills of Farmington, the more suburban vistas of West Hartford, and finally, the bustle of downtown Hartford. The old cliché about rolling up the sidewalks at 5 no longer really applied, as a large number of restaurants, bars, and theaters catered to a pretty wide range of the region's educated and affluent core, from college students to professionals.

Marion asked Rick if he had ever considered working in the city's booming insurance sector. "Ha, are you kidding me?" he answered, grinning sideways at her. "You know I can barely keep a straight face at my banking job. Why do you ask—is insurance your secret love?"

"Oh, yes, I want to be like Wallace Stevens, and work for the Hartford while writing poems in my spare time," she said, smiling at him mischievously.

"Besides," she added, "don't you think insurance is just so ... so sexy? All those numbers and probabilities and actuarial tables?"

Marion finally burst out laughing and smacked Rick on the knee.

"Is it true he wrote poems in his head while walking to work at the Hartford?" Rick asked.

"I don't know," she replied, tickling the inside of his thigh suggestively. "And I never figured out who might be the emperor of ice cream."

Just then, Rick turned a corner onto Main Street, and pulled up near the front of Brown, Thomson & Company. "I thought about making a reservation here," Rick said. "But as you probably know, this place has become better known for its singles action than for its food, and I don't want to have to fend off all those yuppie frat boys hitting on you, so I picked someplace else. But I just love the architecture."

Originally a department store, Brown, Thomson & Company was designed in 1876 by Henry Hobson Richardson, and now stood as a classic example of a unique architecture style named after him: Richardsonian Romanesque.

"Look at the exquisitely crafted arches in the brownstone. I just love it."

"So you like literature and architecture," Marion smiled. "My kinda guy. Ballet and art and poetry too?"

"All very sexy. And I know Hartford has a very good ballet company, but I am leaning more toward modern these days. You?"

"Modern is good. Ballet is good. But if I'm leaning toward anything, it's the sexy guy who is my date tonight."

"Well, I hope you'll like the restaurant I chose. It's upscale like Brown Thomson but smaller and more intimate."

Rick shot her a glance and smiled. "I'm looking forward to getting to know you better tonight. I think you have a beautiful mind," he said, touching his finger to her forehead, "along with beautiful everything else."

Marion nestled into Rick's shoulder and looked at him with her big green eyes. "I'm looking forward to getting to know you too," she said. "I'm sure the restaurant will be fine."

"Deal," he said, reaching his right hand up to run it through her hair.

Simsbury, Connecticut

Back in Simsbury, pints were flowing freely at O'Laughlin's. The two tables of Avon teachers and their friends were mingling. Steve, Sam, Joe, Mark and Terry, all well-acquainted Avon bachelors, were busy catching up. Tom and Nathalie had gotten up to dance. Tiger and Cody were up playing darts. That left Kevin and Marcie alone to resume their flirtation, although Kevin was never one to be too forward.

"So you went to Hartford with Nathalie," he said, legs crossed casually, pint glass tucked into the folds of his Aran sweater. "What did you study?"

"I majored in history with a minor in feminist studies," she said a little shyly.

"That's great," Kevin said. "Don't stop until you've kicked enough asses to change a few things in this world."

"Oh," Marcie said, lowering her face a little. "I've got much more to learn … and I'll be going to grad school, but I think I'll work better as a behind-the-scenes researcher and facilitator than an in-your-face ass-kicker." Looking embarrassed, Marcie covered her cheeks with her hands and said, "I can't believe I just said that."

"See?" Kevin said. "It'll be fun to see you kick some ass now and then."

"Well, who's talkin' about kicking ass over here?" said Cody loudly, sitting back down in his chair. "All I do know is that Tiger here kicked my ass pretty good at darts."

"Just talking about the many good uses of education," Kevin said, smiling. "Marcie's planning on going to grad school."

Tiger picked up his half-full pint glass and chugged it down. "What, they offer an advanced MRS degree?"

Marcie frowned at Tiger, who burped loudly and said, "Little joke. Sorry to offend."

Cody and Tiger clinked glasses, then Cody said, "Oh my friend, you need a refill." He poured from the pitcher unsteadily, spilling a large puddle onto the table. Just then Tom reappeared and snagged the pitcher from Cody. "Allow me," said Tom. "Steadiest hands putting, steadiest hands pouring."

"Steadiest hands wanking," added Tiger.

Nathalie, still bouncing along to the music, grabbed Sam's hand and started leading him to the clearing where people were dancing.

"Are you sure this is a good idea?" protested Sam.

"I'm sure we're just dancing," Nathalie replied. Tom looked like he was trying to hide his slight irritation. "Let him stew a little. It will be good for him to wonder if he's the best the bachelors have to offer."

"We shouldn't stay up here long," Sam whispered.

Nathalie spun him around so she was facing away from the tables and Tom couldn't read her lips. "You are better, you sexy little bastard. In a couple of ways." With that, she glanced down at his crotch.

At this point, Sam was afraid tempers would flare. He pushed her arms away and led her back to the table with one hand, releasing it at her original seat next to Tom.

"Well, quite a night here," Sam said, trying to sound as friendly and noncompetitive as he could. "St. Paddy's never ends. You know, maybe we should all golf together sometime. Problem is, I suck."

Sam sat back down, and Tom, rubbing Nathalie's shoulders, eyed him skeptically. She was back in Tom's territory now. Marcie was seated directly between Tiger and Cody, looking a little aloof as they drunkenly jockeyed for her attention. She would have gladly given that to Kevin, but ever the wise one, he had removed himself from the fray and was making fun of students with Steve and Terry. Let Tiger and Cody have their standoff tonight, he thought. He would later tell Sam, "Marcie is a lovely young lady. And probably too smart to go out with either of those lugheads. As for me, I've laid enough groundwork for now."

Hartford, Connecticut

In front of the restaurant 36 Lewis Street, Rick paid the valet and helped Marion into his car.

"That was lovely," she said. "Thank you. The only thing better than the food and wine was the conversation. And the anticipation." At that, she leaned over to give him a deep, sensual kiss.

"Shall we go to your place?" he said after they disengaged.

"Or yours, either is fine with me."

Rick cocked his head and moved his eyes from side to side as if weighing two equal options. "Let's do yours," he said finally. "I can stay for a while."

As he drove out of the city toward Farmington and Avon, Marion had the distinct impression that Rick had not really considered bringing her to his apartment. She put the thought aside, instead fantasizing about being wrapped up in his body. They would get there soon.

The air and the woods around Brooks House were still as Marion and Rick got out of the car and walked to the front door. Marion paused there and looked around; the surrounding roads were as quiet as the woods. They went inside, and she made sure the doors and windows were all locked. She poured them each a glass of red wine and took a seat on the sofa. He took his glass and perched on the edge of a easy chair facing her.

"It's hard to believe," she said, "that the school year will be over in what, less than a month? And that I might not be back."

Marion had filled Rick in on a few vague details about her stalker, not as completely or as graphically as she had done with Sam.

"You could always go back to living in your own off-campus apartment."

"I know."

"I think we both have unfinished personal business in our lives," she said finally. "But first things first. I have some unfinished business right here and now."

First, Marion removed her jacket and flung it over her shoulder, then she undid the buttons to her shirt from the top down. Then she stood up and pushed her chest gently, teasingly, against Rick's face.

She reached for his hands, still braced against the chair, and lifted him to a stand. She put both of her hands on his tie and began to slip it out of its knots. "There's something about a gorgeous blond man in a red silk tie," she said. "I've been wanting to jump you all night."

Soon they were in her bed, the pleasure they were sharing in the moment blocking out the uncertainty of the world outside. After the first wave subsided, for a while they rested, embracing each other and occasionally whispering sweet nicknames to each other. They rallied for a second act, and then lay there spent again; this time, Rick looked ready to leave. Marion didn't say a word as he dressed.

She gave him a long kiss at the door. "I'm serious about doing an art and architecture tour of Hartford with you, if you're free and willing," she said. Rick smiled and nodded.

In his Honda, he turned it around in the driveway to face the road. He was about to turn when he noticed a car across the road and down 25 yards or so. He was sure it wasn't there when they pulled in earlier. He thought he heard it idling and then shut off.

Rick waited to see if someone would emerge from the car, which had the nondescript blocky shape of many early '80s General Motors sedans. It could have been an Oldsmobile, a Pontiac, or a Buick.

Besides Brooks House, there was nothing in the immediate neighborhood to stop for. No one got out of the car. Rick backed several yards back into the driveway and turned off the engine. He didn't want to alarm Marion, but she was watching. She let him in quickly.

"I'll stay with you till sunup," he said. "I don't want you to be alone."

Marion pulled him close to her and tried to hide her tears. She was still wondering about his place, why he had seemed vague about letting her see it.

"Is there something you can't tell me?" she said softly.

"No questions," he said gently. "Not yet."

He pulled her tightly to him and kissed her face several times.

When Marion opened her eyes to the first light of Sunday, Rick was gone.

She turned, clutched a pillow to her chest, and went back to sleep.

Chapter 6

Marion didn't teach a class on Tuesday morning, so she tried sleeping late. But her mind began to race, and she gave up trying. She got up, stretched, and took a quick shower. The water cascading on her body made her feel calm and sensuous, and made her think of Rick's touch on her skin just a couple of nights earlier. She turned off the shower and squeezed her towel around her chest for a few moments, then finished drying off and began considering what to wear.

She wasn't sure of Sam's Tuesday schedule, and thought about calling him for coffee. She had new things she wanted to share with him.

Suddenly, Marion's calm feeling was overtaken by panic. From her window, she saw a long black sedan pull into her driveway. Startled, but collected enough to realize she was standing there naked, she quickly threw on a sweater and jeans.

The doorbell rang. She looked through the eyehole and saw a short, plump white women in her 40s, frizzy brown-grey hair tied behind her, and a tall, thin black man in a suit, of indeterminate age, whose steely, intimidating presence was cemented by his dark wraparound shades. They both carried briefcases.

Marion opened the door, and the woman spoke. "Sybil Bouchard, Internal Revenue Service, Hartford office. Are you Marion Maloney?"

"Yes, how can I help you?"

Sybil continued. "And this is Anson Fritz, head of our Hartford collections unit." At that, they both held up badges.

"Do you have a few minutes you can spare going over your case with us?" Sybil asked. "I see you have a table there. We can try to keep this as short and to the point as possible."

Marion opened the door wider and motioned for them to sit. Startled and upset by their unannounced visit, she did not offer them anything to drink.

"So to be clear," Sybil began, pulling a paper-stuffed manila folder out of her briefcase, "Miller Maloney Sloane Investment Partners was primarily made up of the three founding partners, with no other significant stakeholders or high-level employees, right?"

"I guess, yeah," Marion said.

"Any other employees at all?"

"As I recall, at first there was a small office staff, receptionist, secretaries, that kind of thing ... I think Marshall and Mark each had their own secretary."

"And who did the books?"

Marion sighed heavily. "Look, as I have explained before, I had a minor in accounting, and a friend of Marshall's offered us a pretty user-friendly plug-in software. So I set it up. That's basically all I did. I never actually worked in the office. If they had questions about the software, I did the best I could. But I never handled any investments or data entries after the set-up. That was Mark and Marshall exclusively."

"And you didn't notice how they were making these illegal transfers?"

"No, ma'am. You'd have to ask them."

"Them? Well ... " Sybil began.

"OK, then you'd have to ask Mark."

"Speaking of which," Marion continued, "Are you going after Marshall's wife too?"

Sybil sighed. "I understand your frustration, Ms. Maloney. But it doesn't work that way. For one thing, she apparently had nothing at all to do with the company. And after his suicide, we aren't allowed to collect from next of kin."

"And Mark? Have you found him? Is he working? I don't even know," Marion said, throwing her face onto the table and trying to stifle a sob. "This is so unfair."

"So far," Sybil said softly, "We have not. He's elusive."

Anson Fritz, extending a clipboard with a single sheet of paper attached to it, spoke for the first time, in a deep, gravelly voice. Marion lifted her face.

"We'd like to suggest the following schedule of payments. A down payment followed by 15 monthly payments until the debt is cleared up. Interest will continue to accrue, but we're willing to suspend penalties if you keep to this schedule. Don't forget, we have the option of levying your bank accounts."

As they left, Anson Fritz motioned that Marion should keep the clipboard with the payment schedule. Both of their business cards were tucked into the clip.

She watched them pull away in their Lincoln Town Car with government plates. Tears streamed down her face, but at the same time, a resolve grew within her—a resolve that somehow she would fight this injustice however she could.

Marion walked over to her phone to call Sam, but got his answering machine. He was probably in class. Rather than leave him a message, she figured she'd see him later.

On her way to her 1:30 class, Marion did see Sam striding toward her. "Hey," he said, "we never did compare notes on the weekend." They embraced; both the length and intensity of Marion's hug suggested to Sam that she was not OK.

"Lots to tell you," Marion said when they unhooked. "I'm done by 4:30 or so; you free for a chat?"

"Should be." Sensing that Marion needed a caring shoulder, he decided to ask Joe to run the last half of baseball practice.

"Any advice on questions for *The Great Gatsby*? She asked.

"Hmmm," he said. "Ask them how many of them see their parents in the book—nah, just kidding. Ask them if it's ethical to make your fortune in an illegal business like bootlegging."

Marion smiled and walked away. Sam had no idea how close to home his offhand remark had landed.

"By now everyone has finished *The Great Gatsby*, right?" Marion asked her class.

The response was an unenthusiastic jumble of "yeahs" and indecipherable grunts.

This is considered one of the great American novels," Marion said. "Is that the best you can do in the way of enthusiasm?"

Jeff Banks finally spoke up. "Ms. Maloney, we might be more interested if there was more sex and murder. You know, like in *Miami Vice*."

Marion smiled and walked over to Banks' desk, holding a copy of the book above her head. Waving it now in front of Banks' face, she said, "Are you sure you read this?"

Well …" Banks stumbled. "Um … yeah, of course! Front to back and top to bottom!"

"And did you not catch any of the sex and murder in *The Great Gatsby*?"

"Um … sure …" Banks continued to fumble. "Didn't they have big sex orgies at Gatsby's house or something like that?"

"Nice try, dummo," said Charlie Morton. "I think all you know about *Gatsby* is that there were lavish parties at his mansion. All the Long Island socialites would arrive on Friday and party like it was … well, 1922. It was Prohibition, but Gatsby was a bootlegger, and he had booze. One can assume there was sex."

"That's exactly what I said, Charlie Choo-Choo," replied Jeff. "Big sex orgies at Gatsby's house. What more do you need?"

"Well," suggested Chet Hennessey, "you could describe the origes in more graphic detail—"

"Wait, wait, that's absurd," Charlie cut in, "and that's not Fitzgerald's style. He was way more subtle than that. He didn't always spell it out for you. You had to read between the lines."

"Not necessarily when it came to the main characters," offered Alex Van Owen. "We know Tom Buchanan was banging Myrtle Wilson. And Jay Gatsby was banging Daisy Buchanan. Nick Carraway and Jordan Baker? Hard to say. Besides, he might have been gay."

"Or bisexual," chimed in Ms. Maloney. "And while I do appreciate your … ahem … depictions of their sexual behavior, I'd also like to discuss some of the novel's other themes, like the growing sense of alienation some characters felt toward the decadence of the Jazz Age lifestyle, including Gatsby himself. In fact, why did he even host these parties, when he didn't really seem to enjoy them?"

"He just wanted Daisy back," offered Charlie Morton.

"And then there are class issues, and geographic ones too—like Midwesterners feeling ill at ease in Eastern society. Fitzgerald himself was from a modest family background in Minnesota. His parents weren't poor, but when he went to Princeton and fell in love with a wealthy socialite, her parents told him poor boys should not marry rich girls. So he might as well have been poor, as far as his romantic prospects were concerned. And he carried that resentment with him."

"I think you can see a little of that in Gatsby," Charlie said. "Making as much money as he could in a shady business and then acting like the king of Long Island to impress Daisy."

"As for murder, what do you make of the death of Myrtle Wilson?" Marion asked. "Accidental or deliberate?

"That depends who was driving," said Alex Van Owen.

"Wasn't Gatsby driving?" said Ted Swanstrom.

"No, he took the fall for Daisy," corrected Charlie Morton. "And if she was driving, maybe she decided to run down the woman who was having an affair with her husband."

"Ah, that would be murder, then!" exclaimed Marion with an undercurrent of excitement. "What do you think, Banks, is that *Miami Vice* enough for you? And was that the only murder?"

Banks shrugged his shoulders.

"Of course not," cut in Charlie. "George Wilson thought Gatsby ran down his wife and that he was having an affair with her. So he went to Gatsby's house and shot him, then turned the gun on himself."

"OK, well, interesting discussion today," Marion said. "Time's up. Quiz on the book tomorrow—everyone hear that? Banks, do you need to borrow a copy?"

"Nah," he said. "Mine's in my room somewhere, probably buried under my lacrosse equipment. I'll find it. Maybe Charlie can help me go over it in study hall tonight. Charlie?"

"You know my fee."

At 4:45, Marion knocked on Sam's door.

"Come on in. Coffee? Tea? Me?" Sam asked before his straight face gave way to a silly laugh.

"Oh stop it, you silly man," she said. "Silly Sexy Question Man. That's it. That's your name. And you know in another time or place you'd have to watch out for me, you know, robbing your cradle."

"Ha, that's funny," he said. "I'm 26. Old enough to date a woman who's—what are you, 32?" Sam knew Marion was a couple of years older than that, but went for the cheap compliment anyway. "Now on the other end, how far down can I go? What is it they say—half your age plus seven? So that's 13 plus seven is 20. Damn."

"Damn what," she asked. "Damn you still can't fuck that Walker's girl?"

Sam grabbed a throw pillow and threw it at Marion's face.

"What makes you think I was thinking about her?" he asked.

Marion chuckled. "Oh, just a hunch."

Marion picked up the throw pillow and tossed it back at Sam.

"Coffee," she said.

"Coffee?" Sam asked, puzzled.

"You know, before you started making all this flirty sex talk, you were going to offer me something to drink."

"Oh, damn, sorry, I'll start a pot right now. Actually, yes, I was just thinking about Maggie. She's 19. Perfectly legal, by the way. Freshman at Georgetown. I haven't seen her in almost a year, so I think we can cross that one off."

"Oh really," said Marion dismissively.

"What do you mean 'Oh really'?"

"You haven't crossed her off."

"Whatever you say. Well then," Sam continued. "Tell me about your hot date!"

Marion smiled. "It was hot," she said. "But it was also really nice. We dressed up a little. He brought me flowers. We drove into Hartford and talked about architecture, and theater, and ballet, and poetry. And sometimes we just talked about silly stuff. And we had a really nice dinner at 36 Lewis Street. We drove around a little more, and then we went back to my place for the fireworks."

"The fireworks?"

She smiled at him.

"Don't make me explain all over again."

"Oh, ha, that's right," Sam laughed. "The fireworks that set your bed up in flames. You're making me jealous again!"

"Well, it seems to me that if you're looking for a little fire-cracker action yourself, all you have to do is say *la formule magique* and sexual bliss will be at your doorstep."

"Speaking of which, I haven't told you about our so-called bachelors' night out at O'Laughlin's the other night."

For no apparent reason, Marion broke into a fit of laughter.

"What's so funny?" Sam said.

"Oh, nothing really," she said, sucking in her giggles. "It just hit me funny all of a sudden, picturing her, appearing out of the blue, banging on your door, her little French mouth twisted into a pout, pleading with you to fuck her."

"Banging on my door, pleading with me to bang her," Sam reworded, as they both chortled involuntarily.

"Let's see," Marion said through giggles. "Knocking on your door—"

"Pounding on my door—"

"Oh, that's good," Marion laughed, as they both carried on like teenagers with a case of the sillies.

Sam composed himself finally, and poured them each a cup of coffee. "Cream? Sugar?"

"Cream, please."

"I know, you're sweet enough already—"

Marion exaggerated a groan. "I wasn't going to say anything—"

"You were thinking it."

"Tell me about bachelors' night."

"Perfectly ordinary night out—me, Joe Grisman, Steve Morrow, Kevin Doolan. And plenty of pints. O'Laughlin's was busy and loud—there was an Irish band—but it was manageably busy. We were having a good time joking about our favorite wiseass students, and about the headmaster's skill at bedding students' mothers."

"Ah, yes, Mister Mommy's Little Humper. Except he's not little. I'll work on that nickname."

"But then the party grew."

"Hmmm," Marion said, eyes twinkling, "Did you invite some ladies to the table?"

"Ha, don't you wish. No, some more Avon bachelors showed up. And one bachelorette."

"Ha, I knew it. Now you have a stalker too! That is, if you mean who I think you mean."

"Well, she is rumored to be sleeping with Tom Dickleman. He was part of their party, in fact I'd say he was the ringleader. Terry McSweeney and Mark Lehrer were there from Avon, you must know them, right? Nice guys."

"Yes," Marion said. She seemed curious but was suddenly less vocal.

"And there were a few others. Two of Tom's friends from town, Cody Savard and Dave Williams. I guess Dave went to Avon and graduated with Tom. They call him "Tiger," but if Kevin is to be believed that's only because there is an NHL player who also goes by Dave "Tiger" Williams."

"Well, is he ferocious?" Marion chuckled.

"I don't know about ferocious, but he is big and tall. I got kind of an odd vibe from him. Oh, and he and Cody got a little weird when—oh, sorry, I'm telling the story out of order.

There was another young woman in their group. A friend of Nathalie's from college. Marcie something-or-other."

"Was she pretty? Don' tell me you started flirting with her."

"No, but Kevin did. And when Cody and Tiger came back from darts they got funny about it. Rearranged their chairs. In fact, I'd say it was almost a classic cockblock."

"Oh, sounds interesting!" Marion exclaimed. "I almost wish I was there—but not really. I prefer the company I was keeping. Anyway, what did Kevin do then?"

"He just smiled and turned back to our table. Kevin stays above that kind of bullshit. Besides, I think Marcie liked him the best, and he knew it. He'll figure out later how to find her if he's interested."

"So ..." Marion began. "That's not the whole story of your night out, is it."

"Well ... There was one more thing."

"Do tell."

"Tom was up dancing with Nathalie. Then he came back to the table, but she wanted to keep dancing. So she grabbed my hand."

"And Tom?"

"I think he was too busy knocking back pints at first to notice. When he did, he looked a little miffed, but he kept himself under control."

"And did she keep her control? You never know what a sex-crazy French woman is going to do."

"Yes, but she managed to position our bodies on the dance floor so Tom couldn't see what she was saying. Then she told me I was better. In a couple of ways. I'm not bragging. That's just what she said."

"In a couple of ways ... hmmm. Did she get any more specific than that?"

"Well, right after she said it, she made a point of looking down at my crotch."

"Oh, well, good for you then!" Marion was about to say something else, but a curious look crossed her face, and she stopped. Just then, she glanced at her watch.

"Oh, I'm sorry," she said. "It's getting a little later than I thought. If you still want to slip into the refectory before they stop serving—"

"I'd actually rather not," he said. "I'm already thinking of a Plan B."

Marion was one step ahead of him.

"I've got an idea," she said. "I hope you don't think it's too forward. I'm not making a move on you—unless it bothers you that I now consider you my best friend!"

"Not at all!" he said. "The feeling is mutual."

They both stood up and embraced. "Friends always," Sam said. "What's your idea—sending out for pizza and beer?"

"Close!" she said. "Wine for me ... I'm having such a good time talking to you, and I feel so much better than when I got here. But I still have a couple of things to tell you."

They ordered pizza for pickup, and drove out together in Sam's Capri to get the pizza, booze, bottled water and snacks. On the way back, Marion wanted to run into her apartment. She came out with a small bag, and a much larger one with a comforter stuffed into it. "I'm sleeping on your couch tonight," she announced. "Don't ask or question—I'll just feel better. And safer."

"Oh, anytime you want," Sam said. "I'll set you up with some earplugs in case I happen to be humping a sex-crazed French babe."

"Oh, but I'd want to listen!" Marion said before bursting into laughter.

They spread out the food on Sam's coffee table and talked about casual topics, like faculty and students, and the fact that neither of them had made concrete plans for the summer.

Then Marion told him about the IRS visit from that morning, and how her ex-husband had left her exposed to tax obligations after Mark and his friend had used their start-up company to swindle investors out of money. She explained that after the friend committed suicide and Mark began to dodge authorities, the IRS decided to take the easy way out and come after her for the money, in spite of her protests that she had little to do with running the company.

"That's so not fair," Sam said. "You need a good lawyer."

"Working on it," she said.

Then she talked about her date with Rick again, and how it ended on a somewhat disquieting note—how he was about to leave Brooks House when he was freaked out by a parked car just down the road that might have been idling before he started his own car.

"Did he see what make?" Sam asked.

"It was dark. He just said it looked like one of those non-descript GM sedans. Could have been a Pontiac, a Chevy, a Buick ..."

"Then what?"

"If it was idling, it stopped. Just sat there. No one got in or out. Finally, Rick turned his car off and came back in, told me he'd stay with me till sunup."

"Hmmm ... So he was never planning to spend the whole night with you and lie around making pillow talk on Sunday morning."

"And it's pretty clear now that he doesn't want me to see his place. I was going to say 'apartment,' but I don't even know if it's an apartment or a house. He hasn't talked about it."

"Did you ask him about it?"

"I asked him if there was something he couldn't tell me. He said, 'No questions. Not yet.'"

"Hmmm," said Sam. "Well, he's hiding something. We just don't know what."

Marion sipped from her wine and brushed away a tear.

"Jeez, Marion, you've had a long couple of days. I'm so sorry all of this is coming down on you. I'm here for you. We can talk all night, or go to bed now or whenever."

She paused, then spoke. "Tell me what high school was like. Do any of these rich kids remind you of you?"

They talked for a while and drank more wine. Then Sam made sure the door was locked and gave Marion his extra pillow. He squeezed her hand and kissed her cheek. "Night," he said.

Somewhere in the night, Sam had a vivid dream, and woke with a start. Disoriented, he stood up, then remembered that

Marion was on his couch. He walked over to her softly. She appeared to be sleeping peacefully.

Climbing back into bed, Sam remembered the last part of the dream. It was more a sensation than a scene. A feeling of motion. The sound of steel wheels. No fields of wheat this time. Just darkness. And he thought he remembered one other sound—a long, lonesome whistle.

Chapter 7

The final spring edition of the newspaper was coming along nicely; everyone agreed they should be able to put it to bed in one more week. At 6 pm on a late-April Wednesday, the students began to file out as Max Grimsby carefully put away the typesetting equipment. Sam told Joe he'd catch up with him at the refectory.

Nathalie Frelet lingered at the press table, pretending to look over some story drafts. Max shot Sam a knowing look and said, "Don't forget to lock up."

Max and Sam both had keys to the room. Max didn't care what else happened as long as Sam locked it afterward.

Nathalie took Sam's hand and led him to a desk in a windowless corner of the room. "I've been so hot for you ever since Saturday at the bar," she whispered. "But Tom has been very suspicious. I have to be careful."

"And I haven't got much time," Sam said. "I'm supposed to meet Joe over at—"

"Then don't waste it all on chit-chat," she said, slipping off her skirt and panties and sitting on the edge of the desk. "I'm ready for you now. No foreplay necessary. I just want a few minutes."

Nathalie undid his zipper, freed his erection, and pulled him into her.

"And then maybe a few more minutes after that," she whispered, as they both began breathing heavily with the heightened excitement of the sudden encounter. She leaned into him, first kissing his face, eyes, and earlobes, then pressing her lips into his. Sam groaned with pleasure and marveled at the skill with which she swept him under her spell. He held the small of her back with one hand, and reached under her sweater to massage her breasts with the other. Even though he didn't have much time, his instinct was to pace himself, but she didn't let him. Before he knew it, they were clutching each other and catching their breath as if they had just run a race.

"I don't mind quickies at all," she exhaled, pulling up her panties and skirt. "Slow and sensual is nice. Fast and furious is nice too. It's a different kind of high."

"I don't know what to do with you," Sam said. "Please let's be careful about this."

"I'll see you soon," she said, smiling at him. I'll slip out quietly. Give me a minute before you lock up."

On Thursday, during a break between her classes, Marion Maloney parked at her usual West Hartford branch of Liberty Bank, pushed open one of the heavy glass doors, and stepped inside. She walked over to a service desk and removed a withdrawal slip from one of the slots. She filled out her account information, then hovered over the slip for a few moments, thinking. Finally, she decided on $600, and filled that in.

The teller, a woman in her 20s, recognized Marion and smiled. She asked if there was any specific way she wanted the cash; Marion pondered for a moment, then said, "Oh, I guess all twenties."

That left $515.20 in Marion's checking account. Later that afternoon, at a different branch, she withdrew $500 from the ATM.

At her Webster Bank branch, Marion was more nervous. In the parking lot, she took a deep breath and looked around, as if Sybil Bouchard and Anson Fritz might be lurking in the shadows, ready to intervene if she tried to withdraw her money. Bouchard had been as nice as she could expect an IRS agent to be, but there was something about Fritz's steely demeanor and his masking his eyes with sunglasses that unnerved her.

Marion had a little over $2,500 in her savings account. She knew there was a $500 limit per day on ATM withdrawals, and planned to remove that amount at another branch. But she was leery of making too large a withdrawal here, lest someone become suspicious.

"What the fuck," she muttered to herself. "It's my money."

At the service desk, she hesitated, then filled out a slip for $1,250 and presented it to the teller. He looked at the slip, stood up, and without a word, walked it into an office occupied by a woman dressed in a navy business suit, and closed the door behind him. Marion's heart pounded.

A few minutes later, the teller reemerged. Anything over $1,000, we have to get approval, he explained. He processed the withdrawal, and before she knew what was happening, his cash dispenser was spitting out 25 crisp fifty dollar bills. He tucked them into a paper sleeve and handed it to her.

"Anything else I can do for you today?" he asked pleasantly.

"No, we're good," she said.

After visiting a Webster ATM about six blocks away, Marion now had $2,850 cash on her person. She put some in her purse, hid some in the glove compartment, and left $500 in fifties inside the paper sleeve, which she hid under the rear passenger-side floor mat.

By 1:30, she was back in her classroom, handing back graded quizzes on *The Great Gatsby*.

"All quiet on campus this year?" Jerry Spellmeyer asked Sam as he dug into the Asian stir-fry Jerry and his wife Jacqueline had prepared for dinner. "No missing Walker's girls for George to fret about?"

"Oh, Jerry, you didn't have to bring that up," scolded Jackie. "I'm sure Sam has moved well beyond that by now."

"Oh, I'm sorry if I stepped over the line," Jerry quickly apologized. "You have to understand, living with a detective for 30 years, the old cases have their way of popping up in conversation again and again."

Almost two years earlier, Jackie—a retired West Hartford police detective—had been hired by the parents of an Ethel Walker School student named Mallory Harding when she disappeared during May of her junior year. The leading suspect was her boyfriend, Tomas Arpante, an Avon Old Farms day student and a promising baseball prospect who was now attending the University of Connecticut on scholarship.

Tomas was the obvious person of interest, but once Jackie was on the case, she all but ruled him out as a perpetrator because when she interviewed him, he not only seemed as perplexed as everyone else about Mallory's disappearance, he also showed no outward or even subtle sign of being nervous. Jerry loved talking about all the times his wife saw past the obvious and noticed things other investigators did not.

Because Sam had developed a close friendship with a student on his hall named Warren Cochran, and because Warren's girlfriend Annie and her best friend Maggie had been Mallory's closest girlfriends at Walker's, Sam suddenly found himself drawn into the case and patched in to Mallory's inner circle. Once Jackie realized this, she invited Sam to help, and they solved the case together. The fact that Sam and Maggie developed a romantic infatuation with each other threatened his professional reputation but also helped him unlock important clues.

In the year and several months since the case was solved, Sam and the Spellmeyers had met occasionally for dinner. And with Jackie aware that young, unmarried Avon teachers often move on after a couple of years, she had made a point of inviting him over before the school year ended.

"Yeah, it's been a pretty quiet year in many ways," Sam answered Jerry, letting him know that he wasn't offended by the question. "And it's weird how long ago and far away Mallory's case seems now, especially the way it consumed me for a couple of months. I just hope their family has found some peace by now. Jackie, do you still talk to them?"

"Less and less. I think we're down to a Christmas-card relationship by now. And even that's not likely to last. When the outcome isn't a happy one, most clients don't feel compelled to be reminded of it that way."

"And how about you?" Jackie asked. "Warren's still a senior, right?"

"Yeah, I see him around campus. It's different with Annie off at college in Boston. I know he's trying to hold that together, but I'm sure it's tough. I try not to ask about it."

"What about Maggie?" Jackie asked. "You two seemed to hit it off pretty well."

"Yeah," he smiled. "We became pretty good friends. I'm sure there are people who thought it was more than that. But we kept our heads. At the end of the year, we talked about staying in touch and getting together sometime. The longer we go without that happening, the less likely it will ever happen. At that age, you don't know where the road will take you next. I guess that's still true for me."

Sam knew Jackie had been aware of the attraction between him and Maggie, and he wanted to leave the impression that it never crossed the line—which wasn't quite true. What Sam still didn't fully appreciate was how years of detective work had left Jackie extraordinarily nonjudgmental when it came to people's quirks, flaws, questionable habits, and bad decisions. If she wouldn't tell you, Jerry would be happy to. "She's seen it all, and none of it bothers or offends her," he liked to say. "She understands that people go through a lot of different interior struggles, and they won't stay in the neat little boxes we make for them."

Jerry asked Sam how his sports seasons had gone. "Hey, you coached thirds hockey, right? Did you get to see the varsity play? I hear that Leetch kid is really good. Maybe the Whalers can get him."

"Yeah, there's quite a buzz about him. We'll see."

"Oh," Sam added, "I hear Tomas will be playing another year of Cape Cod League, in Brewster, I think. Did you guys get out to see him last summer?"

"Yes," Jerry said. "It was fun." He winked at Jackie. "I think my wife really enjoyed watching him play after proving him innocent."

"Well, I'm going to try to get out there this August," Sam said. "So I'll definitely call you. I'd love to see a game with you guys."

As Sam was leaving, he turned to Jackie. "Retired for good this time?" he said, smiling broadly.

"Oh, you know it," she said. "Retired life is the best. It would take—no, never mind that. It would take hell freezing over. I'm happy gardening and cooking and golfing."

Jerry just smiled.

Marion made sure no one had followed her to Brooks House, and carefully removed all of the cash from her Mazda, stuffing it into her purse. Once inside, she distributed it among several inconspicuous locations. Feeling restless, and having no other plans, she decided to head out to the Kettle & Cork.

She took her favorite seat at the end of the bar, ordered a glass of white wine, and asked for a menu. She thought about her chance meeting here with Rick, when she had brought a copy of Kundera's *The Unbearable Lightness of Being*; how she had managed to finish that book, with so much going on in her life, she wasn't sure. But she had, and so tonight she had brought a different book, *Prelude & Other Stories* by Katherine Mansfield.

Marion ordered two appetizers and a second glass of wine. She was enjoying the book and was mostly engrossed in it; only a couple of times did she insert the bookmark and set it down to have a look around the room. The crowd was modest, mostly couples and small groups. She was relieved that no men approached her.

Knowing Rick had patronized the restaurant before, she scanned the room to make sure he wasn't on the premises. She half wondered if he'd walk in with another girlfriend, or even a wife, and then told herself to stop. He had made a decision not to tell her everything about himself; that was his choice. There was no point in her allowing herself to concoct wild theories about what he was hiding. She had already resigned herself to the possibility that the relationship might prove fleeting. Their two encounters had been sexy and fun, and had restored in her a measure of self-confidence. But previous experiences, especially her marriage, had taught her to be practical.

Marion had enjoyed her quiet evening alone; the downside was that she now hated returning to Brooks House in the dark. *Only a few more weeks*, she told herself. She half wished she could just move in with Sam for the remainder of the year.

As she drove past the school entrance and rounded the corner into her driveway, she saw no cars or anything else suspicious. She quickly went inside and locked the door behind her, including the deadbolt.

"Damn it," she said out loud when she realized she had left the Mansfield book in her car. But she quickly decided to leave it there and take no unnecessary chances.

She turned on her television. Nothing interested her, but the fact that *Night Court* was ending meant *Hill Street Blues* was about to start, and she decided that would take her mind off her fears until she was ready to sleep.

Twenty minutes in, Marion was engrossed in the episode, until a sudden series of loud knocks on her front door made her shriek and jump up off of her couch. Heart pounding wildly, Marion didn't know what to do next, but then the knocking began again, sounding even more insistent than the first time.

She considered calling the police.

Finally, she screamed out, "Who are you, and what do you want?"

After a pause, she heard a voice that was neither loud nor soft, as if calculated to be easily heard without the drama of too much volume. The voice sounded male, but slightly muffled, as if spoken through a mask.

"I have something to show you."

"But who are you?" Marion screamed again. She was on the verge of tears—angry tears. Her adrenaline was pumping.

"Calm down, and come on over to the door, and just let me show you something."

Marion tiptoed closer to the door, but had no intention of opening it. She managed to calm down just enough to speak without screaming.

"You haven't said who you are. So I am not opening the door. And if you don't leave, I will call the police."

"You haven't asked me what I want to show you."

"I don't think I want to know." Marion was speaking through sobs now. "Please just go away."

"Well, how about if I just go over here?"

Marion didn't understand what he was talking about.

"Over where?" she sobbed.

"Over here," he said, and now Marion understood where his voice was coming from—about 10 yards from her door, at a window that was locked, but unfortunately, not completely covered by the blinds. And in the space the blinds left open to the outside, pressed up against the window, was what he wanted to show her.

It was a long, thick, veiny, blood-engorged penis, very much like the one in the photo that someone had dropped off for her. With most of the dozen or so sexual partners in her life to this point, Marion had thought the male equipment was lovely to behold. Not this one. She thought it looked ugly and scary. And huge—too huge.

Apparently, that was a selling point.

"I bet that man of yours can't come close to this," the strange, muffled, but eerily suave voice continued. "Just think of the pleasure I can give you—all those deep places lesser men can't reach."

"Get out of here now," Marion screamed. "That's it—I'm calling the police."

She ran to her phone and began dialing. Then she heard him run from the window and down toward the road. At that point she was sure he heard his footsteps running along the road, to her right, their clomping sound growing fainter until she heard a car door open and close. Almost immediately, the engine revved and rubber tires screeched along the asphalt until the noise was gone.

Marion put down the phone without completing the call. She retreated to her couch and turned off the TV. She got back up and closed all the blinds and turned off all the lights and returned to her couch and just sat there, taking in the stillness of the Brooks House property, the deafening silence you could hear there almost any night, unbroken by stalkers, interrupted only by the occasional wild animal.

A half-hour passed. It was 11. Marion got up and stuffed a few things in a bag. She thought about the cash and decided that since no one knew about it, it would be safe here until she could return in the light of day. She dialed Sam.

"You up?" she asked.

"Yeah. You OK?"

"No."

"You need to talk?"

"I need to get out of here right now."

"Come on over."

Marion unlocked and opened her front door and peered around it. The outside light was on. There was no sound or sign of activity. She locked the door behind her. Her heart raced as she made a dash for the car, clutching her bag. She fumbled with the key trying to insert it into the lock. "Damn," she breathed.

She got the key in, opened the door, threw her bag on the passenger seat, slid inside, and quickly closed and locked the door. But once again, she struggled to slide the key into the ignition. "What the fuck," she sobbed as tears began to stream down her cheeks.

Finally, she got the key in and started the engine. She carefully eased onto the road, then accelerated onto Old Farms Road and into the parking lot nearest Sam's apartment.

Sam let Marion in, and she immediately threw her arms around him and pressed him tightly to her. She buried her face in his chest and sobbed. They stood there a few minutes without speaking. Sam rubbed her back. Finally, he led her to the couch, where they sat, close enough that she could lean her head on his shoulder.

"This is not who I am," she said. "I am not a mess all the time. I pride myself on being a together person. What's happening to me is so unfair."

"Something happened tonight, can you tell me?" Sam asked, reassuringly.

She told him the whole story.

"But you didn't end up calling the police."

"No. I have my reasons. I probably should have, but I really didn't want to deal with that too. It's almost like punishment on top of punishment."

"I think I understand what you mean."

"Can I lie in bed with you? Just to feel safe. No agenda. Sex is the furthest thing from my mind right now anyway."

"Of course."

They lay in each other's arms, soothed by each other's breathing and body warmth. As their breaths grew slower and softer, sleep came easily. Sam's mind wandered in and out of consciousness.

Later, when he thought about it, he couldn't place when Marion's gently diminishing breathing morphed into the sound of steel wheels slowing down and gradually coming to rest at what he felt certain was the platform of a train station.

Chapter 8

If I die on the Russian front …

Late Friday afternoon, two Avon Old Farms vans rolled southward out of Massachusetts on Route 7 and into the hills and dales of northwestern Connecticut. The boys were in good spirits after an 8-2 drubbing of the Berkshire School, and were singing crude songs that Sam, driving one of the vans, tried not to listen to. When he did recognize a line from a song he had sung on his own high school sports buses a mere nine or ten years earlier, it made him wince.

With a week and a half left in the season, and a string of wins and consistent solid play behind them, the boys of the Avon thirds baseball team had already been told by Sam and Joe that they could take Saturday morning off and sleep in. What they weren't told was that Sam and Joe knew that they too would want—and perhaps need—to sleep in.

With Sam, Joe and Steve all on duty the following weekend, this was pretty much their last chance of the year for a big night out in downtown Hartford.

Kevin enjoyed a pint as much as the next guy, but happily offered to take it easy and be the driver. The oldest of the group at 30, he still enjoyed the scene (and the flirtations with interesting women), but did not feel any urge to get drunk, and was good at pacing himself—which also meant he could still hold a conversation later in the evening when many of his "competitors" had become a little slurry.

Sam, Joe and Steve piled into Kevin's Chevy Impala and headed for Hartford, where the first stop was Brown, Thomson & Company, the former department store turned multilevel upscale restaurant and bar. The ground floor, where the bachelors assembled on barstools along an L-shaped, wall-mounted, mahogany-stained bar, was both busy with customers and strangely subdued, as if everyone was trying to keep their conversations to themselves. There was a main bar surrounded with seats, as well as a network of wall-mounted bars and a smattering of tables, mostly two- and four-tops. The conspicuous but carefully spaced leafy plants reminded Sam of his hometown's popular "fern bar," Fitzwilly's of Northampton, Massachusetts.

The initial conversations covered the usual banter about students and eccentric faculty—"Joe Kraft *and* Henry Hitchcock are retiring? That will reduce the median faculty age by 20 years," joked Kevin. The new topic of interest was that Sam seemed suddenly very friendly with Marion Maloney; he quickly assured them it was strictly platonic, and they had a lot of interests in common.

"Oh, I see," cracked Joe, "so you *both* like sixty-nine. Sometimes only one partner actually likes—"

"We're in the most sophisticated bar in Hartford, and your head still managed to find the gutter," Sam retorted to Joe, a smile creeping around the corners of his lips. "But no, we're strictly friends, which is kind of nice. And she's been seeing a guy from West Hartford."

Of the group, only Joe had an inkling that Sam had something going on the side with Nathalie Frelet, and he wisely laid off of it, as she was apparently now officially the headmaster's son's girlfriend.

Knowing they probably wouldn't eat again until the obligatory breakfast on the way home, the men loaded up on the appetizers that were the restaurant's specialty: sauteed shrimp, fried zucchini, loaded potato skins. They drank pints and surveyed the room, noticing two women in casual business attire seated almost across from them, balancing brightly colored cocktails in large bowl-shaped glasses and stealing occasional glances at the Avon men.

Kevin broke the ice. "You work downtown?"

The woman with the pink drink seemed the more chatty of the two; she smiled and said "Yes, what was your first clue?" She chuckled, then continued: "Betsy here works for the Hartford. You know, insurance. I'm in ad sales for the *Hartford Courant.*"

"Oh, then you must know Simon Savard," Sam blurted out, overestimating the likelihood the connection would mean much to her.

"Oh, he's pretty high up, isn't he?" she said. "Editor? I'm just a lowly salesperson. I'm Amanda, by the way. How do you know him?"

Sam really did not want to go into the Mallory Harding case from a year and a half earlier, which would have explained how he met Simon. So he took an easier way out: "He's friends with my boss."

"Uh-huh," Amanda said. "And your boss is? We were trying to figure out what you guys do. We came up with three possibilities: journalists, arts administrators, or schoolteachers."

"You don't look like salespeople or insurance executives," added Betsy, holding a reddish orange drink. "And whatever you do, you must have names—"

"Sorry," Sam interjected. "I'm Sam, and this is Kevin, Joe, and Steve. Good guess—we all teach at Avon Old Farms School."

"Oh really," Betsy said. "What do you teach?"

The men quickly rattled off their subjects, but Amanda looked puzzled.

"What's Avon Old Farms? I've never heard of it. Is it an agricultural school?"

Betsy looked at her friend almost scornfully. "I can't believe you've never heard of Avon Old Farms. It's a very well-known boarding school, and it's only about 10 miles from here. There are lots of boarding schools in Connecticut—Choate, Hotchkiss, Loomis Chafee, to name a few. And the all-girls schools—Miss Porter's, Ethel Walker. I actually graduated from Walker's, but that was like eight years ago."

Sam flinched and immediately decided the Harding case did not belong in the conversation agenda for any number of reasons.

"Well," Amanda said defensively, "I grew up in Michigan, so I wouldn't know any of these schools."

"How did you get to Hartford" Kevin asked.

"College," she said. "Trinity. That's where I met Betsy. Now that you mention it, I recall that she mentioned Ethel Walker. Those schools sounded a little quaint to me, like out of a Victorian novel or something, and I didn't give them too much thought."

Sam came to Amanda's defense. "Growing up, I hadn't heard of most of these boarding schools either, until I went to college, and suddenly every other person was from one."

"Must have been a good private school," Betsy said. "Where did you go—Wesleyan?"

"Nah," Sam said. "Princeton."

"Oh, well, impressive," said Amanda. "Did you know Brooke Shields?"

"What?" Sam said, showing more irritation than he meant to. "Do you know what year it is? Brooke Shields is there now. I graduated in 1980."

"Sorry," he added quickly, "I didn't mean to offend you." Sam looked around at his friends, hoping someone could step in and stop the conversation from getting more awkward than it already was.

Kevin came to the rescue, asking questions that focused attention on the women and their lives, and their jobs, and what they thought about living in Hartford. They appreciated that he seemed interested in what they had to say, but the drinks and the conversation were starting to wind down. Steve mentioned that the men would be going next to the Russian Lady, but the women said nothing committal, and before long, they all were exchanging pleasant goodbyes.

If Brown, Thomson had seemed subdued, the Russian Lady was anything but. As soon as they had their IDs approved and entered the main dance floor, the music and beats washed over the room and left patrons to either shout at each other or wait for breaks between songs, which the DJ generally avoided unless he wanted to make an announcement.

She wants to lead a glamorous life, she don't need a man's touch. She wants to lead the glamorous life. Without love, it ain't much ...

The men ordered pints at one of several bars in the multiple-floor establishment. Steve and Joe went to another floor to see if they could shoot pool without too long of a wait. Kevin and Sam made a brief attempt at chatting, then Sam said, "I'll be back," and went off on a solo excursion to take in the vibe of the bar and try to get a read on the crowd.

Sam found another bar and leaned back against it, savoring the electricity of the crowd and the music. His first pint had gone down easily, and he ordered another. A woman standing next to him, talking with a girlfriend, turned away from the friend, smiled at Sam, and asked "You here by yourself?"

Sam looked at her and smiled back. She was cute, if a little overly dolled up. "Nah," he said. "I'm here with a few friends. I just don't know where they are! You?"

"I'm here with friends too," she said. "Maybe I'll catch you on the dance floor."

She and her friend got up to dance; Sam continued to scan the crowd in between generous swigs of beer.

Loving would be easy if your colors were like my dreams, red gold and green, red gold and green.

At some point, Sam decided to leave his comfortable post and venture on through the crowded, labyrinthine nightclub.

One dark hallway led to a quieter room with velvet banquettes and small tables and a rather small bar. Cigar and cigarette smoke mingled. The patrons in this room seemed unusually wrapped up in conversation for the Russian Lady, probably because you could actually hear what your friends were saying. A black-haired, goth-looking woman glanced up at Sam momentarily, and seemed almost to smile at him, though smiling seemed a stretch for her. He vaguely worried that he was imagining that women were noticing him when maybe he was invisible and they were looking through him.

Reemerging into the large dance room, Sam blinked. He thought he saw a cluster of people who looked like Nathalie, her friend Marcie, Tom Dickleman, Tiger Williams, and Cody Savard talking at the far end of the room before disappearing through a portal to some other space in the massive and, to Sam's increasingly hazy brain, amorphous nightclub. He found a bar to steady himself.

Here comes the rain again, falling on my head like a memory, falling on my head like a new emotion.

Steve, Joe, and Kevin walked up. "You doing OK there champ?" Kevin asked.

"Oh, yeah, I'm fine," Sam said. "Just listening to the music and fending off women."

"Haha," Steve said. "You need a beer? Your pint is running low."

"Uh, yeah, sure," Sam said, although Kevin thought it might be a good time for Sam to pace himself. Just then, the woman from the earlier bar conversation walked up, grabbed Sam by the hand, and started leading him to the dance floor.

"We'll watch your beer," Steve called out.

Sam came back about 10 minutes later, a little sweaty, but feeling more alert. "This place is full of women," Sam said. "You guys found anyone to chat up or dance with yet?"

Joe motioned to Kevin and chuckled. "I don't think Kevin knows how to stop flirting long enough to dance," he said. Kevin just smiled.

"Speaking of flirty conversations," Sam said. "Did anyone else think they saw Nathalie and her friend Marcie here? And maybe Tom and Cody and Tiger? I could swear I saw them from about a mile away."

The others just shrugged.

I can't understand what makes a man hate another man, help me understand ... People are people, so why should it be ...

Before he knew it, Sam was standing alone again. Kevin was talking to a dark-skinned woman with intense eyes. Joe and Steve had gone off again, probably to play pool. Sam grabbed his pint and began wandering around the cavernous club again, this time without any particular plan. At one point, he cut through the dance floor, which annoyed a couple trying to dance suggestively with each other. But another woman shimmied up to Sam and began shaking her hips in front of him, then turning around and grinding into him with her ass. He gently touched her arm to signal he wasn't freaked out, but then slithered safely away.

Suddenly, Sam found himself face to face with Nathalie and Marcie. "So I did see you before," he shouted over the din. "Where are the guys?"

"What guys?" Marcie shouted back. "We're here by ourselves. Did Kevin come out tonight?"

"Last I saw he was over near the bar on the other side. Good luck. He'll be happy to see you if you can pry him away from the other ladies."

Marcie started to work her way through the crowd. Before Sam realized what was happening, Nathalie was leading him forcefully with a hand clasped around his wrist.

"Where are we going?" he asked.

"In here," she replied.

You are an obsession, you're my obsession, who do you want me to be to make you sleep with me?

Using her high heel, Nathalie kicked open a door and pulled Sam into a long room where several women were freshening up their makeup at a mirror. She pulled him a few more yards and pushed him into an open stall, latching the door behind them.

"What the—" Sam began.

"As usual, you're talking too much," she whispered. "Shut up and fuck me."

"This is the ladies' room," Sam objected.

But Nathalie was busy positioning their bodies so he could prop her up against the wall. Sam wasn't even sure he was physically up to it. But next thing he knew, they were thrusting together and trying not to make too much noise. Sam's conflicting emotions, coupled with the sensations of Nathalie's body wrapped around him, fully clothed except for the one place where they were now hopelessly joined in a rising crescendo, made him delirious.

The women in the room didn't seem to react much as Sam stumbled past them. He checked his fly once more to make sure he was safely put away. He realized his clothes might look disheveled, but he had to get out of the room. He slipped into the darkness of the club and made sure no one he knew saw him. He couldn't remember where he had left his pint.

And I know I was wrong when I said it was true, that it couldn't be me and be her in between without you.

Sam shuffled unsteadily around the club, trying to gather his increasingly disjointed thoughts. He bought another pint. He was vaguely aware that the stolen quickies with Nathalie, however exciting, were starting to make him nervous. He did not want Tom Dickleman to find out, or even be suspicious.

For the first time all evening, he thought of Marion, and wondered how she was doing. He had told her she could stay in his apartment as long as she liked. But he also had a faint recollection that she had said she might get away for the weekend.

Sam found a men's room, and went inside to pee, then splash some water on his face, and make sure he still looked presentable, and not like he had just had sex in a bathroom stall. This time, he set his pint down on the counter, and re-membered it was there. Just as he was leaving, Joe came in.

"Oh there you are, Sam," he said. "We thought you might be making out with a college chick in a dark corner some-where."

"Ha, not me," Sam said, fully aware that he had been do-ing something far more scandalous. "Where's everyone?"

"Ready to leave if you are," Joe said. "It looked like Kevin might have been on his way to scoring with that Marcie chick, but then the douchebags showed up."

"The douchebags?"

"You know, Tom and Tiger and Cody. I don't mind Tom so much, but there's something about the other two that rubs me the wrong way. And I think they're both still after Mar-cie, though I don't think either one of them has had any suc-cess—and won't anytime soon, if I read her facial expression correctly when they walked up."

Sam half-listened to the part about Marcie. He was ner-vous all over again about Tom, now that he knew he was in the club—and probably was when Sam was banging his girl-friend in the ladies' room.

"Yeah, let's go, I'm ready."

Within a few minutes, the four men had gathered near the exit of the Russian Lady, ready to walk out to Kevin's Chevy. "How you holdin' up there, Sam?" Kevin asked.

I'm good," Sam replied.

You spin me right round, baby right round, like a record baby, right round, right round.

In a few minutes, they were back on I-84, on their way to the Toddle House, an all-night joint on New Britain Avenue in West Hartford. Sam nodded off on the way over and had to be nudged awake by Joe. They took an open booth, and were set up with waters by a waitress whose name tag said "Crystal."

"Coffee?" she asked.

"Yes," the men said in unison. Then they all ordered some variation on the basic theme of eggs, toast, and home fries with bacon, sausage, or hash. Kevin added a stack of pancakes and said it was for the table. "Help you soak up that liquor."

Someone asked Kevin about Marcie, but he didn't seem to want to talk about it.

"Did they leave with Tom and his friends?" Steve asked.

"Not sure," Kevin smiled wearily. "I really didn't want to stick around and deal with their attitude."

Sam was fading, and the room was gently spinning. At one point, he thought Nathalie and Marcie came in, but if it was them, they sat in a booth on the other side of the counter, and he couldn't get a good look. Crystal brought the food, and the men began wolfing it down. "Don't forget to help yourself to pancakes," Kevin said.

Sam was pretty sure Tom arrived a few minutes later, and Tiger and Cody a few minutes after that. Kevin asked Crystal for separate checks, and he, Steve and Joe reached for their wallets.

"More coffee?" Crystal asked.

"Sure, Joe said, elbowing Sam to get him to focus and get out his cash.

The last thing Sam thought he heard inside the Toddle House was a muffled argument between Tom, Cody, and Tiger, with Tom finally saying, "She doesn't want to drive any more. Her car will be safe here. I'll take them both home. They live in the same building, for chrissakes."

Sam was barely functioning, but he felt a vague sense of unease. At Avon, Steve and Joe had to help him out of the Chevy, into his room, and onto his bed.

"Ok, Sam said, waking up, just barely. "I know where I am now. I'll take it from here."

With that, he collapsed onto his back. Joe removed his shoes, and he and Steve left the apartment.

Sam slept deeply. He was too out of it to remember the sensations of anxiety and discontent he had felt at various times earlier in the evening. Whatever he may have dreamed, he did not remember. At some point in the middle of the night, he got up and went to the freezer, and took out a frozen facecloth he had learned to keep there during his younger party days. He rested it across his forehead and went back to sleep.

Chapter 9

Sam Field opened his eyes, removed the damp, folded-up washcloth from his forehead, and flung it in the general direction of his laundry basket. His head was throbbing, and for a moment he couldn't remember what day it was or how he got so drunk. Then something about the previous night came back to him, and he sat up with a start, breathing a sigh of relief when he saw that there was nobody sleeping next to him.

He got up and walked around his apartment to make sure nothing was amiss, and that there was no woman (other than Marion, who was not there) making coffee in his kitchen or reading a magazine on the couch. He checked the bathroom, which looked and smelled perfectly normal. He didn't think he had gotten sick, but he wanted to make sure.

The one scent Sam could smell was Nathalie Frelet's perfume.

Sam sat back on his bed and tried to piece together the previous evening. He knew Kevin had driven them into Hartford, and that they had gone to Brown, Thomson and then the Russian Lady. He tried to reconstruct the Russian Lady; he remembered shuffling around from bar to bar and being caught up amid some drunken grinding on the dance floor. Then it hit him that Nathalie and Marcie had been there, and that Nathalie had dragged him into the ladies' room, against his objections, for a quickie in a stall. He didn't recall seeing Tom Dickleman, and hoped no one else found out that he and Nathalie had been in the bathroom together. He knew they finished the night at the Toddle House, but trying to remember that produced nothing but fog.

Sam's next thought was to get out of his clothes, take a shower, and rid himself of the scents of smoke and Nathalie. He looked at his watch. It was ten minutes before 11. The refectory was out of the question, but he knew a place close to town where he could get coffee and a good, cheap, greasy breakfast, which was always his first step in trying to beat back a hangover. The fact that it would actually be his second breakfast of the morning was beside the point—he needed it.

With no duties or plans for the day, Sam decided, after a shower and breakfast, to lie down on his bed again. He changed the pillowcase first. He looked at his watch again; it was 12:25.

At 2:45 the ringing phone shook Sam out of a deep slumber. He grabbed for the receiver and dropped it on the floor. When he finally managed to pick it up and tuck it between his face and neck, he croaked out, "Hello?"

Marion's laughter greeted him. "Rough night, eh?"

Sam stood up and carried the phone to his table, clearing his throat. "Well, kind of, yeah," he admitted. "I've been sleeping it off. I think I feel much better now. How about you?"

"I had a very lovely night, actually," she said. "Did I tell you I was going to get away from Avon? I think I really needed to do that. I'm at this beautiful old hotel in Essex called the Griswold Inn. It's historic—goes back to the Revolutionary War, in fact. My room is really charming, dinner was delicious, and I had a couple of drinks in the taproom, which was fun. Good crowd."

"Wait—are you with someone? Rick?"

"No," she said, "I wish. I'm here alone. But I'd much rather be here alone than in Brooks House alone."

"You shouldn't ever have to do that again," Sam stated firmly. "Please just stay with me these last couple of weeks until the year is over."

Sam momentarily wondered how it would look if faculty and students realized Marion were coming in and out of his apartment all the time, but, he thought, it seemed they were already seeing what they wanted to see and thinking what they wanted to think.

"I might just have to do that," she said. "But I also might stay here an extra day or two. I've already talked to Dean Hitchcock about it."

"Oh, OK … Is the inn expensive?"

"Nah, not at all, actually," she said, then hesitated.

"What is it?"

"Oh, nothing, I just don't think I've told you much about my past. That's OK, there's not that much to tell, but I did have a life before I met Mark and got sucked into his world—"

"Well, I figured you had a life, most people do!" Sam said. "I just haven't asked you much about it yet."

"Well, I did have friends when I was living in West Hartford, some from home, some from UConn. One of my good girlfriends was in the hospitality industry, and had taken a job as a manager at the Griswold—I called on a hunch, and she's still here. It's downtime before graduations and weddings, so they didn't have a full house. You might say she took care of me."

"Well, that's good," he began. "So you're there until—"

"Why don't you just come down for the night?" Marion blurted out. "We'll have fun. I'll give you a little tour of the harbor and the yacht clubs. And there's an interesting historical museum. We can have dinner in the hotel and just hang out. I miss my best friend already, and I'd love to see you."

Sam mulled it over, though there wasn't much to mull. Especially after the wild and weird Friday outing in Hartford, Sam already craved the comfort of quiet time with Marion. He was aware that his feelings for her were unusual, even hard to place—but he felt safe with her, and also felt that somehow they could navigate their emotions without becoming sexually involved or insanely in love with each other.

He also realized he had absolutely no commitments for an entire day and a half. "That sounds great," he said finally. "I'll do it. How do I get there?"

"Oh, that's wonderful," Marion said with delight. "In Farmington, pick up I-84 west toward Waterbury, but get off right away at the New Britain exit and follow signs for Route 9 south. You're basically taking Route 9 the whole way. Get off at Exit 3, and take Main Street into the village. You can't miss the inn. It'll take you about an hour. I'm so glad you're coming."

"OK," he said. "It's a little after 3 now. I've already showered, so I'll just pack a bag and be on the road by 3:30 or so. See you soon!"

As Sam cruised down Route 9, he listened to music, sipped hot coffee, and let the angst he felt about the previous evening fall away. Near Wesleyan University in Middletown, the highway ran alongside the Connecticut for about two miles, and he contemplated the majesty and might of the river, as he always liked to do. When he began to see signs for Essex, he felt an almost giddy sense of anticipation, not only to see Marion, but also to have a new adventure—hopefully a relaxed and calming one—at a historic New England inn.

Sam pulled his Capri in front of the Griswold on Main Street, and Marion emerged from the handsome, sprawling, white colonial structure, which had seen several additions since its days as a revolutionary outpost. They greeted each other with a hug.

"Follow me," she said, walking around the building and motioning Sam toward a parking area. "You can park over there. Why don't you leave your bag in the car for now, and we can talk a walk around by the docks before dinner."

Sam got back in the Capri and parked, and Marion was waiting for him when he got out.

"Let's go this way," Marion said, pointing down a street called Novelty Lane. "I walked around a little yesterday. This is the Essex Yacht Club," she said, pointing to a building overlooking the river.

"Not much going on, it looks like," Sam said. "Where are all the yachts?"

Marion laughed. "It's not quite season yet, so there aren't many. We'll see a few when we walk by the docks over in the North Cove. As for this yacht club, I think it's mostly here for social purposes."

"So people who own yachts can stand around holding their gin and tonics with one pinky raised, and talk about how their kids are doing at boarding school?" Sam laughed. "Not a crowd I'd want to mingle with."

"Speaking of the crowd you *do* mingle with, you haven't told me about your night out yet!"

"Oh, I'll get to that, don't worry ... What's this up ahead, the Connecticut River Museum?"

"Nice little museum, I hear," Marion said. "The concierge recommended it. I haven't been. Local shipbuilding history, stuff like that. I think it's open Sunday, if you'd like to check it out."

"Perhaps—we'll see what we feel like doing," he said. "I'm in no hurry to get back tomorrow. And my attendance at Sunday evening chapel has fallen way off this year—Lord have mercy." They both laughed.

They continued to walk slowly around close to the water's edge, following Pratt Street around to the Dauntless docks on the North Cove, commenting on the quiet grandeur of the river.

"See, there are a few more boats there," she said. "But I don't think they generally dock them here all winter."

"What do they do with them?" asked Sam, who knew as little about the world of boating as he did about professional wrestling.

"Haven't you seen people who have a boat in their driveway, or backyard, covered with some sort of tarp? Or shrink wrap? I don't understand it, myself. I asked my brother once—he has lived in Rhode Island most of his life, and he's never gone out on a yacht or a sailboat, let alone own one.

He said a boat is basically a hole in the water you pour money into.”

“What does your brother do?”

“He's an accountant in Providence. I guess a facility with numbers runs in the family. I never wanted to pursue it, though, I was always more interested in literature, and poetry, and art.”

“But not boats.”

“Ha, no. But then there's my ex-husband. He always wanted a boat. He even dragged me with him to shop for one once.”

“Oh really, shopping for a boat? Was that fun? Katie and I used to go to Montreal and shop for clothes and furniture we couldn't afford.”

“Well ...” Marion seemed momentarily lost in thought as she considered the passage of her relationship with Mark from innocent and fun to a series of disappointments to an outright catastrophe.

“We had some good times together,” she said. “But that day—” It suddenly was becoming vivid in her mind— “was right around the turning point. He was becoming obsessed with money, and with status, and living a life that would impress his friends and business associates. I guess he thought that if they saw him doing well, they'd think he could turn their investments into gold.”

“But you never bought the boat.”

“We argued over it. He wanted to pay it off in installments. I told him there was no way we could afford it. Then again, he can't read a balance sheet.”

Past the Dauntless docks, Marion motioned up North Main, and said, "There's one more thing I want to show you before we go back to the inn."

They slowly walked several more blocks, arriving at the entrance to a relatively small but lovely graveyard called River View Cemetery, tucked into the shoreline of the Connecticut.

"Isn't this adorable?" Marion said.

Sam laughed. "It never occurred to me before to call a cemetery 'adorable'—but you're right, this one is cute, and I do like cemeteries."

"Are you familiar with the Rural Cemetery Movement?" she asked him.

"Well, no, actually."

Marion smiled. "Okay, time to give the history guy a little history lesson."

"This little plot isn't part of it," she said, "but it's a movement that took hold in the nineteenth century, as people's attitudes toward death changed from the pessimism of the Puritans to something a little more hopeful, even uplifting—like the soul might actually have immortal life."

"Do you think that?" Sam asked.

"Not sure," Marion said. "I grew up Catholic, but I recovered, and stopped worrying about getting into heaven. And I think cemetery design, and helping people make a physical and spiritual connection to nature, is more interesting anyway, even with God's name all over the headstones."

"I'm not offending you, am I?" she said.

"Ha, no, and my parents took me to the Unitarian church, so there wasn't much to recover from."

"Well, practically speaking, cemeteries in cities tended to be crowded into small urban plots, and the idea, borrowed from English landscape design, was that a cemetery could be located a few miles out of town where land was more plentiful, and designed like a park, with hills and gardens and walkways and statues and so forth. So families might come and spend a few hours enjoying the space, maybe even bring a picnic."

"Didn't they already have public parks for that?" Sam asked.

"No!" she exclaimed. "Most public parks came after that—which is one of the reasons they stopped building these beautiful rural cemeteries. Have you been to Cedar Hill Cemetery in Hartford?" she asked him.

"No, but I think that might just have to be our next date!" he said.

As they turned back down North Main, Sam slipped his hands into his jeans pockets, and Marion slipped her arm into his, leaning her head into his shoulder.

"You are amazing," she said.

"Wait—you're the one who knows all this history. I'm just listening."

Marion smiled at him. "Do you realize what you just said?"

They continued arm-in-arm until the inn came into view.

"I'm not making you nervous, am I?" Marion asked him.

"No, not nervous," he replied. "Maybe that's the problem."

"Problem?" she said, looking mildly concerned.

"No," he replied quickly. "There is no problem. In fact, the problem is that there is no problem."

They both laughed. "Being with you is like having a boyfriend," she said, "without the work."

They laughed again, then hugged, and then she suddenly tickled his sides, causing him to laugh unexpectedly and jerk his body backward.

"Whoa," he said. "What was that?"

"It just seemed like the right thing to do," she giggled. "Let's go get ready for dinner before I have another laugh attack."

"My bag is in the car," he said.

"I'll head up to the room. You don't have to check in or anything. Oh wait, they will need your name and license plate so they don't tow you away."

"I'll tell the desk you're my husband," she added with a chuckle.

As he was leaving the building, she called out, "Room 232."

Sam and Marion sat across from each other at a candlelit table. Out the window they could see the last daylight in a red-streaked sky. Marion had insisted that the jeans and maroon sweater Sam had driven down in were fine; she too wore jeans and a sweater, hers black merino wool. Most of the other diners were dressed similarly casually.

For the first time, Sam noticed a piece of jewelry Marion had put on, an elegant silver chain necklace with a beautiful, oval-shaped turquoise pendant.

"You look lovely tonight," he said, smiling at her. "And I really like your necklace."

"Oh, thank you!" she replied. "A friend made this for me. It's a traditional Navajo or Pueblo design, I think."

The dining room itself was more cozy than elegant, with plenty of wood, and bookshelves, and framed photographs celebrating the river's history. They ordered cocktails and a shrimp appetizer while looking over the menu. A feeling of calm well-being settled over them. Sam lifted his glass.

"Cheers," he said. "Here's to an amazing friendship."

"And your best friend," Marion said, "is ready to hear about your crazy night."

"And I was just feeling so calm and peaceful," Sam laughed.

"I take it those words don't describe the Russian Lady," she said. "I know, I've been there before."

"Actually, first we went to Brown, Thomson. Much more sedate."

"Rick and I talked about going there. But on weekends it seems like more of a business-class pick-up joint than a restaurant."

"I'd say that's pretty accurate. And Kevin started right in, flirting with two women who worked in sales and insurance, and dressed like it."

"And the rest of you joined in?"

"I did. You know me, I can handle a conversation. Sometimes I think Joe and Steve would rather watch sports or shoot pool. But for all the conversations I've tried to start up in bars like that, it seems like most of them don't go anywhere. Maybe I expect too much."

"I think you may be on to something—you do expect too much. Like signs of intelligent life. So, if all you expected was to get laid, you'd be like the rest of the dorks who go to those bars in their pinstripe suits and think that alone makes them sexy. Thank heavens you're not like that!"

The server took their orders: sirloin steak for Sam, the halibut special for Marion.

"And I didn't expect to get laid at the Russian Lady," Sam said, watching Marion's face for a reaction. "But I did."

"You *what*?" she exclaimed. "Why you little slut. That's the last time I'm letting you out alone ..."

Sam was a little taken aback, but then Marion laughed so hard she had to cover her mouth with her napkin to keep from spitting her drink onto the table.

"I'm kidding. I'm impressed. How did you do it?"

"I did nothing," Sam said, smiling.

"Wait a minute—you were kidding? You didn't get laid?"

"No, I got laid. But I didn't do anything. In fact, I tried to stop it. But it was no use. Nathalie pulled me into the ladies' room, pushed me into a stall, and wedged us together against the wall. She's ... out of control."

"Oh ... my ... god," Marion said. "She knows what she wants and just goes right after it. Was she part of your group? Did anyone see?"

"I didn't even know she was there. She went with her friend Marcie. And then it turned out that Tom and Tiger and Cody were there. And I didn't even know that. And Tom and Nathalie are an item now. And so I was banging the head-master's son's girlfriend in the bathroom."

"Holy shit," Marion said.

"And no, I don't think anyone saw. The girls doing their makeup must have heard, but maybe that's just a typical Friday at the Russian Lady."

"You're probably right about that. Well, was that it for the excitement? Not that a public fuck in a crowded nightclub isn't enough excitement for one night!"

"Nah, we left soon after. Went to the Toddle House to eat, except I was drunk and I don't remember much of it. Except—"

"Except what?"

"I don't know. Again, I don't remember details, I just re-member feeling uneasy about the other group. Something seemed off."

"The other group?"

"Well, Nathalie and Marcie supposedly went out by them-selves, but I swear I heard them with Tom and Tiger and Cody at the Toddle House, and they might have been arguing about something. That's all. Too hazy."

"Well," she said as the entrees arrived with the glasses of wine they had ordered. "Hopefully they all got home safely and slept it off."

For a little while, the two enjoyed their food, and quietly made up absurd stories about the other people in the dining room.

Then Sam said, out of the blue, "I'm done with her."

"Her?" Marion said. "You mean Nathalie? Or were you thinking about that Walker's girl again?"

Marion laughed impishly.

"Stop it," he said. "You know I mean Nathalie. I guess the sex was hot while it lasted, but this is not how I want to live."

Marion suddenly straightened up, and a look came over her face that was both earnest and curious.

"How do you want to live?" she asked.

"You know," he said, "I've been thinking about that a lot lately. I'm 26, I'm single, I'm living on a little claustrophobic campus that might as well be a snow globe. I'm not writing. I like the students, and I think teaching is important, even noble, but ... I don't know. I think I want something more. Am I spoiled? Should I reach higher? Or are we all supposed to humbly take our place in God's little plan—except I really don't think I believe in God anyway, so that doesn't make any sense, does it."

Marion smiled at him. "You signed a contract for another year, didn't you."

"Yes. And I'll stay another year. But that's it. I look at someone like Joe Kraft—"

"Oh, I'd almost say Joe Kraft is happy. Or maybe content is a better word. He's been here so long. And he gets to spend every summer at the ocean."

"He's single too—has been for as long as anyone can re- member. Do you think he prefers it that way? But he can't admit to anyone who he is. George would freak out if he had a boyfriend. And I'm sure it was even harder when he was a young man. So why did he choose this life?"

"I don't know," Marion said. "I can't make other people's choices. Sometimes I wonder if I can make my own." She looked Sam in the eyes with an unusually penetrating gaze.

"But I'm determined to," she continued. "And I won't be back next year. It breaks my heart though."

Sam thought Marion was about to burst into tears, and he began searching for something comforting to say, but then she continued.

"You know I want to write poetry," she said. "Can I live off of that? Of course not!" Her burst of laughter mingled with an almost-sob. She sighed heavily. "So I'll have to figure out something to do, some kind of work that makes me feel fulfilled. And obviously, it can't be here. Oh, god. I'm becoming a mess again. I'm sorry."

"Don't be sorry," Sam said. "Don't be sorry about anything."

The server appeared. "Anyone interested in dessert?" She handed them two menus.

"You know what I'd really like," Marion said to Sam, "is to have another glass of wine and sit by the fire for a while in the tap room. And pretend I'm living in a fairy tale that's never going to end. A good one. Not the scary one I've been living in!"

They moved to the tap room and found two seats near the fire.

Sam finally decided to ask a question he had thought about asking, then decided to avoid. "When was the last time you felt really, really happy?"

Marion looked at him and cocked her head to one side. "You really want to know?"

"Well, I asked, didn't I? Am I not going to like the answer?"

"Hmm," she said. "I suppose it might scare you."

"What?" he said.

"The last time I was really, really happy was right now."

Sam smiled. "You know, I'm having a great time too. But I mean before this."

"OK then, when I was walking with you in the cemetery."

They looked at each other, then both burst out laughing.

"I can't help it," she said. "This has been, like, the greatest day ever. Now I'm going to tell you a funny little thought I was having. Then I'm going to tell you a serious decision I have made. Are you ready for them?"

"OK, tell me the funny thought first."

"OK, but I admit, I feel like I sound a little like Andy Rooney on *Sixty Minutes*. Have you ever really thought about the phrase 'sleeping together'?"

"Well, um, I guess, or … no, not really. People just throw it around. I think it actually means 'having sex.'"

"Ha!" she exclaimed. "Exactly! Your friend tells you he or she slept with so-and-so, except they didn't necessarily actually sleep with so-and-so. Half the time, someone went to someone's room and they had drunken sex, and if they didn't both pass out, one of them snuck out and went home before anyone actually slept! I've often wondered about that. And then if you do sleep in the same bed with someone, but you don't have sex, you can't call that sleeping with him, because that would mean you screwed when you didn't actually! Isn't that funny?"

Marion began to laugh, and could barely stop. "I crack myself up sometimes," she exhaled.

Then she got a serious look on her face, and said, "You and I are going to sleep together tonight. You saw that big king-sized bed, right? Bigger than your bed, where we've already slept together. Except we didn't have sex then, and we're not having sex tonight."

Sam held his hands out, and said, "I never thought or expected—"

"I believe you," she said. "But I actually have given this a lot of thought. I don't expect much more from Rick. You don't have anything real going on with Nathalie, or the Walker's girl, or your ex. So it would be so easy for us to fall into bed together and say 'Fuck it, let's see where this goes.' But I like it where it is, and I don't want to ruin it. If we screw, we'll ruin it."

"Agreed."

"I'll tell you what I am going to do, when we get upstairs and get ready for bed. I'm going to kiss you once. And I'm going to tell you I love you, and mean it."

"And I'm going to tell *you* I love *you*, and mean it," Sam echoed.

"And then we're going to turn the light out," she said, "and turn away from each other, and dream of some nonexistent place where all our dreams come true."

Chapter 10

Sam opened his eyes, and immediately realized where he was, on a king-sized bed on the second floor of the Griswold Inn. He remembered that bedtime had gone exactly as he and Marion had planned; that they had allowed themselves one tender kiss and an exchange of "I love yous," then turned away from each other to go to sleep. But somewhere in the night, one thing had changed.

Marion, now sleeping soundly, was facing Sam's back, and her arms were draped loosely around him.

Sam gently moved her arms, stood up, and walked to the bathroom in the sweatpants and T-shirt he had slept in, grabbing his jeans and a fresh T-shirt and boxers on the way. He took a shower and washed his hair, put on the fresh clothes, and emerged, wiping his hair with a towel. Marion was now sitting up in bed.

"Good morning, dear," he said to her cheerfully.

"Good morning to you," she replied. "Did you sleep well?"

"Like a baby. In fact, I have no recollection whatsoever of you snuggling up and putting your arms around me."

Marion smiled sheepishly.

"That's okay," he said, smiling. "No judgment. No long-term emotional damage."

She laughed. "That's what I love about you."

"And," Sam continued, "If you choose not to confess what motivated that sweet little gesture of affection, that's your call."

They smiled at each other; it seemed to Sam that she was content to leave it a mystery. Or maybe she had done it without realizing it, which would indicate that no explanation was necessary or even possible.

Then Marion's face seemed to cloud over.

Sam looked at her quizzically. "You okay?"

"I got scared," she said finally.

"Scared?"

"Scared."

"Scared ... because?"

Another pause.

"I'll tell you later. Look, it's going to take me a few minutes to shower and get dressed. If you'd like to go downstairs and grab some coffee, I'm sure they have plenty of that. Probably the Sunday *Times*, too. I think they serve a Sunday brunch, but it's only 10, and that might not start for an hour."

"That sounds good. I think I'll head down. Take your time."

Sam grabbed a black sweater and walked downstairs. He found the self-service coffee and made himself a cup, then sat outside on a long bench and enjoyed the brisk April air. The sunshine warmed him up as he thought about what Marion had said. He had no doubt she would explain it to him in her own good time, but he pondered the possibilities anyway.

Of course she had every reason to be scared of the stalker, as well as the financial threats from the IRS. But there was something else she and Sam hadn't really talked about yet—something that was almost upon them. Until this weekend it had seemed more distant, especially with the more pressing matters before them. But all of a sudden, this other something was bearing down on them, like a train that had been out of sight and out of earshot as it rounded the mountain, but now was visibly and audibly steaming toward the station.

Marion's words from the previous evening came back to haunt him all at once:

I can't make other people's choices. Sometimes I wonder if I can make my own. But I'm determined to. And I won't be back next year. It breaks my heart though.

The words "I won't be back next year" stuck in Sam's own heart like a dagger. What would that mean for their friendship? He realized his emotions were starting to go all over the place, which he had been determined to avoid. He was not supposed to fall in love with her. And he still convinced himself that their relationship was just a friendship—albeit a very special one, even a highly unusual one. But—especially after their very special Saturday together—he could not bear the thought of having it taken away just like that.

Suddenly, Sam realized that his inner conversation was getting out of hand—especially without Marion's explanation. "That's it," he said out loud. "Just stop right there."

Two teenage girls at the other end of the bench, who had sat down without Sam noticing, looked up at him.

He waved his hand dismissively. "Sorry. Talking to myself."

He stood up and went back inside.

Sam and Marion grabbed a Sunday *New York Times* and brought it to their table. They ordered food and pulled out their favorite sections.

"I have an idea," she said, sounding playful. "Let's sit like an old married couple, reading the *Times* over brunch and barely talking to each other except to comment on a wedding or ask for help with a puzzle clue. We'll give it 30 minutes and see if we get bored with each other."

"I think it would take more than that for me to get bored with you," Sam said, "but sure."

They did just that for exactly 30 minutes, reading the paper, commenting infrequently. Then Marion said, "Time's up! Honey, I want a divorce!"

They both laughed. Then Sam said, "I think you're stalling."

"Stalling?"

"Stalling to keep from telling me what you got scared about."

"Oh, right," she said. "After we're done here, let's walk to the river."

Marion's overall demeanor today seemed darker and more pensive than any vibe she had given off on Saturday, when they both had seemed nothing but delighted with each other's company, and charmed by each new shared moment the day brought them. For the first time all weekend, Sam began to feel a vague sense of dread.

They found a dock to sit on. Marion leaned into Sam and clutched one of his arms with both hands.

"The short answer is I'm scared about everything," she said. "The stalker, the IRS, leaving my students and my friends at the school. Everything."

"Is there a longer answer?"

Without warning, tears began streaming down Marion's face, and then she buried it in Sam's sweater. She sobbed softly for a good five minutes while Sam stroked her hair. Finally, he spoke.

"It's okay. Everything is going to be okay," he said. But he didn't believe his own words, and he doubted she did either.

"But what if something happens," she said through tears, "and I have to go away, and I don't see you again for a long time? Or forever?"

"Don't be silly. We'll keep in touch. We'll find each other."

"But what if we don't? What if we can't find each other? What if something terrible happens to one of us?"

"Why do you say that?"

"I don't know, sometimes I expect the worst. It always seems that way with me. Let's not talk about it anymore."

They stood up and walked around town, holding hands. Sam tried to make chit-chat, but Marion had fallen mostly silent, except for intermittent sobs. Back in the room, she finally spoke.

"I'm in a terrible way today," she said. "I don't want to burden you with this. You should probably go."

Sam wanted to plead for more time, but he didn't want to seem suddenly like a clingy boyfriend.

"I'll get my bag together," he said. "But I don't feel any burden. And I'm in no hurry. If you want me to go, I'll go, but if there's anything I can do to comfort you a little while longer—well, you are my best friend."

They both sat on the bed, a few feet apart. Sam offered his hand. She held it with one hand, and wiped her cheeks with her other one. Her tears subsided, but the darkness that clouded over her face did not.

"Thank you so much for being here," she whispered. "I don't know how—" she began, then cut off her thought.

"There you go again," he said. "I know you probably don't mean to, but you're making me awfully confused with the things you're saying. Yesterday I thought I understood you. Today nothing makes sense."

"My life doesn't make sense," she said, looking away.

"Well, I'm here to help," he said. "At this point, I guess that's all I can do."

They sat silently for several minutes. Marion finally spoke.

"And I can't stand what I'm doing to you. If you stay much longer, I think we're both going to break into pieces."

Sam zipped up his bag and walked to the door of the room, ready to leave. Suddenly, Marion ran over to him and clutched him around the waist, trying to stifle another sob.

"I don't know what's going to happen," she said. "Kiss me again before you go. Kiss me like you mean it."

"I meant it last night. But I mean it more than ever now."

She pulled his mouth to hers and kissed him fiercely. Sam felt drunk with emotion. When she finally broke away, she noticed his tears.

"Now you're crying too," she said. "Oh god, I don't know how I got to this place in my life. But I can't stay in it. Don't be surprised by anything. Now go, but just promise me one thing."

"I don't understand half of what you're saying today," Sam said through his own tears, "but I'll go now. What do you want me to promise you?"

Marion turned the knob and opened the door, pulling both of them into the hallway. She clutched him one last time, then turned away.

Looking back at him, she sobbed, "Find me. Promise you'll find me," before closing the door.

Sam drove back to Avon in a fog of emotion, not caring when he felt the occasional trickle of tears on his cheeks. At times he spoke out loud. *"I don't know what's going to happen*—what the hell does she mean by that? What isn't she telling me?"

"And what about school? She said she might take a couple of extra days, but is she not coming back at all?"

Sam felt helpless—and profoundly lonely.

About 10 minutes from Avon Old Farms, Sam took his water bottle and splashed water onto his face, hoping somehow he would not look like he'd been crying. He made it to his apartment without having to stop and talk to anyone, but when he got inside, his phone light was flashing. There were two messages from Joe Grisman. "Call me as soon as you get in. It's urgent."

"What the hell?" Sam wondered, dialing Joe's number.

"Gotta talk to you in person," Joe said. "I'll be right over."

Joe came in and quickly shut the door behind him. He looked as white as a ghost.

"Remember Nathalie's friend Marcie Merrifield?" he said. "She's dead. Murdered."

"What?" Sam exclaimed, horrified.

"Dead in her bed. Smothered or strangled, and probably raped."

"Holy fucking shit. You're not making this up? No, I guess you're not making this up. This is terrible."

"You remember she was with Nathalie at the Russian Lady Friday night, and she and Kevin talked for a little while. Then they were at the Toddle House. Marcie wasn't answering her phone all day Saturday, so Nathalie finally went to her apartment Sunday morning and found her dead."

"Oh my fucking god," said Sam, his heart pounding. "How's Nathalie?"

"She's a wreck, of course. Not that I've seen her. Tom has. He's a wreck too. Nathalie already gave a statement to the West Hartford police."

"That's bad enough," Joe said, "and I feel terrible for her, but for us, it gets worse. Everyone is a person of interest. Everyone who saw her Friday night. Nathalie, Tom, Tiger, Cody, Kevin, Steve, me, you. Everyone."

Sam's brain was still trying to process that this sweet young woman he barely knew was no longer alive.

"And what does that mean for us? Have you talked to the police?"

"Just on the phone. They want us to come in and give depositions. Separately. I'm going in tomorrow at noon."

Joe reached into his pocket and pulled out a piece of paper. "Here's the number."

Just then, Sam had an odd thought. "How's George taking this?"

"From what I've heard," Joe replied, "he's pretending it didn't happen. It's going to be hard to keep that up with his son in the mix. Those of us who rode to Hartford and back with Kevin would seem to have alibis, but who knows what they'll ask. Hell, I don't even think we're supposed to be talking to each other. I better get going. I'd call the cops as soon as possible."

Sam sat down on his couch, shaking. In the space of a few hours, he had been thrown two curveballs that almost defied explanation and left him feeling helpless to process. He sat like a zombie for about 45 minutes until he realized it was almost six and he hadn't eaten since late morning. He drove down to 44 and found a sub shop that was open. When he got back, he double-checked his teaching schedule, called the West Hartford police, and made an appointment for one o'clock for his deposition.

For Sam, it was a long night of hardly sleeping. As he lay in bed with his eyes open, he periodically looked up at his digital clock. Three o'clock rolled around, then four, then five. He couldn't even remember if he had nodded off at all. His alarm was set for 7:30. He planned to skip morning meeting and go straight to his first class.

When his alarm rang, Sam woke with a start and looked around. His dreams, what he could remember of them, had been choppy and unsettling. There had been crowds of strangers pushing this way and that. For a moment they were in a nightclub. Suddenly they were Avon students jostling with each other on their way to the refectory, but he didn't recognize any of them. Finally, there were more strangers moving back and forth through what seemed like a long, wide room. At first he thought he was standing in the middle of it, then suddenly he was at a window, and the woman on the other side of the glass was asking him how he wanted to pay for his ticket.

Chapter 11

"Mr. Samuel Field," began West Hartford Police Detective Frank Garrison. "Twenty-six years old. A teacher, coach, and resident of Avon Old Farms School in Avon, Connecticut. This is you, correct?"

"Yes, sir," Sam replied.

"You and some of your friends and colleagues were socializing at various locations in Hartford and West Hartford sometime between the hours of 9 pm and 3 am this past Friday and Saturday, correct?"

"Yes, sir."

"And during those hours, you spoke one or more times with a West Hartford resident named Marcie Merrifield, correct?"

"Yes, sir."

"And you are aware that Miss Merrifield was murdered in her apartment sometime after that, correct?"

"Yes, sir."

"When was the last time you saw Marcie Merrifield alive?" Detective Garrison asked.

"Well, she *was* alive the last time I saw her," Sam replied.

"I understand. When and where was that?"

"At the Russian Lady in downtown Hartford. Somewhere in the middle of the big room where the dance floor is. She was with her friend and my colleague Nathalie Frelet."

"And that was the last time you saw them?"

"Excuse me," Sam said. "I'm sorry. I'm pretty sure I saw them an hour or so later at the Toddle House on New Britain Avenue."

"Yes, and I'm aware that you were there."

"Again, I'm sorry. I wasn't trying to hide anything. My memory from that point on is very hazy. I guess I was pretty drunk."

"You were not driving, of course."

"No, sir, thank you for asking. My friend and colleague Kevin Doolan was driving. And he wasn't drunk at all. But I was in rough shape by then. I think I nodded off a couple of times. I recall being vaguely aware that I thought I saw Marcie and Nathalie come into the diner."

"Now if you were as drunk as you say you were," said Garrison, shifting slightly in his seat, "How did you remember what street the Toddle House was on?"

Sam smiled. "We've been there several times before. It's our go-to spot for breakfast when we go out to the Hartford bars."

"And is there anything else you remember about the Toddle House?"

"No, not really, I mean I sort of remember what I ate."

"Not that, but anything else about Marcie and Nathalie?"

"Well ..."

"Sounds like there is something else. Try to recall what it was, if you can."

"Again, I was pretty out of it. But I thought Tom Dickleman came in with a couple of his friends. I don't remember ever seeing them, but I thought maybe I heard them talking with Marcie and Nathalie. If it was them, they didn't sit near us, more like on the other side of the restaurant, blocked from our view."

"But what did you think you heard?"

"At one point I thought I heard them arguing about something. For the record, I don't consider my recollection reliable, given how drunk I was."

"Anything else from that night? Did you talk to Marcie and Nathalie?"

"Only a little, at the Russian Lady. Marcie me asked if Kevin was in the bar, and I pointed to where I had seen him last. I think she was hoping to see him, and she walked off in the direction I pointed."

"What about Nathalie? Did you talk to her?"

He paused. "Only for a short while." Sam, who was becoming increasingly anxious, decided his statement was essentially true.

"You and Nathalie both teach at Avon Old Farms. What's your relationship like?"

"Good," Sam said. "We get along."

Frank Garrison looked at Sam as though he wanted to ask him something more about his relationship with Nathalie—at least that's what Sam, in his nervous state, thought. But Garrison dropped it.

"Now I understand that Kevin Doolan drove you, Joe Grisman, and Steve Morrow into Hartford in his Chevy Impala, and then Kevin drove the same group to the diner, and then back to campus. Is that what you recall?"

"Well, yes, mostly. I'm pretty sure I nodded off on the way home, and that Joe and Steve had to help me into my apartment and into bed."

"And Kevin was still the driver."

"Yes."

"And he wouldn't have gone back for any reason, like, to meet up with Marcie?"

Sam looked at his interrogator. "Detective Garrison, I pretty much passed out, so I guess I wouldn't know if he did. But Kevin's not like that. Lots of women are attracted to him, but he does things quietly on his own terms. And he would never confront other men over a woman. From what I remember as we left the Russian Lady, he was ready to call it a night."

"Mr. Field, Marcie Merrifield was brutally murdered in her apartment sometime after the night out—probably strangled or smothered during or after a rape or an attempted rape. Do you know anyone who would do such a thing?"

"No sir, not that I'm aware of."

"Okay," Garrison said. "That will do for now. I have your number at Avon if I need to ask you anything else."

When Sam arrived back at Avon from West Hartford, he had one more class to teach, then baseball practice. He and Joe put the players through a few basic warm-ups, then split them into two teams for a casual intra-squad scrimmage. "Make your own calls, just be fair about it," Sam called out to the players.

"How'd it go for you?" Sam asked Joe. "I guess we can talk to each other now."

"Yeah," Joe said. "They'd like to catch us mixing up our stories. But I think our group is going to check. If anyone, they'll take a harder look at Kevin, because people know he and Marcie had a mutual crush. But I think his story will check out okay too. I'm not aware that they've determined a time of death yet, which presumably will affect everyone's alibis."

"Including Tom's, I guess," said Sam.

"True," said Joe. "But now I really am curious who drove whom home that night. Did you notice them arguing about it?"

"I didn't notice much," Sam said. "But I was vaguely aware that I heard something like an argument."

"All I remember," said Joe, "was Tom saying something like, 'They both live in the same building, for chrissakes.' I think he was angling to take them both home. He was probably planning on a good-night fuck with Nathalie. And I almost got the feeling he wanted to make sure Marcie got home all right. Almost like he didn't trust his friends. If you ask me, they all start acting like dicks when they drink too much."

Sam turned to Joe and smiled. "How about when I drink too much?"

Joe laughed. "You don't act like a dick. If you have a little too much, at first there's a sort of abstract quality about you. And that morphs into an I-can't-keep-my-eyes-open quality. I'd rather deal with that than have you punch someone."

As Reese gathered up the equipment and loaded it into the back of Sam's Capri, they all noticed the spindly figure of

Henry Hitchcock approaching them, the May sunlight giving his bald dome a radiant sheen.

"Why don't you hop into the car, Reese," Sam said. "We'll go see what the dean wants."

"Maybe he wants to know if you're getting him Hair Club for Men as a going-away gift," Reese cracked.

"May I see the two of you in my office in about 15 minutes?" was all Henry said.

When Sam and Joe arrived at the dean's office in the administration building, Steve Morrow was already there. "Come in," Henry said stoically, and shut the door behind them.

"In the matter of the unfortunate death of Marcie Merrifield," Henry began, "I am here to inform you that the three of you are no longer considered persons of interest by the West Hartford police. This is good news, of course, but—"

"What about Mr. Doolan?" interrupted Sam.

Mr. Hitchcock looked irritated, and cleared his throat. "I cannot comment on that, as it is a private matter," he said. "Perhaps he too will be cleared shortly, but until he is, please don't share information with him."

"As for the ongoing homicide investigation," Henry continued, "obviously the students are going to find out, if they haven't already. Apparently Ms. Merrifield was good friends with our own Ms. Frelet, and that won't go unnoticed, either. We have only two weeks left in the academic year. I strongly urge all of you to get your final exams and grades in order, and to not engage with the students in any way on this unfortunate subject. Because believe me, there are busybodies here who will prod you for details if they think you'll take the bait."

"Of course," Steve said. "Understood."

"That goes for all of you, I assume," Henry said, casting a mildly suspicious glance at Sam—or maybe it was a preemptive one.

"Yes Sir," Sam and Joe said in unison.

Sam and Joe did eat dinner in the refectory, taking their usual places at the ends of the same long table of students. No one spoke of the murder, or mentioned Nathalie—or for that matter, Marion—neither of whom had returned yet to their classes.

When Sam returned to his apartment, he had a surprise message on his answering machine. He called back right away.

"Hello, Jacqueline Spellmeyer," he said warmly. "Nice to hear from you. What's up?"

"Well, I got an interesting call today from Frank Garrison over at headquarters. I know you sat with him for a deposition in the Marcie Merrifield case. We worked together for years, you know."

"I didn't know. Seemed like a decent fellow. Didn't go out of his way to make me any more nervous than I already was. So obviously you already know about the murder."

"Yes, the murder—and all of the potential Avon connections. By the way, if you don't already know, Detective Garrison no longer considers you a person of interest. So that's good—I hope."

"And why did he call you? Aren't you retired?"

"You would think so!" Jackie exclaimed. "Maybe I should get an unlisted number!"

"Don't tell me—"

"Here's the thing," she said. "He already knows who you are. He knows all about how we worked together to solve the Mallory Harding case. In fact, I'd say he was impressed by our work. He did not intend to say anything to you at the deposition about it—he's very professional, and you were sitting with him as a potential suspect in the case, or at least, a witness. He would not cross that line in the same meeting."

"Okay, so—"

"But guess what? Here we are again, with another crime on our hands—and once again, the universe of potential suspects and witnesses revolves around a boarding school that you know pretty intimately. Only this time, it's all Avon Old Farms, while Ethel Walker has nothing to do with it. And as far as we know, it's teachers, not students."

"So what are you saying?"

"Well, Frank has asked me if I might pitch in."

"And might you?"

"I don't know why I can't just walk away every time something like this comes up. You'd think Jerry would help discourage me from doing it, but he gets too much of a kick out of watching me work on these cases. Such the voyeur. So he ends up encouraging me."

"And where do I come in?"

"Well, Sam, that's the tricky part. And I don't know the answer yet. I think you might be of help, but I have to rule out in my own mind that there's no way you could be involved, or that you're hiding anything. So—"

Jackie paused. There was a hint in her voice of the affection and trust she had long felt toward Sam, but also a professional distance. It almost reminded Sam of how Jackie had to fight off the warm feelings she had begun to develop for Tomas Arpante, Mallory Harding's boyfriend, until she was certain she could rule him out as a suspect in that case.

"So," she continued, "Is there anything else I should know?"

Sam paused. He knew how thorough Jackie was. Would it even matter that he had been screwing around with Marcie's best friend? To Jackie, everything mattered.

"I, um, can't think of anything off the top of my head."

"Well then," she said, "Should you think of something else, you will tell me, right?"

"Yes, of course."

"Okay then, we'll talk in another day or so. Everyone's waiting for an answer on time of death. Good night."

"Good night."

Sam had another call he wanted to make. He had held off trying to reach Marion for more than a day, but he could bear it no longer. He found a number for the Griswold Inn on a flyer he had picked up in the hotel lobby.

A woman answered. "Griswold Inn," she said cheerfully. "How may I direct your call?"

"Well, I'm trying to reach Marion Maloney in Room 232. Can you tell me whether she has checked out yet?"

"Just a minute," she said. "I'll have to put you on hold."

If Sam was on hold for 60 seconds, it seemed like the most agonizing minute of his life.

The voice returned. "It looks like Ms. Maloney is registered to be here until tomorrow," she said. "I'll put you through to her room."

The phone rang five times, then went to a robotic message to try the call later.

Sam called the front desk again.

"Griswold Inn. How may I direct your call?"

"Well, I just tried to reach Marion Maloney in Room 232, but she didn't answer. Is there any way I could leave a brief message for her at the front desk?"

Sam was worried that the receptionist might say no, but she sounded as cheerful as before.

"Sure, go ahead, and I'll write it down and put it in her in-box."

"Just tell her Sam called, please."

"That's it? No number?"

"She has it."

"Okay. All set."

"Thank you."

Now Sam had two things weighing heavily on his mind. One of them, he could do nothing about. He summoned his courage to take care of the other one.

"Hello."

"Jackie?"

"Yes, Sam. What's up?

"I guess I do have something to tell you."

"Go ahead."

He paused. "I am not in a romantic relationship with Nathalie Frelet," he said. "In fact, I believe she is seeing Tom Dickleman."

"Yes," Jackie said. "Go on."

"But I have had sex with her."

"Recently?"

"Yes," he said. "She has been very aggressive about it. But I'm planning to end it, especially now that she and Tom, well, you know. This is not a boat I'd care to rock."

"Yes," she said. "I had already heard suspicions about all of this."

"You didn't say anything."

"I was leaving it up to you. I wasn't interrogating you. But this is important to know. Thank you for coming clean."

"I hope this doesn't change everything. I still had nothing to do with Marcie—"

"It doesn't change everything," Jackie said, not exactly reassuringly. "But I have to put it in perspective, and weigh all the information I do have. I'll let you know if I need to ask you more questions about it. In the meantime, I'll stay in touch."

"Okay, good night."

Chapter 12

"Well, look who it is! A pleasure to see you again, Mrs. Spellmeyer—and to have you aboard this case. You are, after all, the expert emeritus at boarding school mysteries!"

Jackie looked at Frank Garrison and smiled. "Don't get too carried away with titles," she laughed. "Actually, 'retired' works nicely—you do recall that I had my retirement party almost three years ago, right? Or were you golfing that day?"

"Ha, call it what you will. But I'm looking forward to working with you. Here's the file so far. The depositions from Doolan, Morrow, Grisman, and Field are pretty consistent—although your old partner Mr. Field seems to have, shall we say, lost a little mental capacity as the evening wore on. I still believe his statement—in fact, I believe all their statements. The only one I'm keeping on as a person of interest, and probably not for long, is Kevin Doolan. Seems he and the deceased woman had been carrying on a bit of a flirtation. Everyone else says he drove the men back to Avon and had no plans to turn around and go back to see her somehow. I believe them, I just wish I could prove it."

"Did Dickleman or Frelet have anything to say about him?" Jackie asked.

"They both told me they never saw him after the diner. Now you might want to interview Nathalie Frelet again. She was pretty distraught when I talked to her."

"Yes, I will do that," Jackie said. "Now I'd also like to interview Kevin Doolan and Tom Dickleman, if that's okay with you—"

"Not a problem at all. Talk to anyone you'd like. And do ask Frelet if she remembers her friend talking with any other men in the bars that night, especially if they exchanged numbers or anything like that. She was drawing blanks when I talked to her."

"Okay. I also talked to Sam on the phone last night. You had mentioned there were one or two people who thought he might have had something going with Nathalie. Well, he finally admitted to me he had had sex with her. Sam portrayed her as the aggressor, and said he was putting a stop to it. He said that she and Tom are officially an item now, and Sam does not want to be in the middle of that. I'd like to ask him a few more questions about it, to make sure I can trust him 100 percent."

"He was your partner last year, that won't get in the way of your judgment, will it?"

"Absolutely not. He's a suspect first, until he isn't. I wouldn't ask for his help if I had those kind of doubts. You know me, right?"

"Of course, Jackie. I just wanted to hear you say it."

"Now," she continued, "What about Tom driving both of the women home? Did Tom and Nathalie both say that?"

"Yes," Frank said, "which leads me to the two other people I deposed, Dave Williams and Cody Savard. Good friends of Tom Dickleman. Apparently they were at the diner too, and each driving separate cars, and they offered Marcie a ride home. Tom insisted on taking them both, since they lived in the same building in West Hartford, and apparently that's how it worked out. So my understanding is that they both went home after that."

"And home is where?"

"Williams lives somewhere in Avon," Frank said. "Works as an assistant golf pro. Savard lives in Stratford, near his job as a reporter for the *Bridgeport Post*, but stays with his parents some weekends in West Hartford."

"The *Courant* editor's son?"

"That's right."

"And if both women needed a ride home, how did they get to downtown Hartford in the first place?"

"Oh, yes, I almost forgot," Frank said. "Apparently Miss Merrifield drove her own car with the two women, and also drove them to the Toddle House. But she didn't want to drive any more after that—not drunk, Miss Frelet said, but she'd had just enough that she was worried about being stopped by West Hartford's finest. Tom assured Marcie that her car would be safe at the diner. Unfortunately, he could not assure her own safety. They recovered her car Sunday in the Toddle House lot and impounded it."

"Hmmm ..." Jackie poked her pen at her notebook, thinking.

"Ah, looks to me like one of your famous Jackie moments. I can almost hear the gears cranking up."

"Well ..." she began. "A few things. One, did Tom drop off Marcie at her apartment, then take Nathalie home? How close within the building are the two apartments? Close enough to park once for both, or not? Did Tom see that she got in okay? I do hope his mother taught him to do that.

And then what, did he go inside with Nathalie? Did he stay a while? All night? Is it a fair guess that there may have been sex involved?"

"They both agreed he stayed a while," Frank said. "I think they implied that they went to bed together. She said she was asleep when he left. The other stuff I'm not sure of yet—I'm hoping the officers on the scene did a thorough walkaround. But they may have been more focused on the victim's body and on her room. Nathalie discovered the body and called them, but I'm not sure how much she told them."

"Well then, I've some work to do and some questions to ask!" exclaimed Jackie.

"I expected nothing less!" exclaimed Frank.

"One more thing," Jackie said. "These two other men, Tom's friends. Anything about their stories sound odd to you?"

Frank looked up from the file, which was still in front of him. He straightened the pages, closed the flap, and slid the file to Jackie. Then he took off his glasses and held them to the side of his face while leaning back slightly in his chair and looking across at her.

"You know," he said, "I thought they sounded a little odd too—almost odd by omission, like they were trying to slip out of the narrative before anything came up that might put them closer to the action."

"Yeah," Jackie agreed. "Like something's missing. I, for one, would like to know more about the conversation they had about driving Miss Merrifield home."

"Now that you mention it," Frank said, "a couple of things stand out. Talk to Kevin, and maybe Joe Grisman too. I think one of them said it sounded almost like they were arguing about it. I also got the sense from at least one of them that they really didn't care for Tom's friends. Definitely ask Kevin—he's known them longer."

"Okay, well, I'm off!" said Jackie. "Oh, yeah, and the medical examiner—"

"Briefing today at 4," he said.

On a 20-minute mid-morning break between two classes, Sam Field rushed to his apartment and called the Griswold.

"Griswold Inn," a pleasant female voice answered. "How may I direct your call?"

"May I please speak to Marion Maloney in Room 232?"

"Just a moment. I'll have to put you on hold."

The woman's voice returned about 30 seconds later. "I'm sorry, she has checked out of her room and turned in her key."

"You are sure about that?"

"Yes, her key was turned in and her payment receipt signed about 30 minutes ago. She would not have been able to get back into her room after that."

"Okay, I see, thank you," said Sam and hung up. He looked at his watch. It was 10:40.

Sam taught his 10:50 class, mostly prepping his students for the history final. Then he hurried to the refectory, hoping to catch Henry Hitchcock, who was standing near the entrance door, talking to George Dickleman. Sam stood well to the side of them and waited, but the two men were keenly aware of Sam's presence. They both looked at him, stern looks on their faces.

"Is there something I can help you with?" asked Henry, while George kept quiet and eyed Sam suspiciously.

"Well, yes, I think so," answered Sam. "Marion Maloney told me she had spoken with you about the days off she was taking yesterday and today. Did she tell you what day she was coming back?"

"Coming back to the school?" said Henry.

"Yes."

"She isn't coming back to the school," the dean said flatly. "She took a leave of absence for the rest of the school year. And since she's not coming back next year, that's it. She's done here."

"Oh."

Sam felt, looked, and sounded deflated.

"You two apparently had become such good friends, I'm surprised you didn't know," Henry said. "Then again, after five decades, nothing surprises me any more."

"Thank you, sir." Sam was formulating a plan, and he would need to speak to Joe. He went inside, and there was Joe, seated in his usual spot at the end of their table. Before taking his own seat, Sam tapped him on the shoulder."

"Can I see you for a moment after lunch?"

"Of course. Is this about ... um ..."

Joe was about to whisper Marcie's name, but Sam was a step ahead of him.

"No, actually. Something else. Someone else."

After lunch, the two met up outside and strolled toward the middle of the quad. They both spoke in hushed voices. "I'm worried about Marion," Sam said.

"Marion Maloney?"

"Yes," Sam said. "I knew she was taking a couple of days off, but I didn't know she was taking a permanent leave of absence."

"She is? She's done for the year?"

"Yes. But I didn't realize she wasn't going to come back here at all. And she certainly had the opportunity to tell me."

"I know you guys were starting to spend a lot of time together. Were you, you know, like—"

"Like a couple? No, more like best friends. In fact, last Friday, she checked into the Griswold Inn in Essex—you heard of it?"

"Yeah, it's actually one of the most famous inns in Connecticut. My parents took us to lunch there once. Very historic—goes back to the Revolution, I think."

"Right. Well, Marion spent a very peaceful Friday evening there—not like our Friday at all—then woke me out of my hangover-induced slumber on Saturday afternoon to invite me down for an overnight. I hopped in the car and went—we had such a good time with each other, it's almost hard to explain. In fact, after dinner and wine and great conversation, we took vows to never have sex so we could keep the relationship right where it is."

"And so you stayed overnight with her, and you didn't fuck her."

"Nooo! And we slept in the same bed and everything."

"Then on Sunday," Sam continued, "it started to get weird. Not bad, crazy weird, but ominous, very worried weird. 'What if I never see you again?' And 'What if something happens to one of us?' That kind of thing. I didn't know what to make of it. At one point, she's basically telling me she needs to be alone, but holding me with all her might, and kissing me and making me promise to find her."

"Wow," Joe said. "Actually, that does sound kinda crazy."

"I get that it sounds crazy," said Sam. "But you almost had to be there. It wasn't like she had lost her mind. It was more like she knew something was going to happen, like the details were already in place. But I can't figure it out. And now she's gone from the hotel, gone from Avon, and there's nothing I can do. There's only the one thing I have to do, which is where you come in."

"Practice."

"Yep, I'll give you the equipment bag. My last class ends at 2:50, and I'm on the road."

"Wait—you're coming back, right?"

Sam laughed. "Of course. I wouldn't miss our last game on Saturday. I wouldn't miss saying goodbye to my kids. And I wouldn't miss this one last glorious weekend of being masters on duty."

Sam's face turned serious as he continued. "Marion had issues that no one here knew about. I'll explain sometime. I might not find her, but I have to try. Is your car near mine? Let's switch up the bag before we forget."

At three o'clock, Sam drove over to Brooks House. Marion's car was not there. He walked up to the front door, which was locked. There was no sign of human activity.

A few minutes later, he was was back on the road in his Capri, headed for Essex.

An hour later, he was cruising very slowly down Main Street, watching people walk to and fro. He parked in back of the Griswold where he had parked on Saturday, walked into the lobby, grabbed a magazine, and sat in one of the elegantly upholstered chairs. He sat for 15 minutes and watched people. He looked longingly at the staircase leading to Room 232, as if he could somehow set the big antique clock back three days and relive what Marion had called "the greatest day ever."

Instead, he felt time surging forward, as if an entire month would pass in the space of a day. Every time the door opened and closed it ushered in a cool May breeze that sent a chill through his soul. The breeze seemed to whisper to him: *Everything and everyone that once was here has moved on and is being replaced by something or someone else. And then they'll move on and be replaced again.*

It was late afternoon, and new guests were checking in to replace those who had moved on. "If you'd like to join us for dinner," he heard someone say to a registering guest, "the hostess is taking reservations right over there."

Now it seemed like months since he had sat in the handsome dining room with Marion, clinking wine glasses, and having conversations that seemed then like they would never end. Now it seemed like those conversations—and the feeling of contentment that had accompanied them—were long gone and would never come back.

He thought of the big bed in which they had slept side-by-side, warmed not by each other's bodies but by the comfort in knowing each other was there. It was a peace unlike any he had previously known with any other woman, at least not since Katie. He shuddered to think that such a feeling of peace might never come to him again.

And he realized, all at once, that he had to get out of the inn.

First, he drove over to the yacht club, and then past the museum, sights that registered only a faint memory of strolling and talking with Marion. Sam realized he had half-forgotten his original purpose in making the trip—to see if he could somehow find her, still lingering in this quaint New England town that had provided the canvas on which they had created such an unforgettable day. And he knew there was one more place he had to go.

There wasn't a soul in River View Cemetery—unless the souls of the dead were stirring beneath Sam's feet, or flitting through the trees above him. Maybe he heard them whispering in the breeze, or maybe the breeze was all he heard. When he thought about Marion, and how walking through the graveyard with Sam had been one of the happiest times she could remember, he could almost hear her laughing and talking, and he could almost see the smile lighting up her face. As he was walking back to his car, he could have sworn he felt something else, the hand that she had slipped under his arm as they walked back to the inn that day. Marion was not walking the earth as a ghost—that was not possible. But the memories that now dwelled inside him and filled him with longing were very much like ghosts—the sweetness of her hand under his arm, the intensity of their embrace, the fierceness of their parting kiss.

As Sam drove out of town on West Avenue and approached Route 9, he noticed something he hadn't before: a mileage sign. Under the arrow pointing right, or north, it read, "Chester 4." Under the left arrow, it read "Old Lyme 4" and "Old Saybrook 5."

The names "Old Lyme" and "Old Saybrook" were familiar, though he had not been to either place. They sounded like idyllic coastal towns with histories, places where white-bearded mariners gathered in weathered taverns and spun their tales of the sea. Places that held many charms and many secrets, available to anyone who decided to stop and explore, and not just cruise through on I-95 or the Boston Post Road, or on the train.

Sam thought about heading southward himself, but decided to save it for another day. It was getting late. He would miss dinner in the refectory, so he stopped at a diner about halfway home. That night, he slept deeply, as though revisiting Essex and the cemetery had at least brought him some temporary peace, if not answers.

Toward morning, he was in motion again, steel wheels clearly moving beneath him as he slept, and out the window, the first sunlight of morning dancing off a blue-speckled ocean.

Chapter 13

Jackie called Sam at about 8:30 am on Wednesday. "I told you I'd let you know when I got the report from the medical examiner. Crushed windpipe, as in strangulation. Time of death roughly between 3 and 5 am Saturday. The longer they don't discover the body, the less accurate the tools they use to calculate it. But this fits generally with our hypothesis that the victim encountered an intruder not too long after she was dropped off."

"There are signs of attempted forcible rape," Jackie added, "but also signs that she put up a struggle. I'm waiting for something more conclusive on that."

"So I'm off to see Nathalie this morning at her apartment. It's important that I go there anyway. After I talk to her, I'll have a better idea where you fit in."

"Okay," Sam said. "Keep me posted."

Jackie pulled in front of Nathalie's apartment complex on North Main Street in West Hartford. She had told Nathalie she'd be driving a Volkswagen Rabbit, and asked her to wait outside. Nathalie began waving her arm when she saw the Rabbit pull in.

"Hi, you must be Nathalie. I'm Jacqueline Spellmeyer. Very pleased to meet you, and I'm terribly sorry about what happened to your friend. An awful, awful crime, which I do hope to solve in short time."

"Thank you," Nathalie replied softly. "I do hope so."

"First, can you show me where Marcie's apartment was? I asked the building superintendent to meet us there."

"This way," said Nathalie, motioning to one of the building's several entryways. They walked over, and Jackie tried the knob, which was locked. Just then, someone turned it from the inside.

"Hello, Nathalie," said a stocky Latino man with many keys dangling from a key chain hooked to his belt. "You must be Jacqueline Spellmeyer."

"Yes." She held up the temporary badge she had been issued.

"I'm Ernesto Lopez, the super. Come on in," he said, leading them to a first-floor apartment with a small kitchen opening to a modest-sized living and dining area, with the bedroom in the back.

"Please don't touch or move anything. Now I'm pretty sure the crime scene investigation is completed, and they're doing the final cleaning soon. Obviously the body is gone. But that's all I know. I arrived shortly after the police, and they didn't let me stick around long, just long enough to answer a few questions and get a quick look at the body. Terrible crime. Such a lovely girl."

"So, Ernesto," Jackie said, "Please clarify access—there's a key for the entryway door, and a separate key for each apartment, right?"

"Yes, and entry doors in the back with the same lock as the front. Now if a tenant leaves an outside door unlocked, I wouldn't necessarily know. It's frowned upon by everyone, but it happens."

"And no sign of forced entry," Jackie asked, "at either the front or the apartment door? And no windows forced open either?"

"You can check with the police, but I don't think so. And if the entryway door had been busted open, I would have had to get that fixed."

"Okay, well, thank you very much for letting me see the apartment."

Jackie turned to Nathalie as they walked outside. "And how many entryways down is yours?"

"Two," she said.

As they walked, Jackie considered the distance. "Probably far enough apart that Tom would have dropped Marcie off and then driven to your entryway. Did you wait to make sure Marcie got inside safely?"

"Yes ..." Nathalie said haltingly. "I mean I think so. We were a little drunk. Or at least I was. And I was—"

"You were what?"

"Kind of leaning over with my head on Tom's shirt, making sure he knew I wanted him to come in."

"And did he park in front here?"

"No, he parked in the back. There's a lot and the other entryway Ernesto mentioned."

"Oh, I see. So you parked, came inside, and went straight to your bedroom?"

"I think we both used the bathroom first. But from there, straight to the bed."

"Shall we?" Jackie said, motioning toward the door to indicate that she would like to continue the interview inside.

"Sure," Nathalie said, leading the way to two easy chairs in her living area.

Jackie sat down and looked at Nathalie reassuringly. "No judgment here whatsoever. You seem very open and unapologetic about your sex life. Is that an accurate way to describe you?"

"Yes, I'd say so. Especially compared to so many Americans who are more uptight about it. I like sex, and I don't have any shame about that fact."

"So you had sex that night … do you remember for how long?"

"No, not really. At some point I fell asleep."

"And you never went back out of your apartment that night—or should I say morning—and you never saw anything suspicious?"

"I didn't, no."

"And do you recall the time frame?"

"I think we got here a little after 3. I don't have any idea when I fell asleep or when Tom left."

"And Saturday?"

"I woke up around 11, I think, and made coffee and found something for breakfast and sat and watched TV for a while."

"Normally, would you and Marcie get together to chat about the previous night out?"

Nathalie sighed. She felt bad that she hadn't checked in on Marcie sooner, although she realized it would have been too late anyway.

"Sometimes," Nathalie said, "we'd get together and make coffee and have what we call a 'postgame,' where we go over all the things that happened the night before. It depended on how hungover we were, or whatever else we had planned for the day. I did call her sometime in the afternoon and she didn't answer. I went out for a while, then tried her again at about 9 pm, same thing."

"And by Sunday morning, you got worried."

"Yes, that's right—is it bad that it took me so long?"

"No, not at all," Jackie said, trying to assure Nathalie that she had done nothing wrong. "This kind of thing is rare, and hard to foresee. So our brains tend to rationalize for us, to tell us that her absence is normal and temporary, that there will be an explanation."

Nathalie continued. "I woke up much earlier Sunday, like 8 or so. I called her around 8:30. When she didn't answer, I went right over. The door was unlocked, which seemed strange. I walked in, and there—"

"Oh my god," Nathalie said as she began crying. "Sorry."

"It's okay," Jackie said. "That was a terrible and shocking thing for you to have to see."

"I just don't know who ..." Nathalie said, trailing off.

"Well, let's start there," Jackie said. "Now it could have been a total stranger, although apparently there were no signs of a break-in. Now, who else would have a key? The super?"

Nathalie shook her head. "Not Ernesto. Well yes, he had a key. But he'd never do that. He's actually a sweetheart, and very protective of the single women in the complex."

"Who else then? Did she have any recent boyfriends?"

"Hmm," Nathalie thought. "Not really anyone since Rashmi. He left in January for grad school in California. They left on good terms. She tends to pick the quieter, studious types. And he would never, ever do something like this."

"Okay, let's go over Friday night. Did she talk to many men when you were out together?"

"Just a few. She talked to Kevin Doolan for a little while. I think she was hoping he would ask her out. But then Tom and his friends showed up, and they kind of took over the conversation. They can be ... a little overbearing sometimes."

"Which friends? Cody Savard and Dave Williams?"

"Yeah, and they were both vying for Marcie's attention. It couldn't have been more obvious. What should have been more obvious to them is that she's not interested—oh, sorry, *wasn't* interested." Nathalie sniffled. "I'm not used to this past tense thing. It really hurts."

Nathalie fought back more tears.

"Okay," Jackie said. "I'm going to let you go in a minute. There's just one more thing I have to ask you. I understand you have also had a sexual relationship with Sam Field. Is that true?"

"What?" Nathalie sounded surprised, if only because Jackie had that information.

"Well ... yes. So I guess that's out," she said.

"Yes, well, Avon Old Farms is a small place."

"With small minds, sometimes, but whatever."

"What is or was the nature of the relationship?"

"Purely sexual. Maybe three times total."

"And the last time was?"

"Friday night."

"Friday night?" Jackie asked, taken aback. "With everything else that was going on? Where? When?"

Nathalie sighed. "I dragged him into the ladies' room at the Russian Lady for a quickie. Don't look too shocked—that happens more often than you might think. I saw him there, and I knew we were going to have to stop this, since Tom wants us to be more serious. Sam seemed a little drunk, and I thought, 'Why not—one last fuck.'"

Nathalie smiled sheepishly. "As you have observed, I'm pretty uninhibited."

"I always thought Sam was hot," she continued, "but also more interesting and more of a gentleman than some of the grown-up frat boys I've met around here. So I tried to show him I was interested."

"Do you put Tom in that other category?" Jackie asked.

"Well ... he is sort of cocky like his father. The apple and the tree, I guess. I think his friends are worse. But Tom would kill one of us if he found out I was still seeing Sam on the side. Wait—I don't mean that literally. He can be loud and arrogant, but he's not violent, as far as I've ever seen."

"Unlike Sam," Nathalie continued, "Tom was easy to get into bed. Sam had to be pushed. All I had to do with Tom was take him up on his dirty talk."

"Dirty talk?"

"Yeah. A few months ago, before I started seeing him, he used to whisper little suggestions to me as we passed each other on campus. At first I was a little shocked, but after I got used to it, it kind of turned me on. I think he picked up on that."

"What kind of things did he say?"

Nathalie thought for a minute.

"Do you realize your nipples are poking through your sweater?" Or "I bet you'd like it if I reached up under your skirt," Or "If you need some lovin', come on over and get it."

"Hmmm ... Did he not think you'd be offended? No offense to you, but I would think most women would be."

Nathalie tilted her head for a moment as she thought about it. "Hard to say. Maybe he's always been like this, and he's learned that it works some percentage of the time. Of course, I'm not like most women. Maybe he could tell that I was the type who might get a rise out of dirty talk."

"Well, Nathalie, thank you so much," Jackie said, standing up to leave. "I know this has been very difficult for you. My car is right out front, so ... Oh, speaking of cars, there is one other thing. I know Marcie had decided not to drive her own care home from the Toddle House, and that Tom agreed to drive you both. Was there some kind of a discussion before that about who would drive you?"

"Well ..." Nathalie seemed a little reluctant. "I'm not sure if this is anything or not."

"Go ahead, I always want to hear as many details as possible, so I can sort them out later."

"So," said Nathalie, "There was no doubt that Tom was taking me home. But for some reason, Cody and Tiger started arguing about which one should take Marcie home."

"Tiger?"

"That's Dave's nickname. Anyway, they both had driven there alone. They went back and forth on it a few times. I think everyone thought they were both trying to get Marcie into bed. And everyone was a little drunk. That's when Tom decided he'd drive us both home, and pointed out that we lived in the same building, so there was no reason for someone else to drive Marcie."

"Do you think he was protecting her?"

"Hard to say. Are you interviewing him, too?"

"Of course. I haven't scheduled it yet. Okay then, let me know if you think of anything else that might be of help. Here's my number. Are you back to teaching yet?"

"Actually, I'm going back in for my afternoon classes to-day. Dean Hitchcock has been very understanding about all of this."

Jackie returned home to Simsbury, and considered whom she wanted to interview next, writing all the names on her dry-erase board and making a mental checklist of what information she wanted from each of them. In the meantime, she left a message for Sam to call her.

Sam was out all afternoon, teaching classes, helping Joe run the baseball practice, and stopping in for the final session of newspaper club. It was mostly goodbyes and thank-yous, and handing around copies of the final edition for a last critique. Joe was there too; Nathalie showed up just in time to say goodbye to Max Grimsby, who was blissfully unaware of the drama surrounding the others.

After he left, both Sam and Joe offered Nathalie condolences and hugs.

Then Joe walked out, assuming Sam and Nathalie would need another minute.

He hugged her again and ran his hand through her hair. "I will think of you this summer," Sam said. "It's been good getting to know you. It's probably best for all concerned if we cool it this last week and a half."

"I was thinking the same thing," she said, fighting back tears.

As Sam walked back to his apartment, he felt a twinge of emotion for Nathalie, though he couldn't put his finger on exactly what it was. Besides, he was still carrying a much larger emotional weight, one he could feel in the pit of his stomach each time he thought about it.

When he saw that there was a message, he was hopeful. But it was not Marion.

Sam sighed and dialed his phone.

"Hi Jackie. How'd it go today?"

"Oh, pretty well, I think. I think I got pretty much everything I needed from Nathalie, and I got a good look at the layout of the apartment complex and the crime scene, or what's left of it."

"What's left of it?"

"Well, there's not much left to see three days after the murder. Remember, I didn't get called in on this until after the fact. So now I'm sorting through the rest of it, trying to decide the order of interviews. I'll probably try Kevin first, to clear him in my mind, and get anything from him that might be good to know before talking to the other three. I don't know very much yet about Cody and this guy they call Tiger. I'm getting a better sense of Tom. Oh, and I got a new tidbit from Nathalie that I wasn't expecting."

"Oh?"

"And she spoke kindly of you, by the way. Said she was interested in you because you seemed different than the other 'grown-up frat boys'—her words. And she admitted being the aggressor after she couldn't get you to chase her. As long as you two cut it off and Tom doesn't bring it up, I think I can ask you for help, perhaps discreetly at first."

"What was the other tidbit from Nathalie?"

"Oh yeah, get this. She said it was much easier getting him into bed than you. All she had to do was respond to his dirty talk."

"Dirty talk?"

"Apparently he'd make risqué comments and suggestions to her in a low voice as he passed by her on campus. I said most women probably would be offended by that. She indicated she was a little put off at first, but then she was turned on. That's the kind of sexual creature she is, I guess."

"Well," she said, "I'll keep you posted as I slog through this. Have a good night."

Sam hung up thew phone and leaned back on his couch, thinking about the last bit of new information.

"Holy shit," he said out loud. "Holy fucking shit."

Chapter 14

On Thursday morning, Jackie left messages for both Kevin Doolan and Tom Dickleman.

Tom replied 10 minutes later, but seemed annoyed that he was being asked to give another statement to a second person. Jackie quickly and politely explained that she was working directly for the West Hartford Police and that she had been handed the case file by Detective Garrison. Tom accepted that, but told her he wanted to talk to his father first, and decide whether to have a lawyer present.

Kevin also got back to her promptly, and agreed to meet with her for an hour off-campus later that morning during a class break.

"Since we don't have much time, let me get straight to the point," Jackie began. "What was the nature of your relationship with Marcie Mcrrifield?"

Kevin sighed, leaned back, and crossed his arms. The dimples on his cheeks suggested the beginnings of a smile, but that was all. His blue eyes turned upward, then he lowered them again to gaze directly at Jackie.

"You know," he said, "I thought she was a lovely woman. Interesting to talk to, lovely, wanting to do good in the world, maybe a little shy. I'm a little shy too, and I don't like to rush into these things. I'm not generally a one-night-stand kind of guy, and if a woman is taking an interest in me, I don't like to disappoint her with shallow talk and try to rush her into bed. So ... I was taking my time. I've seen her out a few times.

It seems I'm always about to ask for her number when these other guys crash our conversation."

"Crash? Is that what it feels like? And do you mean Tom, Cody, and Dave—should I call him Tiger?"

"Everyone calls him Tiger. And 'crash' is exactly what it feels like. One minute they're not there, the next minute they're in your face. And they can be so loud."

"I've known them all since we were here together as students in the '70s," Kevin continued. "Tom has always been a little full of himself—his father's son, if you know what I mean. But it was worse then. I can tolerate him now. On occasion—not too often—I have golfed with him or had a couple of beers."

"And not with Cody and Tiger?"

Not as often. The three of them together are a little much. And if there are women around, well ..."

"Yes?"

"I think they think they're being witty and charming with the sexual jokes and innuendo," he said. "I just find it crass."

"Did you all graduate the same year?"

"No, they were all '77, I think. I was '75, along with Terry McSweeney. We both went off to Boston College and somehow ended up back here."

"And where did the other three go to college?"

"Well, Tom and Cody were both legacies at Yale—you know Cody's father is the editor of the *Courant*, right?"

"Yes, I know Simon."

"And Cody is now a reporter at the Bridgeport Post. Tiger, on the other hand, went to Central Connecticut State. I think he wanted to come back and work here, but George, shall we say, declined to hire him. Now he's an assistant golf pro at Tunxis Country Club. Not that he minds that life or anything, but I think he's always had somewhat of an inferiority complex around the other two. Which, if nothing else, make him that much louder."

"Hmmm ... Well, okay. Before you have to get back to class, one more important subject. So back to Friday night. You saw and talked to Marcie at the Russian Lady, right?"

"Yes, for just a little while."

"Did she seem happy to see you?"

"She came looking for me."

"But you didn't get her number?"

"I was being patient, waiting for the right moment. I didn't realize the other men were even in the club. And suddenly there they were. You might say they killed the mood."

"And you gave up?"

"That's not how I would put it," Kevin shot back, then quickly smiled to cover over his irritation at the question. "I do things my own way, in my own good time. The last thing I want is to be in a pissing contest with any of those guys."

"Who else seemed interested in Marcie? Not Tom, right?"

"No, he has Nathalie now, apparently. Cody and Tiger both tried to impress Marcie, both Friday and when we ran into them recently at O'Laughlin's. She wasn't really showing any interest, but that hardly stops them—especially Tiger."

"Oh?"

"Well ... How to put this ... Cody's a little smarter. He also lives a little too far away. He'll play the game for a little while and then leave it at that. Tiger can be a little ... well ... thick. And when he doesn't get his way, he gets more visibly frustrated."

"And I hear they both wanted to drive Marcie home?"

"Yeah, well, that's what it sounded like from the other side of the Toddle House. Do the math—pretty girl, horny men, everyone's a little drunk, and she lives alone less than two miles from the diner. Quick easy score, right? Tom was the only one who had his head on straight that night. Or maybe it was because he was already getting laid. Either way, I was glad his common sense won out. I was thinking at the time that that might have saved Marcie some trouble. But obviously, something terrible happened in spite of what I thought."

"And you don't know what or who?"

"And I left and went home and didn't see anything after that, so I can't speculate."

"And you absolutely did not go back there yourself, right?"

They both stood up, as it was time for Kevin to get back to class. He looked directly at her, trying not to reveal his pain, but to make sure she knew he understood the gravity of the situation.

"Now that we both know each other a little better, I think I can safely say that I absolutely did not, and also that you absolutely believe me."

They shook hands, and Jackie smiled. "Kevin, it's been a pleasure. Thank you for all your help, and enjoy the rest of the school year as best you can."

After lunch, Kevin waited outside the refectory for Sam.

"Hey Sam," he began. "I just met with your old buddy, Jackie Spellmeyer."

"Oh, yes, of course, I knew she was planning to meet with a number of people who were involved that night out. She visited Nathalie in West Hartford yesterday."

"Glad to see Nathalie's back in class," Kevin said. "This must be especially tough on her. Are you helping Jackie on this case?"

"Maybe just in the background. Depends on whether I have anything to add. What's up?"

"Well ..." Kevin motioned in front of them to indicate he wanted to walk away from the cluster of students in front of the dining hall. As they walked to a quieter spot, he began.

"Here's the thing. I was very honest and open with Ms. Spellmeyer," Kevin said, "but considering where we work and who's involved, I also have to be very careful with anything I say that goes into the record with my name attached to it. And there are a few things I might be more comfortable telling you as background."

"Hmmm ... I guess I have to be careful too, but maybe it's a good idea to launder the information through me, and I can funnel it to Jackie to use as she sees fit—if that makes sense."

"It does. Can you go out for beers tonight? If you can, I thought I'd bring along Terry McSweeney. Obviously you know him pretty well from being his assistant on thirds hockey."

"Sure. Just call me later to say when and where."

Sam went to his apartment to call Jackie. As he dialed, he thought about Tom's "dirty talk" and how that paralleled

Marion's experience, and also about how he was getting some kind of new information tonight. He decided to keep it all under wraps until he had that new information.

Jackie answered, and Sam asked how the meeting with Kevin went.

"Very well," she said. "Seems like an honest and insightful fellow. I trust him, and I am no longer considering him a suspect. That leaves only three other people we do know, plus the possibility of a total stranger, and, well, let's not go there yet."

"Kevin gave me some good background on the three men—now I just need to talk to them all. Tom is deciding whether he wants a lawyer present. Tiger lives and works nearby—I just have to get a message to him. Cody lives in Stratford, but if I have to drive down there, I will."

A sudden thought crossed Sam's mind. "Find out what each of them drives. Make, model, year. Sorry to be so cryptic, but if I think there's anything there, I'll tell you."

"Well—okay! We are in this together, I hope—"

"Of course we are. I don't want to embarrass myself if it turns out to be a stupid hunch. Please humor me! Meanwhile ... Do you have a minute? Or maybe 20?"

"I can do 20, probably no more than that. I still have to make some calls, you know."

"I seem to be in the middle of another mystery, and I could use some expert advice."

Sam proceeded to tell Jackie most of the Marion Maloney saga, leaving out the dirty talk on campus, knowing he probably would have to bring it up later. He told her about the strange and scary visits to her residence at Brooks House, and the delivery of crude messages and photos there. He also told her about Marion's predicament with the IRS, and the fact that they were coming after her for tax liabilities from her ex-husband's company because they couldn't find him. He also detailed the deepening friendship he had formed with her over several sessions of him offering her comfort and an ear. And he described her getaway to the Griswold Inn, her spontaneous decision to invite him down to spend Saturday night with her, and a more vague account of Sunday's strange emotional turn. He did mention her mysterious pleas to him to "find me."

Finally, he explained how she had checked out of the inn on Tuesday and begun an extended leave of absence from Avon that she hadn't told him she was taking.

"Wow, that's quite a story," said Jackie. "So she's a first-year, single teacher?"

"Second year," he corrected. "She was hired partway through last year to replace someone."

"And you've only recently gotten to know her well? How personal is this for you—are you in love with her?"

"No, it's not like that," Sam protested, sounding more defensive than he had intended. "Okay, I do have strong feelings for her. Completely platonic. Like brother and sister and best friends all rolled into one. But my feelings aside, I'm also worried about where she is."

"One more thing about your relationship—it sounds like you have spent a couple of overnights with her. Is there sex involved?"

"None whatsoever. In fact, we promised each other not to go in that direction because we like the friendship right where it is."

"Uh-huh," Jackie said.

"I'm serious," Sam replied.

"Well, okay, I'll take your word for that—not that it's necessarily important in the big scheme of things. But you can't find her, and she hasn't reached out for—what has it been now, four days? And to you, she's practically a missing person, but legally, she is not that at all. She left Avon, and also the Griswold Inn, on her own accord, and in her own car. Sometimes people simply want to get away from everything, at least for a little while. Maybe cutting all contact is part of the strategy for getting her head into the right place."

"Well, you're reassuring!" he said.

Jackie laughed and then quickly apologized. "I'm sorry, I don't mean to take this lightly. It's obvious that you're worried about her—and that you miss her. One thing I would do, in case she does turn out to be officially missing, is start making a list of anyone you can think of whom she has mentioned—parents, siblings, girlfriends? And did she have any other recent boyfriends or lovers? Any other co-workers you think she'd call? You could try the post office or the school mail room to see if she's having anything forwarded, like paychecks, but I would hold off on that because you are really not legally entitled to that information. Same with phone bills."

"Oh," she added before saying goodbye, "there's always her ex-husband, but if the IRS can't find him, good luck. Anyway, give it a few days. If what you described is true, she's probably missing you too, in which case there's a good chance she'll turn up."

Kevin and Terry decided on pizza and beers at the Route 44 restaurant where Mario Arpante cooked. All of them knew Mario's son Nico from school—he was a junior, and a very good soccer player—and his older brother Tomas had been the prime suspect in the missing persons case that Jackie and Sam solved, clearing Tomas' name.

And they brought a surprise guest to the party, the good-natured Cuban soccer coach Juan Ortega.

"So here we are," Kevin said. "One Cuban, one Black, one Irishman—and what are you, Sam Field?"

"Oh basically a mutt," Sam replied. "Some English, some Scottish, some French—"

"Ah, no wonder Nathalie has taken a shine to you," winked Juan. "I've seen the way she looks at you."

"Oh, but she's taken now," insisted Sam. "Tom has her pretty well locked down."

"Really?" Juan said. "Well, we'll see!"

"Now Terry and I," Kevin said as they settled into their seats and poured pints from a pitcher, "We went to school with Tom, Tiger and Cody for our junior and senior years, which were freshman and sophomore for them. So we knew them as they were just coming of age. Juan knew them the whole time."

"And what were they like?" Sam asked. "Was Tom spoiled because he was the headmaster's son?"

"Now first of all," Kevin reminded Sam, "this is all off the record, or deep background, or whatever it is you call it in the news business—aren't you thinking of going into that eventually?"

"Yes," Sam said, "and I've already dabbled in it, which is why I offered to advise the Newspaper Club. But yes, let's call this deep background, which means I won't reveal your names to anyone, but we might use the information if we can get confirmation elsewhere."

"So then," Kevin said, "You might say that Tom was a little cocky because he was the headmaster's son."

"A little cocky?' asked Juan in his gruff baritone.

"And while we're on cocky," added Terry, "don't forget little mister 'My father's the editor of the *Hartford Courant.'*"

"Although Cody didn't lord it over everyone quite the way Tom did," said Kevin.

"Now what about Tiger?" asked Sam. "What were his bragging rights? He always seems pretty loud and full of himself when I run into him in the local bars."

"Um ... slightly different story," said Kevin. "I think you have to understand who his family is and what his insecurities are." Kevin looked hopefully at Juan, who was usually happy to take the role of school psychoanalyst.

"Well," Juan began, "I'm not sure how deep a dive I want to take here, but I do know that Tiger's family was never affluent by Avon standards. He came to this school on a football scholarship. Good golfer, too, I mean look at him, how tall and strong he is. It's funny, though, somewhere along the line he learned to get his golf swing under control—unlike other aspects of his behavior.'"

"Was he a troublemaker here?" asked Sam.

"Oh yes, big time," said Juan. "Aided and abetted by his friends he was trying to impress. Nowadays, I don't see him enough to know if maturity has kicked in. From what I understand, he's still insecure—and loud. With a temper. Funny, you could compare him to Tomas Arpante—working class, good athlete, insecure about his own worth. But Tomas handled it differently. He was a quiet kid, introspective, hardworking, and he grew up faster. And he's doing well in baseball, both at UConn and in the Cape Cod League. He'll be back there this summer, which means he's still a pro prospect."

Which Tiger isn't," Terry interjected. "He played football at Central Connecticut, decently enough, I hear, but that's pretty much the end of the line. Not a draft pick, definitely not on the NFL's radar. And he's back here working as an assistant golf pro."

"Now, you did mention bragging rights—" Terry continued until Kevin cut him off.

"I think that silly little story can wait," Kevin said. "The pizza's here, and we have to tell Sam about the incident. We agreed to that, right?"

"Yes we did," said Juan. "Way, way, way deep background."

"I'm not even sure my black ass wants to get involved in this," Terry said. "Were there any blacks on the faculty then? What about students? If there were, I'm surprised they didn't scapegoat someone. I was away at college, thank god."

"Well," Kevin said, It was pretty well known who was on the course that night, and the police case was over practically before it began anyway."

Juan looked at Sam. "Are you confused yet? You should be. Let me explain."

"One June night in 1977, about a week after graduation, Tom, Tiger, Cody and a couple of other kids from the town went out to Farmington Woods after all the tee times were over for the day, supposedly to golf nine holes or some such thing. The team golfed there, and even though the school year was over, Tom and Tiger had the run of the place. Well, they played a few holes until they were pretty far into the woods, and then the party started. A few girls showed up, maybe a few more boys."

"And then the groundskeeper arrived for his shift at sunup," Juan continued, "and found a town girl passed out in a golf cart, her clothes a mess. She had been raped, and pretty badly bruised. While the club bridges the towns of Avon and Farmington, its official location is in Avon, and so Avon police had jurisdiction. And who do you suppose has the Avon police in his pocket?"

"Uh ..." Sam said, tilting his head to think. "George?"

"Bingo!" exclaimed Juan. "So the evidence was bungled, no charges were ever brought, and the school and the club, and even the local media, did the best they could to sweep it under the rug. Cody's father kept the *Courant* from covering it. The girl was an exchange student from Germany, and she went home."

"So," Kevin said, "Somebody—or maybe more than one somebody—got away with rape eight years ago. And our boys were at the center of it."

"I don't know what you can even do with that," Kevin said, but there you are—and Terry is getting restless. Go ahead, tell your story about what Tiger has to brag about."

"Well," Terry began, a smile creeping around the corners of his mouth, "one of my bros from New Britain played football at Central Connecticut with Tiger. One day, they're all showering together, when he notices it. And don't pretend we don't notice these things, especially at that age. At some point he asks me, 'Mac, didn't you go to Avon with Tiger Williams?'"

"Uh-huh."

"Did you ever shower with him?"

"Not that I recall. What the hell you getting' at?"

"I ain't never seen a white boy with a tool like that. Mac, the guy had a fuckin' snake. A fuckin' *snake*."

Terry burst out laughing, while Kevin and Juan just shook their heads, as Juan paid the bill.

"That one's *not* off the record," Kevin laughed. "Use it however you see fit."

Sam just stared straight ahead.

Sam's worries about Marion kept him awake a long time. He finally fell asleep, and was groggy when the alarm went off, so he hit the snooze button. And like so many times before, that's when he had the vivid dream.

At first, he watched out a train window as he passed a seemingly infinite series of tall, snake-like penises waving in the wind. But before he knew it, they had changed into lush waves of grain, rippling like liquid gold in the fiery morning sunlight.

Chapter 15

First thing Friday morning, Jackie Spellmeyer drove down to New Haven. Cody Savard had agreed to meet her there at a café he knew from his Yale days. His shift at the *Bridgeport Post* began at noon, but it was a short drive, and meeting in New Haven saved Jackie a few minutes.

In khakis, penny loafers, a blue Oxford, and bowtie, with a wave of neatly feathered blond hair swept effortlessly across his forehead, Cody was almost overdressed for his job as a reporter, but Jackie guessed he was cultivating a well-studied persona. And once he started talking, it was clear what other well-studied persona he was imitating—his father's.

Not only were his answers peppered with appeals to their shared social and professional status—"Surely you agree that I, like you, would never demean a hard-working member of our service class?"—they also sometimes flipped her assumptions back on Jackie or, especially, her presumed detective partner. "So you're asking if Tom or Tiger or I might have entertained the thought of sampling a pretty young woman's charms because she was too drunk to resist. If one of us, then why not Kevin? Or Sam?"

"Well for one thing," Jackie said, "I hear Sam was too drunk that night to get into his own bed without help, let alone follow Miss Merrifield to hers. And the reason I brought it up to begin with is that apparently, there was some discussion at your table of who would be driving Marcie home."

"Ah, well, then, somebody in Sam's party was not too drunk to overhear us—or to *think* they overheard us. Maybe we were discussing something else, but someone—perhaps someone who was jealous that *he* was not driving Miss Merrifield home—decided that he heard something other than what we were actually saying."

Jackie ignored Cody's challenge to Kevin's integrity, and responded with: "The one line Kevin and Joe agreed on was Tom saying, 'They both live in the same building, for chrissakes.' "

"Well, then, Tom had it all taken care of, didn't he? The perfect solution. Tom drives both of the girls home, and everybody's safe and sound."

"Somehow, I don't equate being raped and strangled in your own bed with 'safe and sound'," Jackie shot back, growing impatient with Cody's glib evasiveness.

Cody sighed. "All right, Mrs. Spellmeyer," he said, striking a marginally more conciliatory tone. "I understand there's a mystery to solve here, and that you have to ask these questions. For my part, I tend to play these flirting games as sport—old habit from my Yale days, I suppose. Anyway, I've started seeing someone from the advertising staff at the paper. I still go up to hang out with my old buddies now and then, but not as often as I used to. And Tom, well, it looks like he's got a regular thing going now with Nathalie."

"And Tiger?"

"Tiger might be interested—excuse me, Tiger *might have been* interested in Marcie. He sure didn't want Kevin cramping his style. But you know what else? If there's an argument, he does what Tom says. Tom is the Alpha Dog as far as Tiger is concerned. And if Tom says 'Go home,' Tiger goes home."

"And as far as you know, he went home that night?"

"Well, we left the diner, and Tom had both the girls. Tiger got in his car and drove down New Britain Avenue toward I-84 to go back to Avon. I saw his car go in that direction. Tom headed up South Main Street toward the apartment complex. I was behind him several blocks before I turned left toward Westmont, where my parents live."

"And you were driving?" Jackie had just remembered Sam's request.

"Yes."

"Driving what?"

"My car."

"Which is?"

"A 1984 Jeep Cherokee. Why?"

"Oh nothing, I just like to get all the details."

They paid and walked out together. "Thank you, Cody. This has been very helpful. Please give my regards to your father."

"Of course." And with that, Cody climbed into a black 1984 Jeep Cherokee.

Sam returned from a brief pregame baseball practice at 4:15 pm and found a message from Jackie.

"Met with Cody in New Haven. Interesting. Not always as helpful as I'd like—talks in circles, tried to reflect suspicions back on your group, especially Kevin. Full of himself like his father, also shares his gift for smooth talk that you can never quite be sure is honest. Said one interesting thing about the relationship between Tom and Tiger—basically, that Tom is the Alpha Dog. Whether that's true or not, those are the two whose stories we need to break down somehow. Oh, let's see, 1984 Jeep Cherokee. I know you have a busy night on duty. Talk to you Saturday."

Sam and Joe had looked over the sign-up sheet—about 25 boys—for the new movie *The Breakfast Club*, and decided to take them to Beefsteak Charlie's first. Joe had called the restaurant with a count. The boys loved going there, and didn't mind that they had to pay for themselves. The ones on scholarship were subsidized quietly by the school.

Sam had showered and was dressing when his phone rang at 4:45. It was Kathy Martin, the headmaster's personal assistant. As Kathy began speaking, Sam started to tremble.

"George won't want anything to do with this, especially so close to graduation and with Marion already excused from the rest of her contract. But I thought you might want to know that I took an odd call from someone at the Old Saybrook Police Department a short while ago. They found a Mazda 626, registered to Marion Maloney under her Avon address, in a beach parking lot. They said it was observed to be there at least two days and appears to be abandoned. Police searched the immediate area today and found nothing—including no signs of foul play."

Kathy continued: "A couple of people here told me not to worry about informing George except for a basic briefing. He'll say it's no longer an Avon matter anyway. But I've also been told that you and Marion had become close friends. I thought you'd want to know. Here's the number of the Old Saybrook PD."

"Thanks, Kathy," Sam said, his voice shaking. "I will call them right away."

Sam immediately called the number.

"Old Saybrook Police, Officer Gregory speaking."

"Yes, my name is Sam Field. I'm calling about the abandoned vehicle registered to Marion Maloney of Avon."

"One moment please while I transfer you."

A new male voice came on the line. "Hi, this is Officer Dan O'Reilly. Can you tell me a little more about who you are and how you found out about the vehicle?"

"Sure. I'm a faculty member at Avon Old Farms, and a colleague of Marion's. More importantly, I'm probably her closest friend here. That's why the administration office called me with the information."

"Okay, and can you tell me when and where you last saw her?"

"Yes. On Sunday, in Essex. She was staying at the Griswold inn."

"And what is your relationship to her?"

"Colleague. And friend. Very close friend."

"Boyfriend?"

"No, nothing like that. More like brother and sister. Listen, I have to go meet my students for an evening activity. I'm free tomorrow beginning early afternoon, and I was wondering if I could drive down and give a statement. Also, is the car still there? At a beach, I heard?"

"Yes, Harveys Beach," O'Reilly said. "It's in the parking lot, where it had been sitting for at least two days. The beach is not open yet for the season. We'll have to move it soon, but not before detectives conclude a preliminary investigation. We'll probably tow it to a local garage soon."

"So, may I come down tomorrow?"

"Yes. Come here first. Thirty-six Lynde Street. L-Y-N-D-E. Ask for me, Dan O'Reilly, and if I'm not here, someone else can take your statement. You are allowed to bring an attorney, if you wish."

"Thank you, Officer. I don't anticipate needing one. I'll see you tomorrow around two, give or take."

It was almost 5:30. Sam hustled over to the main parking lot, where Joe was already loading students onto two midsized vans and checking their names off on a clipboard.

"Ah," Sam said. "I see that some of my favorite clowns are here. I know we have Reese Gilmartin for one more year, but Banks and Hennessey, aren't you graduating?"

"I'll let you know after I see my grades," deadpanned Hennessey.

"Pete Staley, Nico Arpante, Charlie Morton ... Nice to see you all," Sam said, checking off the last few boys to climb into his van. "We'll be at Beefsteak Charlie's in about ten minutes. Before everyone rushes into the restaurant, we'll gather in the parking lot to check you off. And Joe can tell you about the shrimp rule."

"The shrimp rule?" asked Banks loudly. "Like, do we have to be a certain height to get in there? *If your head touches this sign, you're allowed—*" at that point, the boys in the van burst into laughter.

After they parked, Sam went inside to alert the staff that the large Avon party had arrived, while Joe gathered the boys together to check off the names and read them the shrimp rule. "The salad bar comes with every meal and is all-you-can-eat," he said, "except for the cooked baby shrimp. Everyone gets a small plate they can load up once. After that, no more shrimp."

The staff at Beefsteak Charlie's had seen Avon students completely wipe out their supply of free shrimp one too many times, a problem they never had with the spinach or cucumbers.

The dinner was fun, and sparring with the students temporarily took Sam's mind off the new twist in Marion's disappearance. Reese asked Sam if he could have any extra shrimp Sam could fit on his plate. Sam smiled sideways at him, and after they sat down, and when no one else was looking, Sam shoveled about half of his shrimp onto Reese's plate.

The two vans left Beefsteak Charlie's and headed toward the movie duplex that was showing *The Breakfast Club* and *Police Academy 2.* Joe had picked up the tickets in advance, according to the sign-ups; 20 for *The Breakfast Club* plus tickets for Joe and Sam, and five for *Police Academy.*

Sam found the movie mildly interesting, and occasionally funny. At first, he complained to Joe that the five high school students in Saturday detention were flat stereotypes, and later, that the bumbling assistant principal and wise janitor were a little contrived. None of Sam's or Joe's opinions stopped them from trying to match the characters with similar people at Avon.

If the movie didn't especially move Sam, the soundtrack's signature song—which played during both the opening and closing credits—certainly did.

Don't you, forget about me/Don't, don't, don't, don't/Don't you, forget about me

Will you stand above me? Look my way, never love me
Rain keeps falling, rain keeps falling, down, down, down

When he got back to his apartment that night, Sam couldn't get the song out of his head. He realized that Marion's disappearance—especially after their emotional weekend together—had opened a painful wound inside of him. And the song's anxious plea for clarity over an uncertain future just seemed to twist the knife, especially when Jim Kerr's rich tenor swelled passionately at the all the right climactic moments.

Don't you, forget about me/Don't, don't, don't, don't/Don't you, forget about me

As you walk on by/Will you call my name?

Sam had a sudden thought, and looked at his watch: almost 10:30, a little on the late side. But he thought he recalled Jackie and Jerry being 11 o'clock news watchers.

"Hello?"

"Jackie, it's Sam. Am I calling you too late?" He thought he heard a TV in the background.

"No, you're fine. Something must be up—is it about Marcie or Marion?"

"Marion. She really is a missing person now. George got a call from the Old Saybrook Police, though he didn't take it, of course. His assistant called me, because she knew we were friends. Marion's car was found abandoned in a beach parking lot. Not open for the season yet. Been there at least two days."

"Hmmm … two days is the bare minimum for considering a vehicle to be abandoned. Sometimes people just leave a car somewhere they think will be safe for a few days. But this still doesn't add up—actually, very little of her apparent behavior over the last several days adds up. From what you've told me about Marion, it doesn't seem like something she would do unless she had been forced out of the car—or unless she had a calculated plan. If it's the latter, why? Where would she be going from there?"

Sam shuddered as he had a momentary memory of the ending of Kate Chopin's *The Awakening*.

He quickly recovered from that chilling thought. *Not possible. Not Marion.*

But where was she?

"Hey," Sam said, recovering from his mental zigzagging. "Here's why I called. We have our last baseball game tomorrow at 10, and then I'm driving down there. Probably leave about 1 pm. I've already talked to the police. Would you like to tag along?"

"Hmmm," she said, mulling over the offer. "There are only two problems."

"Only two?" Sam asked.

"Yeah ... One, the girls and I have a tee time at Rockledge. They could still play and I could catch up with them next week."

"And two?"

"Two ... No one has hired me to work on this case yet."

"Maybe there's a connection to the Merrifield case."

"I don't see one, not yet," she replied.

Sam just smiled and waited.

"I'm a few miles farther away," Jackie said. "I'll meet you in your parking lot at 1."

At the morning alarm, Sam hit the snooze. Before he knew it, he was standing on a beach as the sun came up. He looked around and saw two women, both wearing apparently identical long, flowing print skirts and frilly white tops with half-sleeves. They were both barefoot; they both had reddish-brown hair; he could not see either face. One began walking toward the sea. He watched her for a moment.

When he looked back, the other woman had begun walking toward the road. He decided to follow her. She arrived at the road and turned toward what appeared to be a village. Behind her by about 30 yards, he decided to walk faster to catch up. But he never gained any ground. The narrow, crooked streets suddenly filled up with people. He lost her and then spotted her again, walking in a slightly different direction. Again, he lost her, then spied her on a different street. Now she was wearing shoes and carrying a suitcase.

She appeared to enter a building, but when he got there, he couldn't find her amid all the people. He looked up and saw two signs, written in tile, one at each end of the building. One

said "NORTHBOUND," the other, "SOUTHBOUND."
Then the signs vanished as sunlight flooded the room.

Chapter 16

Nathalie Frelet slipped out of her tank top and dangled a bare breast in Tom Dickleman's face, gently slapping him with it as he slept. A few moments later, he mumbled something incoherent and then opened his eyes to take in what was going on. Suddenly laughing, he grabbed her by both breasts and pulled her on top of him, taking turns kissing them. Meanwhile, she fumbled with his boxer shorts until he was free for action, as he had already responded, involuntarily, to her surprise assault. She sat straight up and gripped him, allowing herself to settle into place even as Tom reached up with one hand in a vain attempt to slow the encounter down to a gentler, more romantic pace.

"Wait," he said, "don't you want me to—"

"Not necessary this morning," she said with a sly smile. "I'm ready for you. I just wanted to start the day off with a bang before you had to rush off to your practice or match or whatever."

Tom looked at his watch as she began to increase her motion. "I'm good on time," he said, as the last word caught in his throat and he gasped involuntarily. "My god," he said finally. "You are something."

"I am?" she said. "Tell me what you like best about me." With that, she leaned over and gave him a long slow kiss.

"I like it all," he said, struggling to maintain control. "Everything you do is so ... so ..."

"Yes?" Nathalie asked mischievously, slowing her motion again to tease him even further.

"Oh, god, it's no use," he said, and within another minute or so, the wake-up call was complete.

Tom lay back and caught his breath, while Nathalie rested one side of her head on his chest. They lay there for a couple of blissful minutes before Tom suddenly said, "Oh damn," and sat up on his elbows. He looked worried.

"What is it?" she asked, concerned.

"I ... I just remembered ... I have something I wanted to talk to you about. It's very ... um ... well ... I don't know where to start."

Now Nathalie sat up. "Is it about us?"

Tom looked at her and smiled. "No, actually, it's not. I don't know about you, but I'm very happy to be with you. Are you happy too?"

"Of course," she said, lowering her upper body again so she was lying tight to his chest, head to one side again, squeezing him and whispering, "There's nowhere else I'd rather be."

Had Tom been in a position to see her face, he might have detected just a wisp of doubt in her words.

"Okay, then, as I said, this is not about us." Tom paused, stroking her hair. "This is a new one for me. ... Um ..."

Tom was clearly struggling to form his thought into words.

"What is it, honey?"

"Oh, I don't know. Maybe it would be best if I don't talk about it after all. I do trust you, but since it's not about you or about us, maybe I'll just wait and see ... It's nothing. If it turns into something, I'll tell you. Okay?"

The Avon thirds baseball team took the field as the first two Choate batters took warm-up swings. The abandoned car story had not made the local news yet, and the school administration had not shared the information, apart from Kathy Martin's phone call to Sam, who by now had passed the story on to Joe, asking him to please keep it quiet until it broke on the news.

"In the meantime," Sam said, "as you can imagine, I'm too distracted to steal signs today. I trust you and Reese can handle that duty without me?"

"I don't know, Reese," Joe called over to him. "Do you think you can help me steal signs this morning?"

"I don't know, Coach," the boy replied. "You know me, I'll probably just get distracted watching the third-base coach scratch his ass."

Beavers ace Carlton Beaumont kept the Choate hitters off-balance until he gave up a two-out single in the second. Joe and Reese began to watch the third-base coach intently, looking for the one-two combo of the trigger and the actual steal sign. But they never tried for the steal, and Beaumont got the third out. As the baserunner chugged back to grab his glove, Reese observed, "Look at him. No wonder they didn't try to steal. That guy runs like a penguin on Xanax."

Choate's leadoff batter began the third with a walk, and on the first pitch, he stole second. "Did you see that?" Joe asked Reese. "I think he touched his cap, but I missed it after that." Reese just shook his head.

The batter then singled home a run, and now stood off first base with a significant lead. Joe and Reese watched more intently.

"Cap," said Joe. "Now armpit. Now back to cap." The batter took a called strike; the runner didn't move.

"Okay, try again," said Joe. This time, the runner stole second, after the coach touched his cap and then his shoulder. "Okay Reese, I think I got it."

Over the next two innings, with Joe picking up the signs, and Reese providing the chatter, Beaumont picked off two runners. But by the top of the fifth, with Choate leading 2-1, they switched the signs.

With a 1-1 count, Reese suddenly whispered, "Did you see that? He just scratched his ass. And now he's picking his nose!"

Beaumont fired to the plate, and the runner darted to second. "See," whispered Reese excitedly. "Sometimes the blind chicken does find the corn!"

"We never said you were blind," Sam pointed out.

"But you laughed at me for noticing when the coaches touched themselves."

And Reese was right. The coach's trigger was scratching his ass, and a finger in his nose was the actual steal sign. After Avon picked off two more Choate runners, and then came back with two runs in the bottom of the seventh to win 4-3, Reese couldn't stop beaming and bragging about his superior sign-detection skills.

Sam, trying not to show his growing anxiety over the trip he was about to make, turned to Reese and smiled. "You done good, kid. You done good."

"I can drive," Jackie shouted over to Sam from the window of her Rabbit as he emerged from the quad and began walking toward his Capri.

"You sure?" he shouted back.

"Get in and stop fussing," she laughed.

"You know how to get to Old Saybrook?" he asked.

Jackie turned sideways and shot him a look that said, *Do you realize how many years I've been working as a detective in this state?*

As they pulled out of Avon Old Farms and headed toward the highway that would take them to the Connecticut shore, Jackie stayed focused on several turns she had to make in fairly rapid succession. At one point, she looked over at Sam. "You okay?"

"Yeah, well … I guess I am feeling pretty anxious. It helps a lot knowing we'll be down there in an hour to see for ourselves. And I somehow don't …"

"Don't what?" Jackie sounded puzzled.

"I don't know," he said. "I guess I should be freaking out more than I am. She's gone missing, and her car is abandoned at the beach. Doesn't that sound like one of those scary made-for-TV movies?"

"I don't know, does it?"

"But I'm just not getting a scary vibe—not yet. More like a 'What's she up to?' vibe. And the two men I'm most scared about have been otherwise preoccupied this week."

"Speaking of which, I have a couple of new tidbits from Tom."

"Tiger still hasn't responded to a couple of phone messages," she said. "At least Tom is talking to me. Very interesting—he hinted that he might have a little more information—he just didn't say what. And he said he needs a day or two. Oh, and I do have another car for you. As I told you, Cody drives a Jeep Cherokee. Tom drives his father's 1982 Saab; George gets a new one every three years."

"And Tiger?"

"I suppose I could have asked Tom. I guess I didn't want to let on why I was asking. Hell, I even don't know why I'm asking!"

"Ah, okay," Sam said. "Tiger's car will tell me if I'm on to something or not. And if you can locate this Rick Larsen guy and his bank branch on Monday, maybe I'll try to catch up with him later in the day. I think it's probably 'E-N'—she did say he looked Swedish. But it could be 'O-N,' I don't know."

Jackie laughed. "Don't worry, it won't take me long to find him either way," she said. "Now since we should be able to get in a few minutes with the Old Saybrook Police, and it's possible they've collected more information on Marion, what else do we know—and what else would we like to know? You say she has a brother in Rhode Island?"

"Yeah, it doesn't sound like they were super close, but not estranged either. I hadn't given him much thought before—now I think we'll want to talk to him. I wonder whether the local police would have tracked him down. She also has a father in Florida, apparently much older. I did not get the impression they were close, or even in touch."

"And friends?" asked Jackie.

"Well, she did assure me that she had a life before she got married. She's from West Hartford, I think, and went to UConn. Sounds like she had some friends from both places. Oh, here's something—she got a good deal on her room at the Griswold because she remembered she had a friend who had worked as a manager there, and on a whim, she called. And she was still there. I didn't get a name, but I would think it wouldn't be too hard to track it down."

"And then there's the husband," Sam continued.

"What's his name?"

"Mark Miller. The company was Miller Maloney Sloane Investment Partners. Swindled investors, closed abruptly, and left behind a tax bill. Marshall Sloane offed himself, and Marion's ex can't be found."

"Did she tell you anything else about him?"

"Just that he wanted to impress clients by pretending he was richer than he was. Wanted to buy a boat that they couldn't afford."

"Here we go," Jackie said.

"Here we go what?"

"Old Saybrook, 2 miles."

"Oh, keep your eyes out for a sign for Harveys Beach. I don't think there's an apostrophe."

"So if I see a sign for Harvey's that does have an apostrophe, should I ignore it?" Jackie deadpanned.

"Funny."

"Anyway, we get off of Route 9 here. This is 154, and we're about to be on the Boston Post Road, otherwise known as U.S. Route 1. Do you know what that is?"

"I don't know," Sam replied. "The first road ever built?"

"Not exactly," said Jackie. "But it is the longest north-south highway in the United States. It runs from Fort Kent, Maine, at the Canadian border, to Key West, Florida. Most of the way, it parallels Interstate 95. And the railroad tracks, here in Connecticut at least. Oh, and here's Lynde Street, so we go to the PD first."

At the front desk in the reception area, Sam said, "I'm here to see Officer Dan O'Reilly."

"Just a minute."

A dark-haired, athletic-looking man in his early 30s stepped into the reception area and announced himself as Officer O'Reilly.

"Sam Field from Avon Old Farms School," Sam said. "I called yesterday about the abandoned car at Harveys Beach. And this is Jacqueline Spellmeyer, semi-retired West Hartford Police Detective."

O'Reilly looked at her for a few seconds, then said, "Wait, I know your name. Didn't you solve that missing persons case at the girls' boarding school last year?"

"Yes, with plenty of help from Sam. Now it looks like we're a team again."

"Okay, well let's get you both checked in and through security, then I can take statements. And then we can go have a look at the car, and I can tell you what we know so far."

O'Reilly took them to a small conference room where Jackie explained that she had been hired to help with a West Hartford murder case, and how the two cases seemed to overlap with several common witnesses and suspects from Avon Old Farms School—as well as the missing woman, a teacher there. She also explained that the murder followed closely after a night of partying at Hartford bars, and named the relevant people who were out that night, including Sam.

"Okay then, first things first," said O'Reilly. "I need to vet Sam Field's involvement in each case. First, the night out and the subsequent murder of Marcie Merrifield."

"Fortunately for Sam," Jackie began, "he was dropped almost immediately as a person of interest. The violence does not fit his profile at all, but more importantly, from a detective's point of view ... Let's just say he has an iron-clad alibi."

"And the Marion Maloney case? I understand you have described yourself as her best friend. Are you sexually, or otherwise romantically, involved?"

Sam shook his head. "No, I'm not," he said. "It's just funny how that's the first thing everybody asks me."

"Well," O'Reilly countered, "It does help to establish the potential emotional involvement of the witness—and in your case, would-be detective."

"Understood. For the record, we're best friends, not lovers. As for my emotional involvement, I'd be lying if I didn't admit that yes, I am very emotionally involved. I'd also like to think that makes me all the more motivated to figure out where she's gone."

"Hmmm ... I suppose that could make sense," said O'Reilly. "Now can you fill me in on Marion's allegations of stalking, and the IRS problems one of you mentioned?"

Sam gave a brief outline of each, and O'Reilly took notes.

"That should do it," the officer said. "Any questions?"

"Yes, I have a couple," said Jackie. "I understand your officers did a search of the area, and found nothing, including no signs of foul play. Is that right?"

"Yes," O'Reilly said. Nothing unusual, nothing out of place at all. If it weren't for the car sitting there, it would have looked like no one's been there all winter."

"How thorough a search? Any surrounding areas?"

"Not like you see in movies, with six lines of people combing through a field, no, nothing like that."

"And the car itself? Locked? Unlocked? Keys? Anything inside?"

"Unlocked, actually. And nothing at all inside. Not even the keys."

"All right then!" said Jackie. "Can you lead us there?"

Jackie followed O'Reilly's cruiser to Plum Bank Road, where they turned into a parking lot in front of a relatively small beach. Everyone got out.

"Here's Harveys Beach. Over there is Great Hammock Beach. Otherwise, the shoreline is dotted with houses, with an occasional beach or marina. Behind us, some wetlands and wildlife areas. Look around as you see fit. Oh, and I almost forgot."

O'Reilly fished a scrap of paper out of his pocket with a name and a Rhode Island phone number. "A record search turned up this guy. Michael Maloney, a brother living in Providence. I called him, and he didn't have much to say. Hasn't seen her in two years. Said he'd call if he thought of anything."

He handed the paper scrap to Jackie, then climbed into his cruiser and rolled down the window. "Keep in touch," O'Reilly said before driving away. "Obviously, we'll both be interested in any new information."

Sam and Jackie both walked circles around the Mazda, looking at it, in it, and all around the ground next to it. At one point, Jackie said, "This is her car, of course, right?"

"Yes."

The car appeared to be in good shape—no dents at all, and very few scratches. No bumper stickers, no college stickers, just registration and inspection, and an Avon Old Farms parking permit. They opened the doors. On the passenger side, there was one brochure for the Griswold Inn. Otherwise, nothing—no purse, no keys, no torn-out notebook pages, nothing. Not even an empty coffee cup. After going through the registration and insurance materials in the glove compartment, they looked under floor mats, under seats, and inside the seat crevices. All of this, and Jackie found one pen.

She also found the tab to pop open the trunk. Inside, Sam did find one curious item: the large bag with Marion's comforter inside, which she had brought to Sam's the first night she decided to stay over. "I'm gonna take this," he said. "I don't want it disappearing."

Jackie was about to push back and suggest he not interfere with an investigation scene, then decided that the local cops had already had plenty of time, and weren't doing much investigating anyway.

Sam threw Marion's bag into Jackie's backseat, then walked down to the water. Harveys Beach faced almost due west, but if he looked to his left across the Sound, he was looking directly at the lights of eastern Long Island, where the Hamptons and Sag Harbor and Montauk soon would beckon the summer throngs of well-to-do, including his old advertising bosses at Young & Rubicam who gave everyone Friday afternoons off between Memorial and Labor days.

Looking out at the Sound, with the summer playland of the affluent behind it, he tried one last time to imagine Marion pulling a Kate Chopin and striding out into the deep to kiss her ill-fated life goodbye. And once again, he could not picture it.

Sam walked back to the parking lot, where Jackie was slowly pacing around the perimeter, her eyes canvassing the handful of houses and yards abutting the beach, as well as a few grassy areas and bluffs.

"Find anything?" he called out.

"Nah … Pretty clean and quiet. No blood, no weapon, no signs of a scuffle. I knew of one case where they stuffed a body into a burlap sack and dragged it and pushed it into a landfill, hoping it would be quickly bulldozed and forgotten about. And the bag itself left a clear outline of the path it took. Not to mention the flies and critters that showed up for the feast."

She looked up at Sam. "I'm sorry, I didn't mean to gross you out. Or make you worry that this could have happened to Marion."

"I'll get over the trauma. But seriously, then, what else could have happened—in terms of a crime, I mean?"

Again, Jackie looked at him, trying to gauge how fragile his emotions might be. "Oh, and I'll ask Officer O'Reilly to make sure someone checks around the car doors for things the naked eye might not notice—someone else's fingerprints, clothing fibers, et cetera. But as far as crime goes, I see a very narrow window of possibilities, the most likely of which would be some sort of kidnapping where they held her at gunpoint and persuaded her to get into their car without a fight. If she was already out of her car, say, taking a walk along the beach, that would explain why her keys weren't in it. I'm not saying that's likely, but we can at least run a search to see if anyone has committed crimes like that in the area. And show her photo around to other police departments in the region."

"Okay," Sam said. "I guess I'm ready if you are—but I'd like to make one more stop."

As Jackie turned the key in the ignition, Sam said, "Reset your mileage meter."

And after about two miles, he said, "Turn in here," and they were in front of the Old Saybrook Amtrak station. "See?" he said. "Very walkable."

The handsome old station had been built across the tracks heading in two directions, one set toward Providence and Boston, the other toward New Haven and New York City.

Sam stood in the middle of the station in a half-reverie, then turned to Jackie. "You know that Bob Seger song 'Roll Me Away?'"

"Nope," she said. "My daughter left the house not too long after 'Night Moves.' Since then, our radio has three channels—classical, NPR, and the Red Sox."

"I could sing a few bars—"

She shot him a look that said, *Pul-lease...*

"Okay, I'll just quote."

"Stood alone on a mountaintop/Starin' out at the Great Divide

I could go east, I could go west/It was all up to me to decide"

"See? Think about it. Nothing else makes sense. Nothing happened to her at that beach. She just needed an excuse to make it look like something did. She didn't even try very hard. But she wanted desperately to slip her own skin and start fresh. She had been planning this and was committed to it. When I think about it any other way, nothing she did makes sense. When I think about it this way, everything makes sense. Even the fact that she started to fall in love with me a little bit and had to send me away from the inn with a tear-filled plea to 'Find me.' Okay, am I crazy?"

"Well, you might be. Then again ... Should we be looking at train reservation records?"

"No. I don't know how often you ride Amtrak, but you don't have to make a reservation. You can walk on the train and buy your ticket with cash. That's what she did, if she's trying to slip away unnoticed. What we should be looking at is her bank withdrawals."

"Good point. Another job for Monday! I might have to persuade her brother to officially hire me. I think I'll go there tomorrow. Although ..."

She paused.

"What?" asked Sam.

"If I can make the case that the two cases are connected because the killer might also be the stalker, I should be able to get my hands on her bank records."

"So, do you like the song parallel? That might have been her big decision—whether to go east or west."

"Wait a minute," Jackie said, "You can't go east or west from this station."

"What do you mean?" he said. "These tracks run east to west. Connecticut is a perfectly shaped rectangle. That way [pointing]—to New London—is east. That way—to New Haven—is west."

Jackie burst out laughing.

"I'm sorry. I'm not trying to make fun of you. Remember when I explained Route 1 and I-95 to you? They are both north-to-south highways that run from Maine to Florida. And these tracks that run alongside them are north to south. In Connecticut, it doesn't look that way. But see that sign over there that says 'Southbound'? That takes you to New York City. And 'Northbound?' that takes you to Boston."

Suddenly, he remembered.

That's the way it was in my dream.

"Um ... Well ... Okay, I guess you might be right," he said, sheepishly.

"But," he added, "don't you think we've kinda gotten way off the point?"

Chapter 17

On Sunday morning, Jackie had three calls to make. The first was to Michael Maloney in Providence. She went to call him at about 9:45, then hesitated—if he's from a Catholic family, which she thought was the case, maybe he's at church, or about to leave. "I don't mean to sound ignorant," she called out to Jerry, "but aren't Catholics supposed to go to church every Sunday?"

"Every week," he corrected. "They can also go on Saturday. You've seen those signs out front with three, four, five, six mass times. And if they're heading to Fenway for an afternoon game—well, you know which religion counts more."

"And they might also be lapsed," she added. "Besides, since when is this my problem? Jerry, have you ever seen me hesitate to pick up the phone and call someone?"

He lowered the Sunday *Globe* sports section to his lap and thought for a second. "Well, yes, I have," he replied. "But only for very good reasons, like giving a family enough time to absorb their grief. Whether or not they are in the habit of going to church is not one of those reasons."

She dialed the number, and after two rings, a man answered.

"Hello," she began. "This is Jacqueline Spellmeyer, detective with the West Hartford Police. I'm trying to reach Michael Maloney."

"This is him. I presume you're calling about my sister."

"Yes, the Old Saybrook police gave me your number. A colleague and I have been working on a separate case that may be connected. We came down to look at the car yesterday, and talked to one of the officers."

"So you have questions? Go ahead and ask, though I'm not sure how much help I'll be. Marion and I have not kept in good touch."

"Well ... Can I drive over there and meet with you for an hour?"

Michael paused. The apparent disappearance of his sister upset him—to a point—though he was skeptical that all they had to go on was a supposedly abandoned car. And if it turned out that there was no actual problem, and she was safe somewhere, he would have preferred not to be inconvenienced by it.

"Okay, I guess? When? Today?"

"Are you available today?"

"Actually, it's probably one of the better days. I'm just catching up on some work, and Margaret is driving Andy around to look at a few colleges in Massachusetts."

"Your wife and son?"

"Oh, sorry, yes. Our only child."

"Are you right in Providence?"

"Yes, East Side, near Brown."

"I know the neighborhood well. And I'm from Warwick. How's one-thirty?"

Jackie's second call was to Ernesto Lopez, the superintendent in Nathalie Frelet's apartment building.

"Ernesto? This is Jackie Spellmeyer. You may recall that I came earlier in the week to meet you and look at the apartment where the young woman was murdered."

"Yes, I do remember. How can I help you today?"

"I just wanted to call and see whether you had found or learned anything else about that night, any reports of anything suspicious, new pieces of evidence, anything of note the cleaners found in the room, and so on."

"No, nothing else I can think of. No suspicious activity, and I think the cleaning is complete."

"Okay, so that's it? You'll call me if—"

"Oh, wait, Mrs. Spellmeyer. There was one small thing. I didn't think too much of it at the time. A tenant, another young woman, came to me looking for a new key for her entryway. Same entryway as Miss Merrifield. Apparently she dropped hers after she opened the door one night and just left it on the ground. And then it wasn't there in the morning."

"Wait, why didn't she just pick it up?"

"I guess it got stuck while she tried to pull it out, and she got impatient. Then it sort of flew out into the grass, but she wanted to hurry inside. It was late—maybe 2 in the morning."

"Hmmm," thought Jackie. "Do you remember which night?"

"Definitely the weekend, Friday or Saturday. That's why she was out so late. Oh, and another reason she wanted to hurry inside was she didn't like the look of a man who was coming up the walk."

"Interesting," Jackie said. "Do you think you could have her call me?"

"Sure—I'll ask."

Jackie's third call was to Sam.

"Hey Sam. You're still on duty today, right?"

"Yeah, I have to drive the boys around, wherever they'd like to go—mall, bowling, Walker's, Porter's. Reminding them I better not catch them drinking or smoking weed. And looking the other way while they make out or whatever in the woods or in empty classrooms."

"Or whatever?"

"Ha, it's kind of funny, when I got here, I was more of a prude about that. Now I'm more like Juan Ortega—[imitating his hoarse baritone] *You think you can stand in the way of biology?*—I wonder why I don't just hand out condoms."

"You probably should hand out condoms."

"Anyway, yeah, I'll be in a van most of the day."

"Okay. Here's a quick rundown of my latest. I called the super in the apartment building—a woman in Marcie's entryway needed a new outside key because she dropped it after letting herself in, and didn't pick it up because she was scared of a man who was walking up the path."

"The same night?"

"Waiting to hear from her. Meanwhile, I already got in touch with Marion's brother, Michael. He acts like he doesn't know her very well, but he made time for me today. So I'm driving to Providence. Anything you'd like me to ask?"

"Yeah, ask him about her friends before she got married. High school, college, holidays in West Hartford when they still had their mother and father—whatever he might remember. Ask what he thinks of Mark. Did he go to their wedding, at least? And is there anywhere else she's ever mentioned wanting to live?"

"Not bad, now you're thinking like a detective. I'll fill you in. Then I have to turn my attention back to Tom and Tiger."

"Oh ..." Sam trailed off.

"Oh what?"

"I actually meant to bring this up yesterday. I realized something when you told me about Tom's dirty talk to Nathalie in the quad. She may have liked it, but someone was whispering the same kinds of things to Marion, and it scared her. That was the beginning of the stalking she described. She just refused to tell me who it was."

"Well, that sounds important, doesn't it," she remarked, a little scoldingly, as if to say, *Why didn't you tell me this before?*

Defending himself against the unspoken question, Sam said, "We weren't working on Marion's case yet. In fact, it didn't qualify as a case, according to you."

"Okay, eyes on the ball. I have to get going to Providence. Enjoy your day driving the kids around! We'll catch up later."

"Wait, there's one more thing I forgot to tell you."

Jackie sighed. "Maybe you should keep a little notebook in your back pocket."

"And this is something they call 'deep background' in the news business—"

"Yes, I know what that is," Jackie interrupted, impatient to get on the road.

"I'll make this quick. When I met with Kevin, Juan, and Terry, they wanted to tell me a couple of things that Kevin was afraid to put on the record because of his job. The most interesting story took place one evening just after Tom and Tiger had graduated from Avon, and they were playing golf with friends at Farmington Woods, which turned into a party out on the back nine after it got dark. Apparently a groundskeeper showed up for his morning shift and found a girl passed out in a golf cart. She had been raped and badly bruised, but the Avon cops bungled the evidence, and no charges were ever brought. Guess who has the Avon PD in his back pocket."

"Gee, I wonder."

"Food for thought. Talk to you later."

Jackie easily found Michael's modest townhouse on George Street near Brown University. He greeted her at the door with a soft voice and a soft handshake. He stood not quite 6 feet tall, with short brown hair and a mildly receding hairline. Except that he wore no jacket, he looked like he was dressed for the office.

"Cup of tea? I have some hot water going."

"Sure."

"So," he began, placing a cup of hot tea in front of her at the kitchen table, "Here's why we're so far apart. I was born in 1941, 44 years ago. Marion wasn't born until September 1951. So she's 34. And when I left for college in 1959, she was still in grade school."

"Where did you go to college?"

"Right over there," he answered, pointing toward Brown, which was just a few blocks away. "I majored in economics and finance, then I picked up a masters in accounting at the University of Rhode Island."

"Did you go home summers to West Hartford?"

"Not always. I tended to get internships. And I really liked it here. After my MSA work, I landed a good job here, and Margaret and I bought this house. We met at Brown."

"Mom passed away in 1969, while Marion was still at UConn. She was 64. Dad was about eight years older, and he didn't want to keep the house any longer. He had siblings in Florida, and moved down there soon after. I remember Marion helped him pack up his house, and run the yard sales, and finally she drove him down there. Funny thing about all that time they spent together, I think it made them closer than they ever had been."

"Oh, why weren't they close?"

"Hard to say—again, I wasn't around much. I don't think my father understood her. Nor my mother, for that matter. Marion was always the dreamer, the poet. They just lived on separate planes. And she has that dark Irish melancholy."

"I have to say, Michael, you seem to know more about your sister than you were letting on."

He smiled weakly. "Well, maybe, I suppose you could say that. I do love Marion, you know. But I'm afraid I may have exhausted my knowledge of her already."

"Well," Jackie said, "We'll see about that. Now if she wasn't that close to her parents, and didn't have siblings around, what did she do with herself all those high school years?"

"You mean besides reading every book she could get her hands on? Well, she did have a small group of friends in high school. Not exactly the average crowd. Sort of a cross between hippie and bohemian. It was right around that peace and love time, you know. Three or four of them, I think—but one in particular. I remember her the best because she was the most exotic looking. Beautiful black hair, and a darker tone to her skin. Always wearing interesting clothes and jewelry. When I did come home during Marion's high school years, they were inseparable. And then the friend went to RISD for a year—you know it?"

"Rhode Island School of Design."

"Yeah, it's also a few blocks from here. Marion came down to see her a few times, and they'd stop in to say hello. The friend wanted to be an artist. Actually, I think she is an artist. Somewhere. All I know is that she left RISD and moved away."

"You recall her name?"

"Oh, no," he laughed. "And good luck getting me to conjure that one up!"

"Well then, let's talk about her husband, Mark. You knew him?"

"Not well."

"Well enough to form an impression?"

Michael sighed. "I think the impression I formed was, it's too bad I don't know my sister well enough to say he's not good enough for you."

"Something about him bothered you."

He thought for a moment, looking off toward the space above him and to his right, as if trying to re-form an image that had faded over time like an old photograph. Finally, he shook his head.

"They met at UConn. Must have been 12 years ago, at least. I think I met him when they first met, and didn't get much of a read on him. Seemed superficial. Or maybe the meeting itself was superficial. I don't know. Then they got married, what, maybe in 1975? She would have been 24. I guess that's old enough, but she didn't foresee that he didn't have the acumen or the character to run a business, especially one that involved other people's money. I recall a vague impression that he just wanted to be rich and would take any shortcut to get there."

"I also recall from one later visit that he seemed obsessed with boats, or with the idea of owning one. Tried to convince Marion they should buy one. He actually asked my advice, as an investment—wrong person! They're not an investment, like a house. I think they're a colossal waste of money."

"Back to the wedding. Did you go?"

"Yes. And with Dad unable to make the trip, I walked Marion down the aisle."

"Do you have photos?"

He cocked his head and thought for a moment.

"Well if I do, they'd be over here."

Michael led Jackie into a room that looked like his study. "There are a couple of photo albums on the bookshelf, all our family vacations, milestones of Andy's childhood, and so on, I think. Margaret takes everything else and sorts them into manila envelopes, which would be in one of these drawers here."

"Well, let's look!" Jackie said. "And I won't keep you much longer."

About halfway through the first drawer they checked, Michael came upon an envelope marked "Marion's Wedding." He pulled it out.

"What a lovely young woman," Jackie remarked. "I had only seen one photo—in last year's Avon yearbook. Looks almost the same, maybe some added depth to her face, from life experience. I love her chestnut hair, and the way her green eyes sparkle. And Mark ... well, he's handsome, I guess. I can see what attracted her."

Jackie shuffled through the photos. They appeared to have received the standard photographer's set: couple at the altar, couple alone, couple with parents (Mark's only), couple with siblings, each alone with his/her attendants, and one of the entire wedding party. Jackie pulled out the photos of the bridesmaids and stared at them intently, then flipped them over, then back, then over and back one more time.

"Well," she said. "I think we've found our girl."

"Our girl?" Michael said, confused.

"Look, the one with the darker complexion. Beautiful. With mesmerizing eyes. If you look on the back, all of their names are marked. Her name is Ariana."

"Yes," he said, suddenly getting it. "That's her!"

"The artist, you said."

"Yes, Bello. Ariana Bello. It just came back to me, like you opened up a secret door."

"Maybe I did! Look, may I take a few of these to make copies, and I'll mail them back within a day or two?"

"Um ... I don't see why not."

"Just two more questions that I can think of. Did Marion ever talk about any places she'd like to live, besides West Hartford?"

"Oh, gosh, it's been so long since we talked about stuff like that—about anything, really. She mentioned Italy once, because she was reading a book about it. I think she'd go anywhere that attracts artists and bohemians."

"And your father—should we tell him?"

Michael shook his head sadly. "He's not doing well. He probably wouldn't even remember her. And if he did, why make him upset?"

"One more thing. I'm working on this because it dovetails with the other case I mentioned. A teacher named Sam Field is helping. He worked on another case with me, and apparently, he was your sister's best friend at Avon. I also could work on it directly for you, which would give me access to other things. I wouldn't need much beyond expenses. Well, here's my card."

"Sure, let me think about that."

Michael found an empty manila photo and slid in the four photos Jackie had chosen, two featuring Ariana, and two featuring Mark.

He led her to the door, where they thanked each other.

As she walked down the path, he yelled out one more thing.

"Santa Fe," he said. "It's coming back to me. I think she moved to New Mexico."

When Jackie called Sam that evening to go over the game plan for Monday, she told him that her meeting with Michael Maloney had been surprisingly informative. She also told him about the best friend from high school, Ariana Bello, an artist who might be living in New Mexico.

Sam immediately thought of the turquoise pendant Marion had worn to dinner at the Griswold.

With Marion on his mind, and unfinished final exams to be hashed out in the morning, Sam did not get to sleep easily. But he was dead to the world when his alarm shook him awake. As usual, he hit the snooze, and went back to sleep.

In his early-morning dream, first he heard horses' hooves, galloping over the dusty high plains. Then he heard train wheels again; he looked out his window and saw the brown earth give way to desert flowers in a multitude of vivid yellows, oranges, greens, and blues. In the distance, high rock formations loomed like massive, ominous tombstones.

Chapter 18

With his final exams set to begin Monday morning at 9:30, Sam was rushing to get his papers together at five minutes before nine when the phone rang. He picked it up, and Jackie began speaking.

"It's E-N. You know, the Swedish way: L-A-R-S-E-N."

"Oh," Sam said. "The 'Rick' guy. You found him? It's pretty early—is the bank even open? When did you start calling?"

"Haha—just a few minutes ago. I have a friend who works at the main headquarters on Pratt Steet. That's where Rick works, too, it turns out. It helps in this business to know people!"

"Did you get a number?"

"I already had the number. You can have it too, by looking it up in the phone book. But I can just give it to you. Here you go. Two-oh-three ..."

Sam hung up and looked at the clock. He didn't want to be late for exams, but he didn't want to take a chance on missing Rick.

A woman answered. "Good morning. Society for Savings. How may I help you today?"

"Is Rick Larsen there, please?"

"May I tell him who's calling?"

Sam's mind raced. He hadn't planned ahead. Later, he would ask Jackie for advice on how to introduce himself on cold calls. Today, he would have to wing it. In the scant seconds he had to consider his options, he ruled out using Marion's name.

"I'm an old acquaintance from Wesleyan. I'm not sure he'll remember my name, but it's about a loan we discussed."

There was a slight pause, then "Just a moment. I'll see if he's in."

A man picked up. "Rick Larsen."

"Hi Rick, my name is Sam Field, and I'm a teacher at Avon Old Farms School. I'm a good friend of Marion Maloney."

Rick was silent for a moment; when he began speaking, he sounded confused. "So wait, this is not about a loan. Is there some kind of a problem?"

"No problem at your end, not at all," Sam said, "and please allow me to apologize. When the receptionist asked who I was, I guess I choked and didn't know what to say. But Marion spoke very highly of you, and I need to ask you something."

"You did say you're a friend of hers, right?"

"Yes, from Avon Old Farms. I'm Sam Field, a history teacher."

"Sam Field? That name actually rings a bell. I think she mentioned you to me as someone she trusted."

"Yes, that's right. And I don't mean to presume anything about your relationship—I just know you have dated. Did you know Marion has been reported as missing?"

"Oh my god, no—from where? From Avon? I'm surprised I didn't hear. God, that's terrible."

"Not from Avon. It's kind of a long story. Her car was found, apparently abandoned, in Old Saybrook. No sign of her, no sign of foul play. That's all the police have to go on. Hard to tell if anything actually happened to her. So far, not much media attention. But you're at your job. I'm helping a detective on the case, and I was wondering if I could catch up with you after work. You're considered a potentially helpful witness, not a suspect."

"Yes, sure, let me think ... Can you stop by the office on Pratt Street at 3:30?"

"Great. See you then."

Sam rushed off to class, where his students sighed at the realization that they were not getting a reprieve.

"Final exams!" he exclaimed, holding the stack of papers triumphantly above his head. "You know the rules. Push your desks farther apart. No cheating, no craning, no talking, all books on the floor. If you have to leave to go to the bathroom, raise your hand."

In her home office, Jackie dug through some files until she found the one she was looking for: Connecticut marinas.

She combed through the lists and brochures until she found the one she wanted: Cedar Island Marina in Clinton. She dialed the number.

"Is Jeff there? Tell him it's Jackie Spellmeyer."

"Just a moment."

"Jackie, how are you?" Jeff boomed into the phone. "It's been a while. Are you still retired?" he laughed.

"You know me too well. How's it going there? Season in full swing yet?"

"I wouldn't quite say 'full swing,' but it's getting busier by the day. A lot of transients this time of year."

"So yes, retired, and no, not retired. I keep getting pulled back into new cases. And I was wondering if I could pick your brain on something."

"Of course," he replied. "Especially since you've caught me before Memorial Day."

"I need to pick out a dozen or so marinas on the Sound and maybe a little ways up the Connecticut River. I'm trying to assemble a good working list. Let me explain."

"Okay," Jeff said. "I'll see what I can do to help."

"I'm on a missing persons case, a divorced woman in her 30s. Her ex might have indirectly caused her disappearance—I can't prove it, but I'd like to find him. Between you and me, he's a swindler and a tax cheat and a boat lover, and he's probably hiding out under an assumed name. Possibly on the water. But I have photos of him, so we might have a way of tracking him down, if you catch my drift."

"Ah," Jeff replied, mulling over her words for a couple of seconds. "And maybe you're looking to make a list of marina owners to fax his photo to? The resolution might by tricky, but you can try it."

"You are sharp as always, Jeff. Will you help me?"

Between Jeff's thorough knowledge of the state's marina network and Jackie's own files, before long she had a good working list of 16 busy marinas, from Bridgeport to Stonington and from Glastonbury to Old Lyme.

After she had filled in all of the owners' names and fax numbers, she began composing a cover letter. She looked at her watch; it was 10:45. She was scheduled to meet Tom Dickleman and his attorney at 1 pm at the West Hartford precinct.

Jackie arrived early, cover letters and wedding photos in hand, and began combing through the department crime files. She had almost given up when she came across a file in a case initiated by several clients of Miller Maloney Sloane, who claimed that their money had not been invested as per their orders, and was now gone. With Marshall Sloane deceased, Mark Miller vanished, and Marion Maloney (by then separated from Miller) pleading complete lack of involvement in the business, the case had gone cold. But there was one photo of each of them in the file.

Jackie chose the photo of Mark Miller with the best contrast from the wedding, along with the one from the case file, made copies, and set to work sending faxes.

Jackie and Detective Frank Garrison were joined at the precinct meeting by Tom Dickelman and his attorney, Austin Cleary.

"Mr. Cleary," Jackie began. "We'd like to go through some of the testimony Tom Dickleman has given regarding the actions of several parties on the night, or should I say the morning, when Marcie Merrifield apparently was murdered. Now before I ask any more specific questions, does Tom have anything to add to his earlier deposition?"

Austin and Tom looked at each other, and then Cleary spoke. "Why don't we start with your questions, Ms. Spellmeyer, and we'll see where that leads us."

"First of all, can you rehash the argument—or discussion, if that's what you'd prefer to call it--you and your friends had at the Toddle House over who would be driving the young ladies home? And why was Marcie leaving her own car in the diner parking lot?"

Tom cleared his throat. "Marcie had already said she didn't want to drive anymore and risk getting pulled over. I offered to take them both—Marcie and Nathalie—home."

"I understand they both lived in the same building."

"Yes, I believe I pointed that out after the other two started arguing—"

"Tiger and Cody?"

Tom looked again at Cleary, who nodded for him to continue.

"Look, everyone knows I'm seeing Nathalie, so that wasn't an issue. I think the other guys maybe saw an opportunity."

"An opportunity?" Jackie repeated.

"Look, Ms. Spellmeyer," interjected Austin Cleary. "The dynamics of the situation might suggest certain, shall we say, motivations, but it's not my place to speculate on anyone else's thought processes."

"But they both offered, until Tom finally said he'd take both women home." Jackie continued. "At least two other witnesses agree that you said something to the effect of, 'They both live in the same building, for chrissakes.' Is that right, Tom?"

"Yes, that is more or less what I said."

"And then everyone went on their merry way?"

Tom sighed. "I drove the girls up South Main Street toward their apartment complex. Cody was behind me at first, till he turned off toward his parents' house in Westmont. As far as I know, Tiger headed out of town on New Britain Avenue."

"But you're not sure."

"That would be the way he would get back to Avon."

"But you are not 100-percent positive he actually drove that way."

"I didn't see him after that."

"Now if I may, Mr. Cleary and Mr. Dickleman," Jackie continued, as Detective Garrison watched, satisfied as usual with her performance in steering the case forward. "I'd like to present a few observations I have pieced together from various interviews. You may comment, or not, as you see fit. We have taken all the original persons of interest in the murder of Marcie Merrifield and narrowed the field one by one. We no longer feel we have reason to suspect Kevin Doolan, in spite of his romantic interest in the deceased. Nor do we feel you are a suspect, Tom—and we do appreciate your cooperation. Now, barring a break-in by a total stranger, that leaves Cody Savard and Tiger Williams."

"Cody did meet with me, and although I found him to be a bit flippant and full of himself, he also did not seem, in the end, a likely suspect. That leaves Tiger Williams, who does give us serious reason for concern. One, he did seem to have a particular interest in Marcie. Two, he has not been at all cooperative with us. Three, he might fit the description of someone who was seen lurking around Marcie's entryway early the morning in question. Four, he might have a history of aggressive behavior toward women. Any comments on any of that?"

Tom looked at Austin uneasily, then answered.

"No," he said.

"Okay then, now I'd like to draw your attention to an old case I've been made aware of, even at the risk of objections on the part of those involved, and their attorneys."

Tom shifted uneasily in his seat; Austin Cleary looked confused.

"About seven years ago, in June, there was an after-hours party at Farmington Woods golf course—right around the time Tom and Tiger graduated from Avon—at which a young women was raped and later found passed out in a golf cart. Apparently, there were Avon students or graduates involved, including Tiger Williams. No charges were ever filed, so technically, the case isn't closed."

Tom Dickleman and Austin Cleary, obviously caught off-guard, just stared straight ahead.

"I'll leave you on that note, but I'd like to have you come back tomorrow for a formal hearing at 11 am. We have issued a summons to Mr. Williams be here also, or face contempt charges. Good day, gentlemen."

Rick Larsen met Sam in the lobby at 3:30 and suggested a bar around the corner.

Rick ordered a Maker's Mark; Sam ordered a pint.

"So I guess I'm still confused," Rick began. "The police found her car abandoned?"

"They got a call from a neighbor who said it had been sitting in the beach parking lot for at least two days. They searched the car and searched the area, and found no signs of foul play. Jackie Spellmeyer—she's a West Hartford police detective I worked with on another case last year—drove down to Old Saybrook with me. We searched the car, and the area, ourselves, and found nothing."

"On the phone, you sounded skeptical yourself whether anything happened to her."

"Well ..."

Sam hadn't made up his mind how much to divulge to Rick.

"You do know about her stalker, right?" Sam asked.

"Yeah, she told me, and there were a couple of strange incidents around her house the two times I was there, including a suspicious parked car that hadn't been there when we arrived."

"Did you get the make of the car?"

"Too dark and shadowy. All I got was an outline. Looked like one of those boxy General Motors sedans.

"You went on two dates total, right?"

Yeah—the first one, actually, was more like a pick-up. I think she'd tell you the same thing."

"She did tell me the same thing." Both men laughed.

"But to answer your question," Sam continued, "first of all, we had become very good friends—she apparently trusted me more than anyone else at the school. She'd stay on my couch if anything weird happened at Brooks House. But in spite of that, she was very elusive with me about her leave of absence from Avon and what she planned to do next. Like she was keeping a secret or something."

Rick just shrugged his shoulders.

"Speaking of secrets, I think she felt you were keeping something from her. If it's not too out-of-line for me to ask—"

"It's fine," he interrupted. "I'm engaged. She had broken it off before the night I met Marion, but then we worked it out. Kim was away for the weekend when I decided to call Marion for one more date. I liked her, and I didn't want her to feel disposable. I guess that also makes me a bad guy, but I never said I was perfect."

"Nobody is. Don't worry about it. But here's the other thing. Marion's stalker is pretty much one of two men. And they've both been wrapped up in a murder investigation—"

"The young woman who was found raped and murdered in her West Hartford apartment?"

"Yes, that one. Terrible. Marion disappeared a few days later, but I don't think those guys even knew where she was, let alone decided to chase her down to the shore to pull her out of her car and do something to her."

"Did you know where she was?"

"Yes. She called me from the Griswold Inn. I had dinner with her there on Saturday. But after that she was very mysterious about what she was going to do next. But back to your dates with her. Did she ever say anything about wanting to go away anywhere? To leave the Hartford area and move to another state or country?"

"Not that I recall. She did mention that she might not stay at Avon. It didn't seem like a done deal, and she didn't dwell on it."

"What did you talk about?"

"Mostly literature. And on the second date, art and architecture, that sort of thing."

"Did she ever talk to you about Kate Chopin's book *The Awakening*?"

"Ha, that's too funny. We did. And we talked about that final scene where she walks into the Gulf—"

"Oh my god," Rick interrupted himself, "You don't think—"

"No, I don't," Sam replied. "But we have discussed the book, and when I saw her car parked right next to Long Island Sound, I thought to myself, she wouldn't, would she? I mean, she does have a lot to run away from, between her stalker and her ex-husband's illegal business dealings. But I thought it over and said to myself, nope, not her."

"You know her better than I do," Rick said, "But I don't see her doing that either."

"Now I could see her parking the car there as a distraction," Sam said. "But there was something too clean and clinical about it. Car left unlocked and almost nothing inside of it. No keys, no handbag, no candy wrapper, no suicide note. Were there any other books or movies she brought up that had desperate characters?"

No, I don't think so ... I mean, lots of books have desperate characters in them, but they're not role models for a secret escape plan—"

Rick stopped mid-sentence, then began again.

"Oh wait, there was one. Canadian author. Atwater. No, Atwood. Margaret Atwood. Can't think of the title. If I recall what Marion said, the protagonist's life is always a mess, whether she's succeeding or failing, so she fakes her own death and moves to Italy. I think Marion said she loved the idea."

"Hmmm ... Well," said Sam finally. "Here's my number. Can I take yours? Let me know if you think of anything else, and I'll let you know if I get any new information."

From the bar, Sam drove six blocks to the Hartford Public Library on Main Street. First he asked the reference desk if they had telephone books from other cities around the country. He was directed to an aisle where there were two shelves of phone books, mostly from around Connecticut, New York and New Jersey. There was also Boston, Providence, and Portland, Maine, along with big national markets like Chicago, Philadelphia, Denver, Phoenix, Houston, and Los Angeles. There was no Albuquerque or Santa Fe.

Sam did not have any better luck with national newspapers. He did find one Santa Fe visitors' guide with some limited information on arts venues and events, as well as programs offered by the College of Santa Fe and the Center for Contemporary Arts of Santa Fe. It also had a list of area colleges and universities. Sam checked the volume out of the library. On his way home, he made one more stop, at Union Station, where he picked up some Amtrak schedules and a national route map.

Back in his apartment at about 5 o'clock, Sam suddenly had a thought. He picked up the phone and dialed the Griswold Inn, this time rehearsing how to introduce himself.

"Griswold Inn, how may I direct your call?"

"May I please speak to the manager on duty?" Sam asked.

"Sure, just a moment."

The phone went to soft classical music, then a woman picked up. "Anne Carruthers. How may I help you?"

"Hello, this is Sam Field. I'm detective from the Hartford area working on a missing persons case, and I'm looking for some information on a recent guest at the inn."

"What is the name of the guest?" Ms. Carruthers asked.

"Marion Maloney."

"And what information are you seeking?"

"Well, Ms. Maloney is the missing person, and I'm trying to find—"

Sam was cut off by a gasp at the other end of the line.

"Marion is missing?" she said. "Oh my god."

"Okay, so you must be the friend who booked her room, then, is that right?"

"Yes, wait, who did you say you were?"

"My name is Sam Field, and I'm—here, let me explain. I am working with West Hartford Police Detective Jacqueline Spellmeyer on this case. I also happen to be one of Marion's best friends at Avon Old Farms School, where she taught until recently."

Anne gasped again, trying to take it all in. "I think you were here too, for a night. I saw your name on the register. What happened?"

"Well Marion checked out that Tuesday, and the Old Saybrook Police found her car—abandoned, they concluded—down at Harveys Beach. Jackie and I drove down on Saturday to talk to the police and have a look around. I don't think they even knew what to do with the case. It certainly hasn't made a splash in the news. Between you and me, I don't think anything happened to her. I believe she's …" Sam trailed off, not sure how much to say.

"It's a long story," he said finally. "I believe she has gone somewhere on her own, and I can't speculate where or why. Nothing quite adds up. But we have to try to find her."

"Well, I sure hope you do," Anne said.

"Look," Sam said, "I don't know how close you two are. If you have any other information you can share, please do. Anything she told you, any plans, any old friends she wanted to go and see. You knew each other from growing up in West Hartford, is that right?"

"Yes. Okay, let me take your number, and if I think of anything, I'll let you know."

"Oh, how about phone calls? Would you be able to see what calls she night have made from her room?"

"Well," Anne said, hesitating, as if deciding whether that was legal or proper.

"Let me get back to you on that one."

"Okay, thanks."

Back in his room after dinner, Sam saw that he had a message.

"It's Jackie. The woman who lost her key called me. Everything the super said checked out. She had the door open, but she had dropped the key, and didn't pick it up because there was something creepy about the man approaching her. Big, tall, swarthy guy, she said. It's coming together. Could be interesting tomorrow morning at the precinct. I can't bring you along, but I'll tell all about it."

Sam sat down, and was poring over the Amtrak route map when the phone rang. It was Anne from the Griswold.

"I'm not even sure I'm supposed to give this out," she said, "so please don't tell anyone. I want you to have it. Besides a few 203 calls in Connecticut, there's one that stands out. Area code 505. That's New Mexico. And I have very little doubt who it is."

"Ariana Bello?"

"My, you're good at this, aren't you. Yes, they were inseparable in high school. But Ariana left West Hartford to chase her dream, something Marion wished she had done. I think she didn't want to leave her father behind. Ariana knew she wanted to pursue art—I think she paints and also makes jewelry and maybe pottery. She might even teach there, I'm not sure. But that's where she wanted to be. Besides the vibrant arts community, it's also in her blood. She always said she was half Mexican with a streak of Navajo."

"And they kept in touch, I take it?"

"Yes."

"Do you think I might find Marion there?"

"Well ..." Here Anne hesitated again. "Assuming she wants to be found."

Sam mulled that over, then said, "In the last minutes I spent with her at the Griswold, Marion pleaded with me, if we ever got separated, to come find her. I didn't know what she meant at the time, but I'm not making it up. *Promise me you'll come find me.*"

"Well, go find her! And call me when you do!"

Chapter 19

At 9 am Tuesday, Sam's phone rang. It was Jackie.

"Oh, good, caught you. Are you off to class shortly?"

"No classes today. Just exams to grade, and one more set to administer in class tomorrow."

"Okay. So you have a second for some updates?"

"Sure. And I can tell you about my meeting with Rick, and a very lucky phone call I made to the Griswold."

"Hmmm," she replied. "If you made the call for a good reason, or even a good hunch, and you got good information from it, it's not luck--it's good thinking. But you'll learn—if you ever go into this business, or into investigative reporting, which is almost the same thing."

"Anyway," Jackie continued, "First a question. What day do you guys get paid? And do you have direct deposit?"

"That's two questions. You know, in college I took a course in interviewing, and one of the things I was taught was to avoid asking two questions at once, because your source might answer only one of them."

"Well," she snapped back, "So far you've answered none of them, and I have to be at the precinct soon."

"Sorry. Just being a wiseass. I think I get it from my students. We get paid every other Friday, and if you have direct deposit, it's in your account when you wake up."

"And when is the next payday?"

"This Friday."

"Okay," Jackie said. "So that means ... the last payday before this one was almost two weeks ago, the same Friday when you went partying in Hartford, and when Marion started her weekend at the Griswold."

"Yes."

"Okay, that makes sense. She made another withdrawal on that Friday, after pretty much cleaning out her accounts a couple of weeks ago. So you were right—at least as far as her walking around with pockets full of cash to spend on things like train tickets."

"Oh, that reminds me," Sam said. "If you're free later, I'd like to stop by and show you that Amtrak national route map."

"What else?" Jackie continued. "On a hunch, I put together a list of 16 marinas on the shore and along the river, and faxed each of them a letter with photos of Mark Miller, just to see if they've seen him living his dream of boat ownership."

"And I have to get going, but here's the best part: I think I may have Tom Dickleman on the ropes, thanks to that golf course rape story you shared with me. I brought it up today, and he and his attorney looked very nervous, and I reminded them that since no case was opened, it's still not closed. Now your friends said Tom and Tiger were both there, right? Of the two, I have my own hunch who the likely perp is. I can only hope I've planted enough worry in Tom's brain that he'll come to his senses and throw Tiger under the bus."

Okay," Sam replied. "Rick Larsen pretty much confirmed what Marion told me about their two dates. But the best info I got was from Marion's friend, Anne Carruthers, the manager at the Griswold. It was a good day for hunches, I guess—I decided out of the blue to call the inn, and I got directly connected to Anne, who had no idea Marion was missing. Don't the papers care about these things?"

"Maybe the Old Saybrook cops didn't give them much to chew on. Not the most thorough bunch—oh never mind. I'm not going to pass judgment. So what else?"

Once she warmed up to me, she really wanted to help. Called me back with Marion's phone records from the inn. One outcall stood out. Area code 505--New Mexico. Anne was worried that giving me the info might be some kind of violation—"

"Probably was."

"So I didn't just tell you that, right?"

"Tell me what?"

Sam just smiled and said, "Thank you."

In a conference room at the West Hartford Police headquarters, Tom Dickleman sat on one side of the table, flanked by his attorney, Austin Cleary, and his father George. Detectives Jackie Spellmeyer and Frank Garrison sat at each end. Dave Williams, who had continued to evade Jackie's efforts to meet with him, had been issued a summons to attend the 11 am hearing or face more serious legal consequences. At 11:05, he walked in with his attorney, Gary Bianchi.

After cursory introductions, Jackie cleared her throat, and turned to address Bianchi and Williams.

"At this point," Jackie said, "thanks to the cooperation of all the other witnesses in the case of Marcie Merrifield's murder, we have a pretty good outline of what went down that Friday night and Saturday morning, who was involved, who was in what car, and how everybody got home. There's just one thing that remains a little vague—we don't know for sure when you, David Williams, left the Toddle House, and more importantly, where you went from there."

Williams held his palms out on either side of him as if to say, *I thought this was all settled.*

"I drove home," he said. "Home to Avon. Everybody knows that."

"Do they?" Jackie replied. "I don't think anybody really saw where you went."

Tiger looked pleadingly at Tom. "Come on, Tom, you saw me get in my car. You saw me drive away, down New Britain Avenue toward the interstate. Didn't you tell them that?"

Tom cleared his throat. "Look, Tiger, I drove in the other direction, up Main Street. I remember you getting in your car, but I couldn't see anything after that. So that's what I told the detectives."

"But it was all settled," Tiger protested. "You had the girls, and I was to go home. That's what we agreed, right?"

"Was it settled, Tiger? How would I know if you did what you said you were going to do?"

"Jesus, Tom, would I lie to you?"

"I don't know, Tiger, would you? I just know you wanted Marcie in the worst way. That's why I insisted on taking her home."

"What the—" began Tiger, until he was cut off by Gary Bianchi.

"Tiger, easy. No need to lose your cool. We do have it in the record that Tom drove Miss Merrifield home, right, Ms.

Spellmeyer? So anything beyond that is just idle speculation, and of no legal consequence."

"Except that you didn't go home, did you, Tiger."

It was Tom speaking; everyone in the room turned to look at him, startled.

"Go on, Tom," said Jackie, hopeful that her chess move from the previous day was paying off.

"I saw you," said Tom.

"You wh-what?" Tiger stammered, his voice rising.

"At about 4 in the morning, after I left Nathalie's apartment, I saw your Oldsmobile Omega leaving the rear parking lot. I pulled up closer to make sure, but there was no denying, with that big familiar dent in the rear fender, that it was you. I was about to get out and talk to you, but you sped away suddenly."

"Thank you, Tom," Jackie said.

Gary Bianchi furrowed his brow and coughed. "Detective Spellmeyer, Detective Garrison," he began. "This allegation is new to me, and I cannot vouch for its accuracy, or lack thereof, without further investigation, including private consultation with my client. I would request several days to a week to respond."

"What's today?" Garrison asked no one in particular. "It's Tuesday, May 14. I would like your response by Friday, May 17. If true, the allegation does take the investigation into new territory."

"You will hear from me by Friday."

The people in the room began shuffling and putting away their papers, sliding back their chairs, and preparing to leave the room. Jackie noticed that Tiger wasn't moving, and that his face, tanned from many spring days on the golf course, had turned a discernable shade of red. What happened next came in such a blurred succession of violent movements that Jackie later would have trouble describing it to Sam.

"You fucking asshole son of a bitch."

The words came from somewhere deep within Tiger's diaphragm, sounding hoarse and guttural and almost otherworldly. Bianchi reached over and tried to persuade his client to shut up and leave the room quietly, but by then there was no quiet left in Tiger's mind or body.

"Some asshole friend you are," he screamed, lunging suddenly across the table and grabbing Tom by the throat, the momentum of Tiger's leap and table slide forcing Tom to the floor, his chair buckling into splinters beneath him, with Tiger landing on top. In such a vulnerable position, Tom, despite his own considerable size and strength, was no match for the bear-like strength of Tiger, who dug his fingers into Tom's neck while his own neck veins seemed to swell almost to the point of popping. Tom tried to fight him off, and to scream for help, but his voice came out strangled.

While the two attorneys and Jackie watched, frozen in disbelief, Frank opened the door and yelled for someone to help with a violent aggressor. What happened next shocked everyone.

Suddenly, Tiger's head jerked back violently, and his body twisted awkwardly to the side, his arms flailing. George, his military training coming back to him in all its brutal glory, had cupped Tiger's chin in one strong hand, and used the other hand and one leg to leverage his control over him until he had both arms crossed behind Tiger's back, held down at first by one hand, and then two hands, and by one painfully stabbing knee. Tiger howled in agony.

Before long he was in handcuffs and being read his Miranda rights, while Frank dictated charges of aggravated assault, and also the murder of Marcie Merrifield. "Forget Friday," he barked at Gary Bianchi. "What he just did was response enough."

"As for the homicide," Jackie added, "with Tom Dickleman's testimony on the sighting of your car, the rest of the pieces of our investigation complete the puzzle. We know from other witness accounts that you had been vying for the attention of Marcie Merrifield. We also know that you had offered to drive her home that night, and that Tom thwarted your hopes by insisting that he drive both Marci and Nathalie Frelet home because they lived in the same apartment building. But you turned around and went there anyway. And now we know that another tenant dropped her entry key on the ground after she opened the door, and left it there in her hurry to get away from an approaching man who fit your description."

"We're not sure how you gained entry into Marcie's apartment; maybe you caught up to her before she closed the door, or maybe you persuaded her to let you in and talk. Either way, once you were inside, there was a struggle and an attempted rape that left her badly bruised. And somehow, in your attempt to subdue her, you strangled her."

Tiger, handcuffed and helpless, had enough left in him for an angry parting shot. "You've always had it in for me," he screamed at George, "because my mother wouldn't fuck you. You thought when I got into Avon, you'd get into her pants, and she wouldn't let you. I overheard her telling you to go fuck yourself. You fucking pig."

George said nothing, but he smacked Tiger's face so hard his lip bled.

"Whoa," shouted Bianchi, turning to Garrison. "How about an assault charge for that?"

"File a complaint if you like," replied Garrison. "From where I stand, he had it coming to him."

As Tiger was led away, he looked at Tom. This time, his voice was practically a whisper.

"I thought we always had each other's back," he said. "I thought you'd protect me."

"I protected you once," Tom replied. "I won't do that again. This is where it ends."

Sam Field finished grading one of his students' exams, placed it on his "finished" pile, and decided it was a good time to take a break. It was a few minutes after 5 pm in Connecticut, which meant that long-distance rates were now on the somewhat cheaper evening schedule. It also meant it was only just after 3 pm in New Mexico.

"University of New Mexico, how may I direct your call?"

"The main office of the art department, please."

"UNM College of Fine Arts. How may I help you?"

"I'm looking for a faculty member named Ariana Bello."

"Is that 'B' as in boy, then 'E-L-L-O-W'?

"No 'W' at the end, I don't think."

"Let me see … Uh … No, I don't see that name on our faculty list."

"Okay. I appreciate your time."

Sam continued his inquiry at other institutions in the Albuquerque-Santa Fe area, including St. Francis, St. John's, and Central New Mexico Community College, with similar results. He finally scored a minor breakthrough when he reached the art department at College of Santa Fe.

"Let's see … no faculty member named Ariana Bello. But I do recognize the name. Is she a local artist?"

"Yes. I thought she might also be affiliated with a college. I'm trying to track her down for … for a possible project here in Connecticut, where she grew up."

"You might also want to try the Center for Contemporary Arts. And there's a big art and craft show coming up Memorial Day weekend. So that's about a week and a half away, if you want to get more information about that. Maybe she's showing. Here's the CCA number."

Sam was thinking about what to ask the CCA when his phone rang.

"You are not going to believe what happened at the precinct today," Jackie said. "I wish we had it on videotape."

"Oh?" Sam replied. "Do tell."

"I'd rather describe it in person. Jerry and I are making stir-fry again. Why don't you come over, and you can also show me the Amtrak map."

As Sam stepped into the Spellmeyer home, he was greeted first by Duke, wagging his tail excitedly, happy to see Sam but probably even happier about the aromas emanating from the kitchen.

"Wait till you hear this," said Jerry. "She asks me why I don't encourage her to stay retired, but entertainment like this is hard to pass up."

"Come on in the dining room," Jackie said to Sam. "We haven't set the table yet so I can use it to block out the action from today's hearing. Jerry, keep the stir-fry on low, and keep Duke from jumping up."

She turned back to Sam. "So on this side, you have Tom in the middle, and his lawyer, Austin Cleary, over there, and George over here—"

"What was George doing there?"

"I'm pretty sure it was because I brought up the old rape case yesterday. Maybe he knew his son had more to tell, and he wanted to make sure we could wrap up the case without damaging his son's, and the school's, reputations. As you have seen in the past, he can be pretty prickly about that. Plus, he seems to have a lot of influence with police departments around here."

"Anyway, it probably was a good thing he was there. So here's what happened ..."

Jackie finished telling the story, and Sam just stared blankly at her for a minute before speaking.

"Holy fucking shit."

"Wow," he continued. "So did Tiger pretty much incriminate himself in the murder by his actions in the hearing?"

"Well, he didn't leave many dots to connect. They've charged him, and now he and his attorney can decide how to plead, and we'll see if it goes to court."

"Who pays for the mangled furniture?" Sam asked, then chuckled loudly. "Interesting, though, that Tiger clawed back at George with the story of him trying to get his mother into bed. All the bad things these men have done, coming back to bite them."

"Well, mostly Tiger. And Tom seemed to hint at the end that he protected his friend one too many times—makes me think about that rape on the golf course all those years ago. I doubt anyone will go back and reopen that case. Actually, I think you said a case was never opened in the first place."

"Shall we eat?" said Jerry, as Jackie set the table and Duke watched expectantly.

"Gee, I wonder who Duke will go to first," said Jackie.

Oh, let me show you the Amtrak route map," Sam said, reaching over to grab it from a side table.

"Now if Marion went west—I mean south—her first major stop would be New York," Sam began.

"How do you know she didn't go toward Boston?" Jerry asked. "She had enough cash on her for Red Sox season tickets. Maybe Bruins too."

"Don't be silly, Jerry," his wife scolded. "Anyway, if she's escaping her current life, Boston would be too close, like one small pawn move on the chessboard. I see her moving more like the queen."

"In terms of evidence," added Sam, "now we have that phone call to Santa Fe."

"Have you tried calling the number?" Jackie asked him.

"Not yet. I'm still trying to make a plan."

"Oh, speaking of which," Jackie said, "I almost forgot to tell you. We're hired. Michael Maloney agreed to pay us a modest fee if we find Marion. More important, he's willing to cover reasonable expenses."

"Hey, that's great!" Sam said. "Well then, let's look at this," said Sam. "From New York, the logical gateway to the west would be Chicago. There are a few ways to go New York to Chicago on Amtrak—I'm not even worried about figuring that part out."

"But here's what I like," Sam continued. "In Chicago, you can board a train called the Southwest Chief. It's a historic route, and practically a straight line to Albuquerque. And it's such a romantic Old West ride. Listen to the towns it connects: Kansas City, Topeka, Dodge City, Lamar, Albuquerque. You can practically see the old wooden train stations, the cowboy hats, the "WANTED" signs. Maybe for an extra fee they hire robbers to attack the train."

Jackie and Jerry both chuckled as Sam waxed nostalgic about the Southwest Chief. More to the point, Jackie now believed this travel itinerary for Marion was, or had been, a real possibility.

How long does that trip take in total?" asked Jerry.

"At least three days, I think, depending on the connections," answered Sam. "The Southwest Chief runs only once a day."

"Do you know," Sam continued, "that there's a city in New Mexico called Truth or Consequences? There was an old radio show with that name, and the town of Hot Springs changed its name to win a contest on the show. Truth or Consequences, I love it."

"I never heard that one," admitted Jackie. "But speaking of consequences, it still bothers me that Tom Dickleman harassed Marion, and not only is he getting away with it, no one besides us will ever know. I think you said you had some thoughts on this."

"Yes, it bothers me too, in general. You know what Marion said when I asked her if she ever thought about calling the police when the stalker harassed her at Brooks House? She said she considered it but didn't really want to. She said something to the effect of, 'It's almost like punishment on top of punishment.' I think I know what she meant. What do you think?"

Jackie sighed, underscoring her years of frustration with the issue. "It's the worst-kept secret in law enforcement. Woman gets raped or harassed. Woman goes to police. Police make woman feel like she's the bad person. There's a reason so many of them don't even report it."

"Do you think that will ever change?"

Jackie pondered the question for a moment. "Maybe someday, if there are more women in positions of power. Or if more women decide to speak out. But how to speak out effectively is tricky. You can have a big rally or protest, or a "Take Back the Night" march. Have you heard of that movement? But what happens if the media don't cover it? Or they cover it for one day and then go back to business as usual? It fizzles. Maybe the whole nature of mass communication will have to change."

"Back to Tom for a moment," Sam said. "I don't for a second think the things he whispered to Marion—or to Nathalie, for that matter—in the middle of the quad were appropriate. But Tom was not her stalker at Brooks House."

"Oh, said with such certainty! How do you know this?"

A few things. Rick said the suspicious car hanging out by the house for no reason was a boxy GM sedan—that's exactly what Tiger's Oldsmobile Omega is. Marion observed, without giving it too much more thought, that the dirty talk—which stopped on campus with Marion around the time it started to work with Nathalie—became much nastier when notes started appearing at Brooks House. At least Tom seems to have limits; Tiger, I have noticed these past few weeks, is far more prone to being crude.

And the photo of the penis. Did you see it? And did I tell you Terry McSweeney's story about a friend who saw Tiger in the shower at Central Connecticut State College? He asked Terry if he had ever showered with Tiger, and Terry was like, 'Why are you asking me that?' And he said "Mac, I showered with him. The guy had a fuckin' snake." That description matches both the dick pic he dropped off and the real-life penis he flashed in Marion's window."

"And not too be too crude myself, but since we are talking about it, you are sure that could not be Tom's penis?"

"I am sure."

"You've seen it?"

"Seen what?"

"Tom's penis."

"No, I have not."

"But you know something about its size."

"Nathalie has seen it. And as you already know, she has seen mine. Do I have to go any further with this embarrassing conversation?"

I'm just trying to do thorough detective work." At that, Jackie burst out laughing. "Don't tell me, Nathalie compared you favorably to Tom. Maybe you're the stalker!"

"Not favorably, really ... just ... comparably. Jeez, I can't believe I'm even talking about this. And if you must know, for the sake of thoroughness, when boys first grow into full-sized males, they are all kinds of angsty about how they stack up. So you know what? They measure them. And they compare what they measure to what the average is."

Sam looked over at Jerry, perhaps hoping he could save him with some comic relief.

"I'll sit this one out, thank you," he laughed.

"Well?" persisted Jackie.

"You know I'm not the kind of person who goes around talking or bragging about this."

At that point, Sam jumped up and started pumping his fists like Rocky Balboa. "I'm average!" he declared. "In fact, I'd say I'm extra average!"

"That makes Tom average too," she said. "Well then, I'm convinced. No more embarrassing conversation. Tiger Williams was the stalker all along. Nice work, detective. I just wonder ..."

"Wonder what?" Sam asked nervously.

"I wonder if Tom Dickleman has learned anything from all this. Probably not. Oh well, I'm not going to lose sleep over it. As for you, will you be taking a ride on the Southwest Chief?"

"As I said, I have a little more groundwork to do. But if I'm reasonably sure she's gone there, I'm going to go find her."

"I'll probably fly, though."

Chapter 20

As Sam Field prepared to administer his last set of history exams for the school year, it suddenly occurred to him that the tumultuous events of the last month or so had pretty much sponged away any lingering thoughts he might have had about Maggie Duchesne.

The sophisticated and strikingly pretty Walker's student, then a senior whom he last saw when she visited his apartment almost exactly a year earlier, was now completing her freshman year at Georgetown University. Despite the intense two-way crush that had inspired several impromptu makeout sessions over the course of her senior year—and a mutual vow to stay in touch—communication between the two had fizzled away like a burned-out firecracker.

Though their liaisons were supposed to be secret, on the Avon campus, they were anything but—even a year later. Reese Gilmartin constantly needled Sam about it, and Nathalie Frelet made several references to "that brunette bitch from Walker's" while trying to seduce him. And despite the now-widespread presumption that Sam and Maggie had been lovers, they both actually had had just enough will power to curtail their questionable behavior before it went too far.

In part because they helped Sam and Jackie Spellmeyer solve the disappearance of another Walker's girl, Maggie and her best friend Annie Green—along with Annie's boyfriend Warren Cochran—had become good friends with Sam. But Maggie and Annie had graduated, while Warren, now a senior and no longer on Sam's residence hall, had seldom crossed paths with Sam in the current year.

At 9:30 am, Sam passed out the exam papers and watched as the students began filling them in. He looked at them and wondered which ones he would still know well next year, which would probably be his last at the school. A vague sadness came over him as he realized he would miss them, but it didn't take long for that to be overshadowed by the return of his anxiety over Marion Maloney. And he decided that today would be the day when he tried the number in Santa Fe that Marion had called from the Griswold Inn.

At about 10:15 am, Jackie Spellmeyer's phone rang.

"Hello, this is Jackie Spellmeyer. Who's calling?"

"Hi Ms. Spellmeyer, it's Marilyn at the Old Lyme Marina."

"Hello Marilyn!" Jackie replied. "I assume you received my fax about Mark Miller?"

"Yes, and I have a couple of questions about the photos you faxed to us. We might have a match with a new customer, but the resolution of these images isn't great. He used the name Mark McMahon when he signed in, and the ID he gave us had the same name. Do those names mean anything to you? Besides that your suspect's name is Mark?"

"Yes, and sometimes people who use aliases keep their same first names if they're afraid that they, or their friends, will keep using them inadvertently. I don't know where he would have gotten McMahon—maybe he's a Chicago Bears fan. Has he rented a slip there?"

"Yes. He docked this morning and came into the office to see what we had available. His reservation officially begins this afternoon at four."

"Great! I'll see if I can get together a little welcoming party for him. So he'll come in off the water, right?"

"I assume so. He left again in the boat."

A little after 1 pm, Sam left lunch at the refectory and returned to the apartment. He looked at the 505 number he had written down. He decided it was time to make an attempt. "It's 11 o'clock in New Mexico," he said to himself out loud.

As Sam dialed the number, he felt a surge of adrenaline along with a tightening sensation in his chest. He hung up the phone and tried to collect himself. Then he picked up the receiver again and slowly began to dial.

It rang one, two, three, four, five times—at which point Sam panicked again and slammed it down.

He took several deep breaths and dialed again. After seven rings and no answer, he gave up.

"At least it didn't cost me anything," he said. Sam thought about the other long-distance call he wanted to make, to the Center for Contemporary Arts in Santa Fe. This time, he decided to wait until after 5 pm when the rates would be lower.

At 4:15 pm, a modest-sized cabin cruiser appeared on the Connecticut River near the Old Lyme Marina, approaching the slip Marilyn had identified as the one reserved by "Mark McMahon." The driver, a dark-haired man in his mid 30s, cut the engine and steered up to the dock, securing the boat with ropes thrown over wooden posts, which he tied upon stepping off the craft. Walking toward the small parking area, he was about to be greeted by a woman who looked to be in her late 20s, wearing sunglasses, carrying a shoulder bag, blonde hair pulled back in a ponytail, with navy blue boat sneakers, jeans, and a fleece-lined navy windbreaker over a pink "UConn Huskies" sweatshirt.

But before they got close enough to embrace, a man and a woman stepped out from behind a vehicle and stepped in front of the man, flashing badges. "West Hartford Police," announced Frank Garrison. "I'm Detective Garrison, and this is Detective Spellmeyer. Are you Mark Miller?"

"I ... I ... No," the man said. "My name is Mark McMahon. Look, I've got an ID here somewhere ..."

"Mark?" the woman asked, looking worried.

"Britt, why don't you wait in the car. Hopefully this little misunderstanding will be cleared up shortly."

"Your appearance matches photographs we have of Mark Miller," said Jackie. "And we believe 'Mark McMahon' is an alias. By the way, you should be aware that using an alias for the purpose of evading law enforcement, or other government agencies, such as the IRS, is a crime."

"The IRS?" he stammered. "I don't know what you're talking about."

Just then, a black Lincoln Town Car with U.S. government plates pulled up, and out stepped agents Sybil Bouchard and Anson Fritz—the same pair who paid a surprise visit to Marion Maloney one morning at her Brooks House residence. "Maybe they can help jog your memory," Jackie said.

The IRS agents identified themselves and showed their badges. "Mark Miller?" asked Agent Fritz.

The boat man hesitated. "As I was just telling the detectives here, they have the wrong name. I can show you my ID that says I'm Mark McMahon—"

Fritz stepped forward, now towering over the man, his height, steely demeanor, and wraparound shades reducing Mark to a simpering bundle of nerves. "Are you sure you want to show us that ID and put yourself in further legal jeopardy?" Fritz asked menacingly.

"Okay then," Mark responded finally. "I'm Mark Miller. What do you want with me?"

Now Frank Garrison stepped forward.

"You're under arrest, Mr. Miller. Securities fraud, mail fraud, tax evasion. I'd say that's a pretty good start. Oh, and Agents Fritz and Bouchard, you might want to get that boat impounded, and also get an assessor to work on determining its auction value."

A West Hartford officer stepped out of another waiting cruiser, handcuffed Miller, and escorted him to the backseat. In the parking lot, a horrified Britt watched it all go down, then scrambled into her car and drove away.

Before they left, Jackie found Marilyn in the marina office and thanked her for her help. "And I'll call Jeff too, but if you happen to talk to him, tell him we couldn't have done it without him."

At 5:05 pm, Sam tried the mystery Santa Fe number again. And again, it rang seven times with no answer before he hung up.

"Well, okay, I'll try again later," he said to himself. "Meanwhile, let's try something else."

Sam dialed the number for the Center for Contemporary Arts. A woman answered.

"CCA. May I help you?"

"Yes. I may be visiting from Colorado, and I heard there's an annual arts festival in Santa Fe over Memorial Day weekend. Is that right?"

"Yes, it certainly is. Would you be coming with friends? Family? There's something for everyone, including children …"

"Can you tell me more about the festival?"

"Sure. There will be more than 75 artists and craftspeople with works on display, from painting to photography to sculpture to crafts and jewelry. There will be music all day long all three days, including local folk and pop artists, children's performers and traditional Native American music. Oh, and food vendors of all types, emphasis on Southwestern, or course."

"Beer and wine?"

"Yes, there will be tents set up; you'll need a wristband. Beer, wine, other spirits, especially tequila."

"And what's the admission price?"

"Admission to the festival itself is just $5 individual, $10 for families of three or more. Of course, all food, drink, and merchandise are sold separately."

"You mentioned jewelry. Do you have a list of the craftspeople who will be showing?"

"Well, I don't know if everything is finalized yet, let me see …"

"Oh, okay, here we are … Jewelry creations by Diego Aguilar, Ariana Bello, Tabitha Claw, Penny Condon, Danielle Daisy—"

"Did you say Ariana Bello?"

"Yes, do you know her work?"

"I have a piece of hers. My wife does, actually. A turquoise pendant. Does she live in the area?"

"Yes, she lives here in Santa Fe. She and another jewelry maker own a shop—Casa Adobe, I think. They both make jewelry, and paint. I think Ariana does some Navajo rugs. And they feature other artists. Ariana is a big supporter of the center, and I think she does some teaching in the local public schools."

"Well, thank you for the information. I think I may drive down for a couple of days."

"Anything else?"

"No, that should do it, thanks."

Sam stopped into the refectory for dinner; end-of-the-year attendance was thinning, and the seating requirements were no longer enforced. Sam sat with Joe, Kevin, and Terry. Neither George nor Tom Dickleman had been seen on campus since the incident at the police precinct and the arrest of Tiger Williams. Even Nathalie had been scarce.

The men asked Sam if there was anything new on Marion's whereabouts. They knew she was officially missing, but also that Sam didn't think she had been kidnapped or harmed.

"You'd want to start a new life too, if you had to go through what she did," was all he said.

"Any idea where she might be?" asked Kevin.

Sam paused. "Yes, I do," he said. "I'm working on it. And Mrs. Spellmeyer and I have been hired by Marion's brother."

"Ah, big time private investigator!" Joe exclaimed. "You getting big bucks for this?"

"Nah, we didn't ask for much. Mostly expenses. Speaking of which, I might be getting on a plane in the next few days."

"You do know where she is," Terry said, smiling.

"Let's just say I have a good hunch," he replied, smiling. "Backed up by some solid detective work."

"Look at you," said Joe. "Who are you—Jim Rockford? Barney Miller? Kojak?"

"Jessica Fletcher?" offered Kevin, to a round of chuckles.

"I'll let you guys know if I'm leaving for a few days. I'll be stopping in here now and then over the summer. But it looks like I may miss graduation this weekend."

When Sam returned to his apartment, there was a message from Jackie. "Another day, another arrest," she said.

Sam dialed her number excitedly, and she answered. "Old Lyme. Woman called me this morning and said a new customer might be the guy in the fax. Hard to tell because the resolution was so poor, but she was right. And he walked right into our trap."

"Did they confiscate the boat? Was the IRS there too?"

"Oh yeah. You should have seen the look on Mark's face. And the new girlfriend—or whoever she was—just ran back to her car and drove away. Something tells me that's the last he'll see of her. Oh yeah, the boat is impounded, and I believe the IRS gets their cut before what's left gets settled among the investors. So if you do find Marion—"

Jackie stopped right there and regrouped.

"No," she corrected herself. "*When* you do find Marion, she should be very happy to learn this."

After Sam hung up, he decided to try the Santa Fe number again. He dialed and waited. One ring, two rings, three rings.

And on the fourth ring, a woman's voice answered.

"Hello?"

Sam was startled, but he collected himself quickly, and decided to keep it simple.

"Hi. I'm trying to reach Ariana Bello."

There was a long pause—too long, it seemed to him.

"I'm sorry, there's no one here who goes by that name."

"Oh, okay, I'm sorry to bother you," Sam said, pacing his words in a way he hoped would dissuade her from hanging up. "What about—is there someone there who goes by the name Marion Maloney?"

The pause on the other end of the line lasted even longer than the first one. "I'm sorry," she said finally. "You must have the wrong number. There is no one here with either of those names. Is that all?"

Now Sam paused. In a split-second of mulling over the tension in their silence, he wondered why, if it really was a wrong number, and if she were irritated or even scared by the call, she didn't just hang up.

"Yes," he said finally. "That is all. Thank you."

Sam sat down on his couch and exhaled a long sigh. He thought and thought, trying to conceive of some way he could break through and reach a more definitive conclusion on the whereabouts of these two human beings. From his brief telephone encounter with Anne Carruthers from the Griswold Inn, he trusted her and was sure she would not give him bad information. Unless Marion herself had dialed a wrong number—and now Sam kicked himself for not asking how many minutes the call was—then this had to be Ariana's number. What else could it be?

Which meant Sam had just been speaking with Ariana Bello (or Ariana Bello's roommate, if she had one), and that she had pretended that was not the case.

What were they hiding, whom were they hiding from, and why?

Marion had made him promise to find her. What was going on? Had she been kidnapped after all?

If this was a puzzle, the pieces did not have an obvious fit.

Sam had no idea how long he had been sitting on the couch and letting the possibilities bounce around in his head like superballs. And when he became conscious of the knocking at his door, he wasn't sure how long it had been happening.

He wasn't expecting Nathalie, who seemed to be settling into her relationship with Tom. And it couldn't possibly be Marion—could it?

Sam shrugged his shoulders and decided to just be ready for anything. He stood up, walked over to the door, and opened it—and found himself staring at the one person he was not ready for.

"Hard to believe it's been a year," Maggie said. "May I come in?"

"Of ... of course. I'm sorry. I don't mean to be rude. I'm just ... shocked."

Sam sized her up. She looked older than he remembered, and ever prettier. She wore stylish black boots that looked like ones you'd see in the city, with jeans and a sleek white blouse. "My, you look lovely," he said. "I'm sorry I haven't called lately. I just figured you were busy with college life. Come have a seat."

"Well, I haven't called either. Yes, I've been busy. Academics, parties, and so much to do in DC."

"And plenty of boys, no doubt."

"Haha, I call them men now. Even though most of them still act like boys!"

"I'm sure. I look at some of the boys who are about to graduate from here, and I think, holy fuck, are they really ready for college?"

"Do you miss me?"

Sam was startled at first by Maggie's question. "Of course I do. You don't know how many times this year I've wished you'd come and knock on my door."

"But you've been busy, I hear."

"Busy? How?"

"Not suffering from a lack of female companionship, I mean."

Maggie looked at him with that penetrating stare and smirk he had become used to the previous year, especially when they danced around their feelings for each other.

"I'd love to know what you mean exactly. But what about you? You can't tell me that you've been partying with all those smart boys—I mean men—without going a little deeper now and then."

"Deeper?"

"I mean, like developing a deeper relationship."

"I'm not actually in a relationship at the moment," Maggie said, crossing her arms.

"Surely you've been, you know, having some ... um ..."

"Sex? Can't you just come out and say it? I'm not 17 anymore—in fact, I'm 19. And yes, I have had sex with a few men at Georgetown. Can you handle it?"

"Wait, why—"

"I'm sorry, I don't know where that came from. I guess I always wonder, if we were still in the same place, if you'd

be judging my behavior. Like when I kissed that boy at the dance—"

"I was not judging you! I was trying to avoid having you see me, so you could have whatever fun you wanted without making me jealous ... I mean ... What I'm trying to say is..."

"Aha! See, you were jealous!"

Maggie's presence in Sam's apartment flooded him with feelings he thought he had finally left behind. And for the moment, it was his yearning to find Marion that he had set aside. As with his involuntary reaction to the familiar scent of Maggie's perfume, he was nearly overcome by his desire to hold her, to meet her lips and tongue with his own, and get lost in the delirious haze of lust they had once flirted with.

"I missed you so much," he admitted, "that I compensated by trying to forget you."

"Well, like I said, it seems you've had plenty of help. Warren and a couple of my other guy friends have kept me updated. Nathalie Frelet—how *tres Parisienne*. Isn't she banging the headmaster's son now? I hear you were getting in on that action. Was she good?"

"What do you want from me?"

"It's just a question."

"In her own aggressive way, yeah, I guess she was good. The key word being 'was'."

"And now Marion, I hear."

"Marion, Marion," Sam chewed on her name as the reality of his predicament came rushing back into his mind. "Yeah, we've been like best friends. Strictly platonic."

"Strictly platonic? Again, not what I hear."

"And how would you know what goes on behind that door over there when you're not around?" Sam snapped. "Think of it, people said the same thing about us whenever you ended up in here and then had to sneak back out. And we weren't even fucking."

"No, we weren't fucking." Maggie's eyes burned with a combination of lust and frustration.

"But the kissing was very sweet," Sam offered. "You have no idea how amazing that was for me."

"And for me," she said. "I just—"

"Just what?"

"I always hoped that some way, at some point, I'd be able to have all of you, even if only one time."

Maggie, who had been gazing directly into Sam's eyes for most of the conversation, suddenly looked away.

"I always wanted that too," Sam said. "Marion and I joked about how you were still too young, according to the half-your-age-plus-seven formula—"

Maggie turned back and faced him, holding back tears. "Can you please not bring up Marion? I really don't need to hear about her right now. Once again, I shouldn't have come. But I wanted to see—"

"Wanted to see what?"

"What do you think?"

"To see if I still had feelings? To see if you still had feelings? Tell me where we're going with this."

"You want to know where we're going with this?" she asked him, her voice breaking. "How about this—do I get do decide?"

Sam looked at her for a long moment. "You know I've always been putty in your hands. I don't think I could stop this feeling if I wanted to."

Maggie stepped forward and kissed Sam's lips gently. He responded, and she began circling her tongue on the inside of his mouth. It didn't take long to get back to where they had left off, making out intensely and running their hands all over each other's backs. Only this time, Maggie knew she was not stopping.

First, she pulled his shirt over his head. Then she undid the buttons on her blouse, stopping only to unhook her bra from behind so that when her blouse fell off, her bra fell with it.

"Let's go to bed," she said, and started to laugh.

"That's a Cure song," he said.

"I know," silly boy. "How about this then—let's fuck."

"You have to be anywhere?" he asked softly.

"Not till tomorrow. Can we take this nice and slow? I want to savor every minute of it."

"Like I said, whatever you say. I'm all yours tonight."

And the world slowed down to a crawl. Nothing outside Sam's little apartment mattered tonight, not with Sam and Maggie lost in the sensations flooding though their minds and bodies. Pleasure came in waves, subsided, and came back again, finally giving way to a sense of peace as they lay there entangled in each other's arms and legs, thankful that although they could not stay together, time and tide had brought them one glorious gift they could share for a few hours.

Chapter 21

Sam and Maggie sat drinking coffee at Sam's kitchen table. Sam wore sweatpants and a T-shirt; Maggie was dressed to leave.

"Do you need to be somewhere soon?" he asked.

"Oh, no timetable, really. I have a few friends to see here, then I'm heading over to Walker's."

She looked up from her coffee and laughed. "But it's pleasant sitting here and talking to you--like normal adults! Besides, I didn't want to just fuck and run, you know?" She placed her free hand over his for a long moment.

Sam smiled. "I hope you had fun. I know I did."

Maggie smiled at him devilishly.

"What do you think?"

"It's funny," he said, "I'd almost forgotten how badly I wanted this. Back then—and it really does seem like ten years ago—when you were alone with me here, in this apartment, I was so tempted. And it was so forbidden. You have no idea what you did to me when you kissed me."

"Hmmm," she said. "Maybe the reason you wanted it so badly was because it was so forbidden. Didn't you wonder if your desire would go away after I turned 18 and graduated?"

"I did wonder that. I guess it never really went away. I missed you and thought about you a lot. But eventually I knew I had to deal with the here and now. And then we kind of fell out of touch. Funny, I did just think of you the other day. Maybe I had some kind of intuition you were coming. You still surprised me, though!"

Maggie smiled. "I wasn't necessarily planning to ambush you like that. But driving up yesterday from DC, I started to feel it. And the idea grew on me. By the time I got into Connecticut I almost couldn't stand it. I stopped once for gas and coffee and a snack and came straight here."

"And you don't feel any guilt about this, even as we go our separate ways, do you?"

"No. Do you?"

"No, I guess I don't. I would have if we had done it last year. Now I sort of feel like ..."

"Like what?"

"Like we were meant to do this. Almost like it's a little gift we've given each other to take away and remember—and to remind us ... um ... that our feelings for each other were real. Or something like that." Sam laughed at himself. "Sorry if that sounds really goofy. Once I start trying to talk about feelings, I start to sound really stupid."

Maggie smiled at him. "It's fun watching you, Mr. Articulate, fumble for words," she said. "But you know, as a guy, you're doing better than most just to even try."

"Really?" He smiled back at her, and something Marion had said to him crossed his mind.

"A friend of mine at Walker's used to talk about how repressed we all are sexually, and that our bodies are wired for pleasure, and that we should learn to enjoy sex in a variety of ways, from casual to married and whatever else in between. As long as it's consensual, and nobody's getting hurt, of course."

"Speaking of which," Sam said, "how are the men at Georgetown? Do they treat you with respect? Do they consider you equals? I've been thinking lately about men who grow up to be sexist pigs, or worse, abusive sexist pigs, and like, where does that come from? Where does it start?"

"Well, my woman's studies professor might say it starts in the crib, with the toys your parents toss in for us to play with." She laughed.

"I would tend to agree," she continued, "Except, how does that explain the differences between different men? Or women? You, for example, came out great. Maybe your parents did a better job than most."

"Well, one, yes, my parents did a great job, I think, and two, no, I'm far from perfect. And three, maybe they forgot to throw me Tonka trucks."

They both laughed, and Maggie leaned in to give Sam a long, sensual kiss.

"Wow," he said when they finally pulled apart. "Careful. You're all dressed and ready to go."

"I know," she said. "I couldn't resist. And you were perfect last night. I'm not going to risk damaging that memory."

"And I wouldn't trade it for anything."

"By the way, I'm sorry I snapped at you for mentioning Marion. I didn't know which way our thing was going, and I guess I selfishly needed all of your attention without another woman interfering. I wanted you so badly—and I got you."

She laughed and ran her hand through his hair. "And I'm happy now. And I do want to hear more about your life. So you can tell me about her now, if you like."

"Well, we do have a platonic relationship—a very close friendship. Except now she's gone missing."

"Missing? Holy fuck."

Sam told Maggie an abridged version of the whole story, from the harassment on campus, to the harassment at Brooks house, to the IRS liability that was her ex-husband's fault. And he told her about the night at the Griswold Inn, which brought them even closer as friends even as they agreed that anything more physical would most likely ruin the relationship.

Maggie's familiar skeptical smirk crept across her face, but this time there was no anger or jealousy associated with it. "Darling," she said affectionately, "that just doesn't sound like you."

Sam thought for a minute. "It's really weird, isn't it. With you, last night, I felt like I couldn't stand another day without making our passion count for something. To take that firecracker and explode it. And we're still going to be friends—I know we are. Maybe lovers again someday, who the hell knows? With Marion, it's practically the opposite. We have to stay friends—I can't explain why, but we do. It's like a cosmic imperative. And I'd do almost anything to protect that. Including not fucking her. I hope that makes sense."

"Well, in its own weird way, I suppose it does. And I do feel awful about what she went through here. Do you think something bad has happened to her?"

Sam told Maggie about the abandoned car that didn't look like a crime scene, and his theory that Marion had gone somewhere to leave all her problems behind.

"And the irony is, little did she know that within a couple of weeks, her ex-husband and one of her stalkers would be arrested, and the IRS would release her from the liability."

"Who got arrested?"

Sam quickly explained about the murder of Marcie Merrifield after a night out drinking and going out for breakfast with Avon boys. "Did you ever meet Tom Dickleman's friend Tiger Williams?" Sam asked.

"Don't think so."

"He's been charged with the murder. And he's the one who was stalking her at Brooks House, I'm sure of it. But not the one who was harassing her on campus—that was a different man she never named."

"Tom?"

"Yep."

"Well, he's the headmaster's son. Who would wish that kind of trouble upon themselves? Almost worse that reporting it to the police."

She thought for a minute. "At Georgetown, we're supposed to be adopting more progressive policies around rape and sexual assault, and how the university responds to complaints. Tell that to any woman who's been raped or assaulted at a fraternity."

At that, Maggie stood up. "Let's try to really keep in touch. Maybe we'll get together again sometime, somewhere. In the meantime, I promise not to be jealous of your other women."

"Yeah, me too. Your other men, I mean. Or boys, whatever you'd like to call them."

"I am hoping to leave the boys behind."

"You want to sneak out, or shall I walk you to your car?"

"You don't have to get up. I'm going to surprise a couple of seniors anyway, before I leave. I won't be here when they graduate on Saturday."

They embraced, and Maggie wiped away one last tear.

"It's a happy tear," she said, before slipping out the door.

Sam drove down to 44 to run a couple of errands and grab some lunch. He went back to his apartment, and decided to nap until the phone rates dropped at five o'clock.

Sam woke up 15 minutes too early, and was unable to concentrate on anything except the phone call he was about to place. So he paced around his apartment until it was time. But he got a result that was becoming all too familiar: seven rings, no answer.

He thought again about the time difference. In Santa Fe, it was a little after 3 pm. Maybe Ariana was at her store. He dialed information to see if they had a listing for Casa Adobe in downtown Santa Fe; they did, on Paseo de Peralta. Sam took down the number.

Sam stared at his phone again and felt the same tightening in his chest as he had the day before. He began to breathe more rapidly as he considered how a phone call to Casa Adobe might play out. Ariana might answer, or maybe it would be her business partner, or a hired employee. He might at least be able to establish that Ariana existed and that he had found her. Maybe he would have a chance to explain who he was and that his intentions were positive—even better, that his intentions were in line with Marion's own desperate plea to him at the Griswold. But what if she wasn't there or couldn't come to the phone? What if she was busy with customers?

Frustrated by his indecision, Sam exhaled a deep sigh that included an audible grumble of anguish. He stood up and paced some more, then came back to the phone. But the number he decided to dial was Jackie's.

"I'm getting closer," he said. "I'm circling in—I think." Sam explained about the phone calls to the arts center and to Ariana's number, yielding the one mysterious back-and-forth the previous evening. He also explained how he was trying to settle on a game plan, but wasn't sure if he should try the store first or not.

"I've also been speculating on what is really happening here," he said. "My hunch is that Ariana really did answer last night's call. But she was evasive and mysterious. If she's protecting Marion, I understand that. But at some point, wouldn't Ariana want to acknowledge to Marion that Sam—the good guy—is the one trying to reach out?"

Jackie thought for a few seconds. "All of that is possible, even likely. But if you do get her back on the line, I think you need a strategy for allowing her to hear you out even if she doesn't want to respond to you at this time. Now here's a question I have to ask—do you think Marion and Ariana ever had a deeper—let's say, more romantic or sexual connection? They were best friends in high school and maybe a couple of years after that. That's the time when girls typically start to explore those feelings, if they have them."

Now Sam was silent for a few seconds. He had not considered that. "It's possible. But she didn't tell me. She really didn't talk to me about Ariana—in fact, she didn't name her when she said a friend had made her the turquoise necklace. You got that info from her brother."

"Oh, and I meant to tell you," she said. "Michael called, and he arranged to pick up her car and pay whatever fees she incurred. So if she does come back, it's here. Well, in Providence."

"And that reminds me," he said. "You mentioned expenses. Do you think he'll be able to help with a trip I might be about to make?"

"So you're taking the Southwest Chief after all?" Jackie laughed.

"No, as I told you, I'd fly. I'm about to check flights and hotels. In fact, maybe I'll do that now, in case I learn something on my next call to Santa Fe."

"I will call Michael and see how he wants to handle expenses," Jackie said. "We'll probably have to submit them later. Do you need help up front?"

"No, I think I'll be okay. I'll keep you posted."

It was 5:45. Sam was not sure what time area travel agencies would close for the day. He checked the Yellow Pages, and found one he had heard someone else talk about. He got an agent on the line, and asked if she could recommend a hotel in downtown Santa Fe that had reasonable rates and was close to shopping and arts districts. He also asked about flights from Bradley Airport, possibly even for the next day. She took his number and promised to get back within the hour.

A half-hour later, his phone rang.

"Sam? This is Mary from Mary Harris Travel. Here's what I've got. For hotels, you can't do better than the Hilton Santa Fe Historic Plaza. Modest rates, and right downtown near shopping and the public squares. As for flights, can you get to the airport for a 7:50 am departure? Great connection in Denver and then an early afternoon arrival in Albuquerque."

"Albuquerque? Is that the best airport to fly into?"

"Almost everybody going to Santa Fe uses it. The Santa Fe airport is regional and has limited options. Albuquerque is 60 miles away, but there's a hotel shuttle."

"Would I still be able to book these tonight?"

"I'll be here till eight."

Sam got to the refectory just in time to grab a quick dinner, and sat down next to Joe Grisman, who was finishing up.

"Hey buddy," Sam said, putting his arm around Joe's shoulders.

"Hey buddy? Go ahead, Sam, we're best friends. Tell me what you need."

"Possibly—I won't know for an hour or so—an early morning ride to Bradley."

"You know what I charge the students, right?"

"Yeah, I probably charge them the same, but they can afford it."

"What's early?"

"Leave at 6:30."

"Call me as soon as you know."

By 7 o'clock, Sam was staring down his phone again, as if he could will it to connect him to Ariana Bello and end the mystery once and for all. At 7:15, he picked it up and dialed.

"Hello?"

"Hello. Is this Ariana?"

Silence at first.

"Is this the same man who called last night?"

"Yes, and if you confirm that you're Ariana, I'll go one better and tell you who I am, and how I heard about you, and how I became best friends with Marion Maloney."

Another excruciating pause, then: "You did hear me say last night that there is no one here who goes by Ariana or Marion, right?"

"That's right. I remember it well. But I don't believe you."

Another pause, as the woman continued to choose her words carefully.

"And why do you suppose it would be in my interest to lie to you about my name?"

"Well, good point. Maybe so I'd finally believe you, and stop calling, and go away. But I don't believe you, and I know you still go by Ariana Bello. In fact, you're listed that way in the program for next weekend's arts festival."

"Oh, so there is someone showing in the arts festival who goes by Ariana Bello. And just how exactly do you know it's me?"

"Because I trust the person who gave me your number. And because of the way you are talking to me. But you do have something to hide. Or should I say, someone. Marion Maloney."

"There's that name again. What makes you so sure I know a Marion Maloney?"

"I'm not sure. Because you haven't admitted it. But you did say there's no one there who goes by Marion Maloney. And I'm thinking, maybe that's because she doesn't go by Marion Maloney any more. Because maybe she has changed her name. Because she is running. Running from bad people trying to do bad things to her. She wants to change her life and start over. And to complete her escape, she decided to ditch the name Marion Maloney. She goes by something new. What that might be, I have no idea."

This time, the silence lasted so long that Sam had to break it.

"You are still there, right?"

"Yes."

"And? You deny everything I ask you, but you allow the conversation to continue instead of just hanging up on me. I find that a little ... interesting."

The woman sighed.

"Okay," she said finally. "Suppose in your world, this is all very real. And it all happened to you. And you had a best friend named Marion. But bad people were doing bad things to your best friend, so she had to get away from it all. And change her life. And start a new life. In a new town. With a new name. Do you find that so hard to believe?"

"No, I don't. I've learned to believe that all sorts of nearly impossible things are possible."

"So why are you trying so hard not to let this supposed best friend of yours have her way?"

"Huh? Because she's not my supposed best friend. She *is* my best friend. And—"

"And what?"

"And she begged me that if we ever got separated, if she ever disappeared, to come find her. It was almost as if she knew something was going to happen. Or if she even planned it all herself. But then she wasn't sure she wanted to be forever separated from her best friend. And she went through with the plan, but with a heavy heart. And maybe her heart is reaching out to mine right now. I can almost feel it."

One last pause.

"Whoever she is, maybe she needs more time."

"Ariana?"

"There's no one here who goes by that name."

"I still don't believe you. But I'm Sam. Sam Field. And I'll be there soon, in Santa Fe. I'll be staying at the Hilton. But don't worry, I would never come to your house without an invitation. I sincerely wish you a pleasant evening."

Twenty minutes till eight. Sam hung up the call, and dialed Mary Harris, and booked a round-trip flight to Albuquerque and three nights at the Hilton. Then he called Joe Grisman and told him the morning flight was on.

Sam could feel his heart throbbing inside his chest. He took several long, deep breaths. He packed a duffel, trying hard to focus so he wouldn't forget simple things like socks or toothpaste. He found a book he hadn't read and stuffed that in. He watched some TV. He set his alarm. And finally went to bed, though his mind was still racing with anxiety and with the uncertainty about what he would do after he arrived at his hotel in Santa Fe.

In the darkness not too far from dawn, he fell asleep, and fell into a world of mountains, sagebrush, and beautiful desert flowers, and then streets lined with adobe houses and Romanesque chapels with bells in high windows and crosses on their roofs, solemnly silent against the blue skies above. Finally, he stood in a colorful plaza surrounded by people walking this way and that, some stopping to look at bins of produce and bread and jam and colorful crafts.

Beyond the farmers' stalls was a woman seated at a table with an antique manual typewriter and several teenagers in front of her scribbling words onto cards. Sam was facing her back, and he wanted to get closer and see her face, but when he tried, he bumped into a bin of chili peppers and grabbed it to keep it from falling off the long wooden table. When he looked up again, the woman was gone, and his alarm was ringing.

Chapter 22

As the airport's hotel shuttle cruised up I-25 toward Santa Fe, Sam marveled at the views: up close, desert plains dotted with sagebrush, and in the background, jagged rocky mountains jutting skyward and glistening with colors from orange to sandstone under the wide turquoise skies. Later, toward sundown, he would be even more awestruck by the vibrant reds that lit up the horizon, a source of artistic inspiration to scores of painters and photographers who called the region home.

He also felt a sense of déjà vu—hadn't he just dreamed these landscapes that very morning?

By the time Sam stood at the Hilton registration desk, his anxiety had given way to exhilaration. He was here, having a new adventure. He was fascinated with what he had seen of Santa Fe. And he could sense that he was ever closer to Ariana, whom he would not recognize, except perhaps by voice, and to Marion, whose disappearance, though only a couple of weeks old, seemed like ages ago. Sam felt confident she was here, though less confident that he would easily find her. And even assuming he did find her, he could not predict how either one of them would handle it emotionally.

Sam was carrying only the one large duffel, so he politely waved off the bellboy, then grabbed a city map and rode the elevator to his second-floor room.

A shower and a change of clothes later, he was on his bed, studying the map. He found the street Paseo de Peralta, though he couldn't tell where to find Casa Adobe on it. He found one other thing that attracted his attention: the words "Santa Fe Farmers Market" at a location on Alto Street. In the lobby, he asked the concierge if she knew anything about the farmers market.

"Well, there are a bunch," she said. "But the one right over there—" she pointed to the west of the hotel—"is the one that seems to be growing the fastest these days. It's only about six blocks from here."

"And do you know when the market is open?"

"I believe it is ... Here, let me check for you. Yes, that's right. Every Tuesday and Saturday from 8 to 1 at the Alto Street Recreation Center."

"Thank you very much for your help."

Sam strolled out of the hotel and onto the streets of Santa Fe. As cities go, Santa Fe was on the small side; with a little over 50,000 residents, it was less than half the size of even Hartford. But as he sized up the bustling human activity in front of him, his quest suddenly seemed farfetched—to find two women, one he wouldn't recognize, and one who was hiding from the world. He gazed out at the sea of people for several minutes, as if either of them might be in his field of vision, and would be magically illuminated by celestial beams of light as soon as he set eyes upon them.

He shook his head at the thought, and began to walk, concentrating on the route he had mapped out to Paseo de Peralta. When he got to the intersection of Sandoval Street and the street he needed to be on, he realized from the map that Paseo de Peralta actually wound around in a "U" and would eventually double back behind his hotel. He sighed, and chose to turn left because it looked more promising in terms of storefronts, and it also followed the "U."

Sam walked a half-dozen or so winding blocks, even making a hard left at one point, and had begun to daydream when he was startled to see the sign for Casa Adobe about 20 yards in front of him.

Now that he had found the store, he had a new dilemma.

He had decided that he wasn't ready to give himself up to Ariana—which meant, among other things, that he needed to avoid talking openly to any woman who might recognize his voice. At the same time, he would not be able to positively ID her without some kind of help. Momentarily paralyzed by his indecision, he finally said to himself, *You came all this way, you have to follow through. Just walk inside and act like any other customer, and see what happens.* Sam looked at his watch; it was 4:45.

Wind chimes over the door clinked lightly as he entered. The store was not particularly spacious, with several glass display cases of jewelry in the center of the room, some paintings hung on one large wall, and the others lined with shelves holding various items, from jewelry to homemade-looking miniature clocks to carved Pueblo kachina dolls. There was a small checkout area with another glass display case and a cash register off to one side. Behind the case, on a stool, sat a woman with dark brown hair, dark eyes, and a light bronze skin tone. At a glance, Sam thought she looked like an exotic blend of ethnicities, including, perhaps, Native American. She looked to be somewhere in her 30s. He took her in quickly and then resumed browsing. There were four other visitors in the store.

At first, the woman seemed not to notice Sam, as she rang out a customer's purchases and wrote something into a notebook. Sam made his way slowly around the store, stopping near the door and glancing at a bulletin board with a variety of pinned messages, from "roommate wanted" to "jewelry classes" to "pop-up poetry slam for teenagers." Sam did a double take on the last one, noting that it was scheduled for 10 am Saturday at the farmers market.

In one corner, three 5-by-7 rugs hung from the wall under a sign "Navajo rugs." They were vibrant, colorful rugs with mesmerizing geometric shapes. Sam stared at them in a momentary trance, until he realized he was being spoken to.

"I have more in the back if you're interested," said the woman behind the counter.

"Uh-huh," he replied, as he quickly strained to disguise his voice. "I might be," he said. "I'll be coming back."

"Did you know that Navajo rugs always have at least one flaw?" she asked.

"Um, no," Sam replied.

"Humans can't be perfect," she said. "Only gods are perfect. The rugs are made by humans."

Sam nodded in acceptance of this new learning. The woman paused and then continued.

"But there may be another reason. Traditional weavers believed a part of their spirit went inside the rug while they worked. So they had to break a line somewhere to create a 'spirit path' and be able to escape."

"Wow," he said. "That's fascinating."

Sam moved to the middle of the store, where he stopped to look over some sterling silver chain necklaces with a variety of pendants; roughly half of them were turquoise-colored stones. A small handwritten card in the case said, "Authentic Navajo jewelry handmade by Ariana Bello."

Just then a woman entered the store and walked directly to the counter area, slipping in behind the woman working there, and dropping her shoulder bag on the floor. She was shorter and more slight than the first woman, also mixed race, but with stronger features suggesting Native American ancestry.

The first woman picked up her own bag and slung it over her shoulder, and said to the other one, "Pretty normal Friday so far; you'll probably get an early-evening hit. I'd stay till at least seven, maybe eight. After that, your call. I'll open at noon tomorrow."

As she walked through the store, she stopped where Sam was admiring the pendant necklaces.

"Those are part of my collection," she said, smiling at him.

The woman continued to the door, and opened it. Then she turned around and faced Sam, getting his attention with a look that was piercing, but not hostile.

"I've been expecting you," she said. "I do hope you enjoy your stay here."

While Sam overcame his initial shock, Ariana Bello turned back to the door and disappeared into the Santa Fe evening.

Sam wandered up Paseo de Peralta, stopping to check out stores and galleries and read restaurant menus. He decided to turn left down Palace Avenue, not realizing that in two blocks, he would come upon one of Santa Fe's grandest landmarks, the Cathedral Basilica of St. Francis of Assisi. The church was closed for the day, but he walked around it, marveling at the Romanesque Revival architecture with its beautiful arches, limestone blocks, and bronze doors. As he prepared to walk away, he noticed how the fiery red sunset and low light played off the lines and contours of the church, as well as the sandy color of the neighboring adobe buildings, creating a soft natural glow that seemed to blanket the city.

On the next block, the Shed restaurant enticed him with its comfortable, low-key atmosphere and aromas of Southwestern food. He found an open seat at the bar, ordered a beer and began perusing the menu.

Sam was hungry, so he ordered food and took in the scene around him. It looked like a Friday post-work crowd to a point, though he saw very little business attire. The restaurant and bar were filling up, but the crowd was not annoyingly loud. There seemed to be people of every age from 20 to 80. While the overall vibe was relaxed, the older patrons looked even more so, many sporting beards or braids, and wearing brightly colored beads over clothing so casual it suggested they had not just come from an office.

When his food came, Sam ordered a second beer. He would take his time and enjoy himself for a little while. But he also realized that if Ariana were to alert Marion that he was here, the only way she could contact him was at his hotel—provided Ariana remembered that he had said he'd be at the Hilton.

On his way out, Sam noticed a large bookcase stacked somewhat chaotically with newspapers and event fliers. He noticed one flier listing musical entertainment and other events at the Saturday farmers market, including "teenage poetry slam hosted by Lacey Oracle."

Sam grabbed that flier and a copy of the free weekly *Santa Fe Reporter*, and walked back to the Hilton. At the front desk, he inquired whether he had received any messages; he had not.

In his room, he turned on his television, but soon got bored and found himself pondering his encounter with Ariana Bello. She had seemed more curious than anything—not overly friendly, but also not terse or judgmental. He decided that she had suspected it was him all along, and perhaps had coaxed him to say just enough to confirm the voice match in her head. The history lesson on Navajo weaving was interesting. And her parting shot seemed to open a new door—a door, perhaps, of acceptance.

The other thing rolling around in Sam's head was the name "Lacey Oracle." It sounded familiar to him in some distant way, but he couldn't figure it out.

A little later, Sam decided to head downstairs for a glass of red wine at the lobby bar. He brought along his copy of the *Santa Fe Reporter*. He skimmed through it with some interest—it looked like they were doing the kind of journalism he admired in the *Village Voice, Boston Phoenix,* and his hometown *Valley Advocate*. At one point he turned back to the masthead page to see how many people the paper employed, though it was hard to tell, as some of them appeared to be just "contributors."

As he flipped the front cover back on top, he noticed that a woman two seats over was watching him. She was a tall, brunette, white woman, age 40 give or take, dressed slightly more professionally than most of the patrons in the Shed, and sipping a white wine. "Is that a good paper?" she asked in a friendly tone.

"I don't know—seems pretty good, from what I can tell, like a smaller version of the *Village Voice* or *Boston Phoenix*, if you know either of those. I don't live here—I'm visiting from the Northeast. I'm Sam, by the way."

"I'm Helen," she said, offering her right hand. "I guess you could say I'm from the Northeast too, depending on how you categorize Toronto geographically. We have a similar paper too—*NOW* magazine. Started a few years ago. I know Alice and Michael, the publishers. Great people. And they do great things for the arts community."

"Are you involved in the arts there?"

"Well, yes, books. I run a small publishing house. I'm here for the publishers' summit."

"Publishers' summit?"

Helen laughed. "Are you staying at the hotel?"

"Yes."

"And you haven't heard about the conference? Didn't you see the signs? They're all over the place. See?"

She pointed to a sign near the entrance to the bar. "PUBLISHERS' SUMMIT REGISTRATION, CONFERENCE ROOM C." An arrow on the sign pointed the way.

"Oh, ah, I see now. Must have missed it before. Did it start today?"

"Not till tomorrow. Runs through Tuesday. I just got here late this afternoon. What do you do?"

"I teach history and coach sports at a boarding school in Connecticut."

"Really! That sounds like fun. You should write a boarding school mystery. There's actually a niche market for that. What brings you to Santa Fe?"

Sam looked at her like one of them must be crazy. "I'm solving a boarding school mystery," he deadpanned.

Helen laughed and almost spit out her wine.

"Are you serious?"

"I'm afraid I am." He paused ... "And I solved one last year too!" They both laughed.

"Well," she said, "If you ever want to start a second career as a writer, look me up!"

"Say, maybe you can help me with one thing. I assume you know a lot of books and authors, right?"

"Well, I should hope so!"

"I saw a name today I can't get out of my head. Like I know it from somewhere. And I'm thinking maybe it's an author or something."

"Well, then, don't be bashful, let's have it!"

"Lacey Oracle."

"Lacey Oracle," Helen repeated. "And what makes you think this 'Lacey Oracle' is an author?"

"I don't know. I was wracking my brains over this. I know I've heard it before. And I associate it with books."

"Maybe it's the title of a book."

"I don't know," Sam said. "I suppose it could be."

"And what a coincidence that would be."

"What do you mean? You know a book with that title?"

"I know a book with the title *Lady Oracle*. By one of our very own Toronto authors. Oh, she's so good. I wish I had her in my stable."

"And her name is ..."

"Margaret Atwood."

Sam rolled that name around in his brain for a minute. and then said, "Holy shit!"

"Well," Helen said. "I seem to be getting warm. Do tell me more!"

"Could it be that simple?" Sam said out loud.

"I don't know," Helen said, chuckling. "Could it? I'd try to answer, except I don't know what you're talking about."

"I was thinking out loud," said Sam, who had been staring off toward the bar lights. Now he turned and looked Helen directly in her eyes. "What's the book about?"

"It's about a romance novelist who is always running away from difficult situations, whether scandal or success. Everything that happens to her, good or bad, seems to bring her trouble. So she fakes her own death and escapes to Italy. I think the escapist aspect was a large part of its appeal. It got some nice reviews, and a couple of Canadian awards. Inside word in Toronto book circles is that Atwood is coming out with a very feminist novel this year that might be big. Another publishing house already has their hooks in it."

Sam had stopped listening after "escapes to Italy." This book had come up in his conversation with Rick; Marion herself might have mentioned it at one point. It all made sense now; he was 99 percent sure who "Lacey Oracle" was.

Snapping out of his mental exercise, Sam looked back at Helen and tried to resume the conversation. "Escapes to Italy and starts a new life, how romantic," he said.

"Yes, as I said, that kind of romantic escapism appeals to a lot of readers, especially women, and especially if they feel trapped in their day-to-day lives."

For the first time, Sam noticed the wedding ring on Helen's finger. He had not been thinking of this bar conversation as a prelude to anything. But he had read somewhere that hotel conferences are ripe with opportunity for adults seeking a temporary thrill without fear of being caught. And he noticed something in the way Helen was smiling at him.

"Are you going to stay for another?" she asked. He paused, and for a brief moment, the two studied each other's eyes.

"You know," he said, "I'd love to. But I've had a long day. And I have a morning appointment."

Helen was still smiling, though she looked vaguely disappointed.

She opened her mouth to say something, but Sam beat her to it.

"I will be here a couple more nights; maybe we'll run into each other."

"I hope so," she said. "It's been nice chatting with you."

On his bed, Sam looked at the poetry slam flier one more time. "Lacey Oracle," he said to himself. "I'm looking forward to meeting you tomorrow."

When Sam woke up the next morning, he could not recall a single dream.

Chapter 23

Sam drank some coffee in the hotel lobby, then grabbed a muffin and croissant from the breakfast buffet, and began to nibble at them while seated at the now-empty bar where he had chatted the previous evening with Helen from Toronto. He ate slowly and tried to settle his nervous stomach.

He looked at his watch. It was 8:45; the farmers market was under way, but the poetry slam was not. This gave him a new dilemma: Should he arrive early and not risk missing anything, or should he arrive after Marion had gotten started, and watch her from a distance to avoid distracting her in the middle of her event? All of this assumed, of course, that she really was Lacey Oracle.

He settled on arriving around 10, but keeping his distance until he felt the time was right. He rode the elevator back to his room and tried reading the book he had brought with him, but just couldn't concentrate. He thought back two weeks to the Saturday he had spent with Marion in Essex, the Saturday she called "the greatest day ever."

He thought about the growing emotional closeness he had felt for her that weekend, and how he sensed she felt it too, and that they were both trying to resist it, if only to keep things from getting messy. Then there was Sunday, when Marion's previously cheerful outlook gave way to something more foreboding. Now it made more sense to Sam that there was a plan already in motion—one she couldn't or wouldn't tell him about—which had the effect of making her sound gradually more incoherent to the point where she had to send him home. And then the dark hints of her disappearing, followed by the words he could never get out of his head:

Don't be surprised by anything. But just promise me one thing. Promise you'll find me.

"Promise you'll find me," he said out loud. "Well, here goes."

Sam paused for a moment to mull that over, then spoke two more words: "Then what?"

Sam took a deep breath and walked into the hallway toward the elevator.

Outside the hotel, Sam was greeted with a clear blue sky. The temperature had barely risen into the 60s, but with sunshine streaming across his back and shoulders as he walked briskly westward, it already felt like 75. A scattering of people strolled through town, and there were some cars on the streets; on the whole, Santa Fe seemed pleasantly calm and Saturday-like.

Sam walked about a half-dozen blocks to the Alto Street Recreation Center. And as he got closer, the crowd noise picked up. Finally, he could see the stalls the vendors had set up in the parking lot to display their wares, along with the trucks they had parked on the outer edges of the space. And he could hear what sounded like a folksinger playing an acoustic guitar.

He slowed to a slow, careful shuffle as he reached the perimeter of the market, and felt a little like a panther stalking his prey as he slithered carefully from truck to truck, peering through the spaces to try to get a picture of how the market was set up. The vendors were arranged in a long horseshoe, most offering fresh produce and baked goods, a few selling jams, cheeses, and salsas, and several displaying handmade crafts. The open end of the horseshoe was the farthest from him, and just beyond it, near the entrance to the stalls, he could see a man singing and playing guitar. To one side, he could make out children playing in a bouncy-bounce, their little heads bobbing into view as they pogoed up and down.

There seemed to be more activity behind them, but Sam could not make it out without walking a little closer. He looked at his watch; it was 10:30.

He decided to come in from the perimeter of the market and peruse the vendors. He did this for 15 minutes or so, until he got close enough to the open end to locate a cluster of people—parents with their children waiting in line for the bouncy-bounce—to use as a shield as he tried to get a closer look at whatever was happening at the far end of the parking lot.

Sam ignored the parents who noticed he didn't have a child with him. Convinced that someone was about to inform him that adults were not allowed in the bouncy-bounce, he kept stepping aside for others to stand in front of him, and saying "Don't worry, I'm not in line."

In the back of the lot, he could now see three tables. On one side, a woman was painting children's faces. On the other, a man was blowing up and twisting balloons together, creating animal shapes in less than a minute each, complete with whiskers or teeth drawn on with a Sharpie.

In between the two was another table, but Sam's hopes and expectations for it were dashed as he walked closer and saw that there was very little activity around it. His heart began to pound. In front of the table, three teenagers, two girls and a boy, were chatting. Behind them, taped to the table, was a sign Sam could not read because the teens were obscuring the view.

He walked up to them. "Hello, folks. Hey, I was wondering, is there a teenage poetry slam happening somewhere here at the market today?"

They stepped aside and pointed to the sign. "That's why we're here," one of the girls said. "But I guess Lacey can't make it today."

The sign read: "Due to circumstances beyond my control, today's teenage poetry slam is postponed until next Saturday's market. I hope to see you then. – Lacey"

"Who is Lacey?" Sam asked. "Has she been running the slam for a while?"

"No," offered one of the two girls. "She started doing this last Saturday. I saw the fliers and was curious. It was a lot of fun, so we came back."

"Or we came back because we won prizes," said the boy.

"Who are you?" asked the second girl.

"Oh, I'm sorry, I should have introduced myself. I'm Sam Field. I'm a high school teacher from Connecticut, visiting a friend in Santa Fe. Our school year just ended. My friend knows I like poetry, and that I've talked about doing something like this with my kids at the school. So I just wanted to check it out. Did you say you won prizes?"

"Those two did," said the second girl. "I'm Rose. That's Will and Cheryl, first and second place last week. I had a killer poem for today that would have cleaned up!"

The others laughed. "What were the prizes?" Sam asked.

"Gift certificates," Will said. "From Collected Works Bookstore. It's a cool store."

"And you guys are into poetry? That's great! What did you write about?"

Both Rose and Cheryl looked away slightly, apparently too shy to say. "Ask him," Cheryl said. He won first place."

Now Will looked down.

"Oh come on," Cheryl said.

Will looked up. "I wrote about a chair," he said.

"Not just any chair," said Cheryl. "You wrote about your grandfather's chair. And how you wanted your mother to leave it at the table after he died, so you would think about him every night. It was beautiful."

Will looked down again, blushing.

"Well, I don't mean to keep you," said Sam. "One more question—did you like Lacey? Did she say anything special to encourage your poetry?"

They looked at each other, then Cheryl spoke. "Yes, she was very encouraging. She reminded us to always own what we feel. And that if we wanted to be poets, whatever we feel in here"—at this, Cheryl patted her hand twice over her heart—"write it down on paper. And don't be afraid of our emotions."

"I love her," added Rose. "She's like the best teacher I never had."

"Well, hopefully she'll be back next week," said Sam, well aware that he would not be back.

He had thought about asking them what she looked like, but he didn't want to sound creepy, and based on what they did tell him, he had very little doubt.

Sam gazed out at the various activities taking place at the market, and shook his head. *I came a long way. And I was sure I was going to find you here. But you're not here. And I don't know where to go next.*

Dejected, Sam left the market and began to wander the streets, more aimlessly than on his previous forays into Santa Fe. Soon he noticed he was hungry, and stopped into a restaurant called Maria's that looked popular. "Traditional New Mexican cuisine and distinctive margaritas since 1950."

Sam walked in, got a table, and ordered. His stomach was no longer nervous, but he felt sad and frustrated. When his food came, he ate slowly and tried to think of a new strategy. *So close, and yet so far. And I don't know where to go next.*

Oh wait. I do know where to go next.

Sam looked at his watch and saw that it was only 12:30. He took his time finishing his food, and took out his map to try to get his bearings. He asked a server for his check, and also if she could identify where he was and direct him to Paseo de Peralta.

"Our address is Cordova Road, but when you go left out of the restaurant, bear left on Camino de Los Marquez. Follow that to Galisteo Street, turn left, and it's about six blocks."

Sam followed her directions, and sure enough, he soon found himself on Paseo de Peralta, approaching Casa Adobe.

He stopped at the door to catch his breath, then slipped inside.

Ariana looked up from her checkout counter. "Well!" she exclaimed. "Looks like someone has a new favorite store!"

"Either that, or someone has too much time on his hands!" Sam replied.

A customer asked if the two kachina figures she was purchasing had spiritual significance.

"Well," Ariana began, "if they're authentic, and if they were made by the Hopi people to give to their daughters, then they represent the katsina spirits who act as messengers between the human and spirit worlds, and bring gifts of song and dance, fertility for the new bride, rain for the harvest, and so on. Their origins were ceremonial, but nowadays, most of them are made for buying and selling, even within that, there are details that separate authentic Hopi kachinas from imitators, generally having to do with the quality of the workmanship."

The woman looked a little confused as she looked over the dolls.

"I'm sorry if that was too much information," said Ariana, smiling. "But I only sell ones that are carved from a single piece of wood, which is the right way."

The woman smiled and said, "Oh, okay, I'll take them," and got out her credit card.

"As for too much time on one's hands," she said, now turning to Sam, "I hope you know there is a lot to do and see in Santa Fe."

"Yes, for one, I went to check out the farmers market this morning."

Ariana paused.

"And was that all you hoped it would be?"

Now Sam paused, and gazed directly into her eyes, hoping to match her intensity with a little shot of his own.

"I'd say it was 90 percent what I was expecting. The other 10 percent—well, it felt like something was clearly missing to-day. Too bad for the kids who showed up. Oh, that reminds me—do I hear that you teach art in the local public schools?"

Ariana just stared back at him for another long pause.

"Well, someone's been doing his homework."

"Oh, I just wanted to mention how much I admire that. Teachers can have such a profound impact on children's lives."

Ariana turned away, trying not to show her irritation that Sam had won a round.

"And you also teach," I'm told.

"Yes, history."

"I have another customer, if you'll excuse me for a second."

Sam waited for her to ring up another sale before speaking.

"As for all the things to see and do hear, I guess I only wish I had someone to see and do them with!"

Ariana paused again.

"You know, you came out here by yourself, without know-ing what or who you would find. I'm not sure what you want from me."

"Your evasiveness is usually a little more artful than that. You know damn well what I want from you. And it's not just me. Did you know that Marion's brother has hired me to find her?"

Ariana looked down and wrote something on her notepad. When she looked up, a lock of her fine black hair fell in front of her face. As she brushed it aside, Sam thought he saw her also brush aside a tear.

"I'm sorry," she said. "I'm just not sure what else we can accomplish in this conversation."

"Well," he said, stepping over to the case holding her beautiful silver necklaces with the colorful stone pendants. "I do love these, and I still might have to buy one. I know someone it would look good on. You are very talented."

"Thank you," she said, unusually weakly.

"And I should get going," he said, moving toward the door. "And I just have one thing to ask of you, a favor, if you can see your way around to it. My guess is that Marion is staying with you. I don't know where you live, and I'm not going to try to find out. The favor is to please make sure she knows I'm staying at the Hilton. Then she can decide if she wants to contact me or not."

"Oh, and tell her the kids from the slam really like her. I talked to a few of them. She's only done it once, and she's already had an effect on them. One girl called her the best teacher she never had."

The chimes tinkled lightly as Sam opened and closed the door. Ariana turned around to face her backroom, and with no one in the store able to see her, she allowed one quick flood of tears, then wiped them away with a tissue.

Sam killed more time walking around Santa Fe. He checked out several stores, and visited the Cathedral Basilica of St. Francis of Assisi. He went back to his hotel and napped. He got up, took a shower, and decided to return to the Shed for dinner. It wasn't quite as busy as on Friday, but still lively. The bartender remembered him. A couple of young women drinking Margaritas smiled at him. It occurred to him that a new friend might be just the thing to take his mind off Marion.

That evening, Marion and Ariana sat facing each other at her table.

"You know I was devastated when Sarah left me," Ariana said.

"Yes, you told me in so many words."

"And then, all of a sudden, you were here. It seemed like a sign. Like a realignment of the spirits. That's the way I look at things."

"You have done so much for me," Marion said. "And I do love you."

"You know I love you too."

The two women looked at each other for a long moment, each trying to fight back the sadness that had descended on the room. Ariana finally spoke.

"Do you know why some lesbians can't or won't have long-term relationships with bisexual partners?"

"I could guess. You tell me."

"Because we're always afraid that one day it will happen." Ariana was speaking almost in a whisper. "In fact, it's practically a given that it will happen. You'll meet some guy and decide to return to the life you've been brought up to accept as more normal. And there's nothing we can do or say to convince you otherwise."

The two women sat silently for a long minute. "I have to take a walk," Marion said, as Ariana lowered her face to the table and sobbed. Marion slipped into another room to quickly change her clothes, and then slipped out of the house without Ariana hearing her.

"So we meet again," said Sam, taking one of the only two available seats at the hotel bar. He called to the bartender. "Cabernet, please."

"Well, hello again," said Helen. "Sam, this is Dan from Chicago," she said, motioning to her right.

"Another publisher, I assume?" Sam said to Dan.

"Yes, small press on the North Side. Mostly detective fiction set in Chicago."

"So," Helen said, looking at Sam, "did you solve your mystery?"

"Oh, yeah, funny you should ask. Almost, but not quite. She gave me the slip today. But she's here. I know she is, and maybe if I can get one more good clue, I'll find her." Sam laughed. "Yep, I'll find Lacey Oracle."

"No kidding! Is that why you were asking me if I knew that name? Who, pray tell, is Lacey Oracle?"

"Right here," said Marion Maloney, standing behind Sam with her hand raised, as if she were taking an oath.

Sam wheeled around on his barstool. "Oh my god! What the—"

"You're sure I'm not interrupting anything?"

"No! Not at all! Oy my god, I can't believe it! You're here! I'm so happy to see you!"

He stood up from his barstool and embraced her, burrowing his face into her shoulder and repeating, "I can't believe it!"

"Oh, sorry, where'd my manners go?" said Sam, disengaging. "Lacey, this is Helen, and this is Dan, book publishers in Toronto and Chicago, respectively. Do you want a glass of wine? I saved this seat for you."

"You did not—you didn't know I was coming," Marion laughed, taking the seat to his left anyway. "Sure, I'll have a glass of white."

"I have a chenin blanc," said the bartender. Marion nodded.

"And Helen here," said Sam, laughing nervously, "suggested I write a boarding school mystery. Isn't that too funny?"

"Well," Helen said. "You remembered! I must have made an impression!"

"I'm sure you did!" Marion replied, quickly adding, "I'm sorry, I didn't mean that to sound catty. Sam and I are best friends, and he has a way with women, and we're always comparing notes—"

"Nothing here like that," Sam said. "But these guys have been good bar company, and Helen actually helped me figure out that 'Lacey Oracle' came from 'Lady Oracle.'"

"You know the book?" asked Marion. "I got a kick out of it. And I loved the escapism."

"Oh yeah, she's my favorite hometown author," said Helen. "I hear she has something big coming out this year. Alas," she sighed, "I did not win the bidding war."

"And what brings you to Santa Fe?" asked Dan.

"Oh ..." Marion replied, pausing. "Just visiting a friend."

She turned and gazed into Sam's eyes. "And now I'm visiting my best friend," she whispered. "I can't believe you. I begged me to find you, and you found me. When we finish our wine, I'd like to talk to you alone. Did you miss me?"

"Are you kidd—"

"Not half as much as I missed you. You have no idea. Let's drink up."

Dan and Helen seemed mildly confused, but exchanged pleasant goodnights without probing any further.

"So I've made one decision tonight," said Marion as she slipped off her barstool.

"Oh?" Sam replied.

"Pay your tab first."

Sam motioned for his check, wrote in a tip and his room number, and signed it.

"Okay, let's go," she said.

"Where are we going?"

"To your room," she said, grabbing his hand and pulling him in the direction of the elevators.

"Well," Helen whispered as he got up. "Someone's getting lucky tonight!"

Sam shot her a smirk, and then was swept away.

"To my room? What is it you've decided?"

"I've decided to ignore what I said at the Griswold. I no longer care what this does to our relationship. It might be for the worse, or it might be for the better. Or—it just might be that in the big scheme of things, it really isn't going to matter."

The elevator closed behind them, and Marion fell into Sam, clutching him like there was no tomorrow.

"I've missed you so much. And I want to make love to you tonight. And I won't take no for an answer. I don't ever want anything to happen where I lose you again and regret that we never slept together. So let's please just take this moment now and make the most of it. We can figure out the rest later."

Chapter 24

Sam opened his eyes first. Marion was still asleep, lying next to him with one leg draped over his, and one hand resting on his chest. Her head was next to him on a pillow. She was breathing softly, with a look of childlike innocence on her face.

Sam replayed their night together as best he could remember. He had never felt particularly drunk, but his memories took on a kind of kaleidoscopic quality, his sensory recall twisted up in shifting visual patterns interspersed with sounds of laughter, then deep breathing, then soft cries of delight. He remembered tender kisses, clothing items flung aside one by one, and fingers gliding teasingly across each other's skin. The lovers' dance came back to him as a slow-motion erotic ballet in soft focus, sensations and emotions tumbling over each other like kittens at play, giving way to dreamy waves of bliss, then peace, then sleep.

He watched Marion sleep for a little while longer, then put one of his hands over her hand on his chest, and gently squeezed. She did nothing at first, but a few minutes later, she rolled toward him, put both arms around his torso, and hugged him tightly.

She still seemed to be sleeping, but Sam sensed that she might be mulling over what to do or say next. The memory of their emotionally turbulent Sunday a mere two weeks ago at the Griswold barged into his room uninvited and sat in the spare chair, waiting to see what would happen.

Finally, Marion disengaged and sat up in bed; Sam did likewise. At first they just looked at each other. Finally, Marion burst out laughing.

Sam looked at her, not knowing what she was thinking.

"Did I miss the joke?" he said. "Was I that bad last night?"

His second comment made Marion laugh all the harder.

"No, darling," she managed to get out between giggles. She took a deep breath and composed herself.

"Seriously, you were amazing. Even better than I expected. In fact, wow—that was great. I'm just laughing because, well, here we are—"

"Here we are ... and?"

"And we don't know what anyone's supposed to say next, do we!"

"Well," Sam offered. "You could say, 'Making love to you made me realize how much I love you and want to be with you. I'll pack up my things and book a flight to Connecticut.' Or you could say, 'Just like we predicted, having sex has completely ruined our friendship. I can't even stand to look at you another minute. So I'm staying here with Ariana, and I'm never coming back.'"

Sam looked at her. He had laid out the bait—however exaggerated—and now it was her turn.

But once again, Marion just smiled and tried to squelch another laugh.

"Okay," Sam said. "Now I'm seriously feeling like I'm reading off the wrong script. Or that someone snuck in this morning and replaced Marion with a pod person."

"Do I seem like a pod person to you? Seriously?" She leaned over and planted a long, sensual kiss on his lips, then returned to her upright position.

"Okay, you tell me. Was that a pod person kiss—or does only Marion kiss like that?"

"Aha! You called yourself Marion!"

She rolled her eyes. "Okay, so we're on your territory now, and to you, I'm Marion. Let's not get hung up on that."

"And," she continued, "I have wanted to be intimate with you ever since the Griswold. And you know what? Whatever I decide to do, I don't think that's going to ruin our friendship. In fact, I think I feel closer to you than ever. What about you? How do you feel about it?"

"I feel the same way, I think—I mean, when I thought about it this morning, I didn't just think about how great the sex was. I just felt warm and cozy, kind of peaceful, like our connection has only gotten stronger."

"I actually thought about all the possible consequences of this before I came to the hotel," she said. "There may be one or two others I worry about. Ruining our friendship wasn't one of them. And I am glad I came here."

"What ones do you worry about?"

Their eyes locked for a long moment.

"Oh Sam ..."

"Okay, I get it, you're still not coming back to Connecti-cut."

"I didn't say that."

"And now you have two people hanging on your decision."

"And who knows, what I decide might not please either one of them. Remember, I'm going to do what I think is best for me now."

Sam sighed heavily. "Yes, I know," he said. "And I agree. And I'm prepared to accept whatever you decide. I just want you to be happy."

With that, Sam got up, went into the bathroom, and turned on the shower. When he emerged 10 minutes later, a towel wrapped around his waist, she said, "I'm going to shower too. I only have last night's clothes—good thing I wasn't in them long!"

Marion smiled playfully at Sam and slipped past him to the bathroom door.

"Oh, by the way," Sam called out to her, "All this hot sex, and I almost forgot, I have so much to tell you."

Marion dried off, but had to circle the bed twice before she found each piece of her clothing. "What the hell happened here?" she deadpanned. "Well, start filling me in! And what time is breakfast?"

"I hardly know where to begin, said Sam. "Should I start with the murder, or the marina sting?"

"The murder?" she gasped. "Whose murder?"

A friend of Nathalie's. I'll come back to that. But between the murder and the marina sting, Marion Maloney is no longer a woman running from trouble."

"And what do you mean by that exactly?"

"Jackie had a hunch that your ex might have a new name and a new boat, and she cleverly found out what marina he was using, and set up a sting there with the West Hartford

Police and—you'll love this—the IRS. They caught him, arrested him for fraud, and impounded the boat, which should sell at auction for well above the company's tax liability. There are other creditors, of course, but guess who's first in line?"

"Wow," Marion said. "Are you kidding?"

"Would I lie to you?" he said, smiling.

"So the IRS isn't looking for me any more?"

"Nope, and neither is Tiger Williams. He was your stalker at Brooks House—more on that in a minute. Now he's in jail on a murder charge. So," Sam smiled, "you can come back to Connecticut whenever you like, and be Marion Maloney again!"

"Well, that's good to know! So tell me about the murder."

"Nathalie had a friend from college named Marcie Merrifield. Did I ever mention her?"

"Maybe," Marion said. "Is this another one of your conquests? I need a scorecard to keep track of you."

"Nooo, nothing like that. Marcie was the lovely young woman Kevin was interested in. But so were all the guys in Tom Dickleman's little rat pack, including Tiger Williams and Cody Savard. And they were all at the Russian Lady that night. Little did I know, when I drove down to Essex to see you on Saturday, that Marcie was already dead. Strangled and raped. Actually, nobody knew until Sunday morning, when Nathalie checked on her and found her dead in her bed."

"Oh ... my ... god," said Marion. "I had no idea."

"So awful. See all the drama you missed?" Sam said. "We were all suspects for couple of days, but then it got whittled down to Tom Dickleman and Tiger Williams. Marion Maloney was also dead, so to speak, and off on a new life as Lacey Oracle, and meanwhile, *poof*, just like that, your two stalkers were being grilled in police stations in West Hartford. So they had little reason or opportunity to stalk you all the way to Harveys Beach. And one of them—Tiger—was charged with the murder."

"My two stalkers? What else do you know about this?"

"I'll get to that," Sam said. "Can we talk about your escape plan now?"

"I guess," she began.

"Better yet, let me tell you what I think I know."

"Sure, why not, you're on a roll today, Mister Inside Information."

"First of all, I think you took two inspirations from literature—Kate Chopin's *The Awakening*, and Margaret Atwood's *Lady Oracle*, and mingled them. The first one gave you the idea to leave your car at the beach, and the second one gave you the idea of vanishing and starting a new life—and even gave you an idea for your new name. Now, knowing you, I didn't believe you would actually drown yourself in Long Island Sound. Police speculated that you could have been abducted in the parking lot, but there were no signs of foul play, and it just didn't look like a crime scene."

Marion smiled weakly. "Once I got to the beach, I realized I hadn't thought through what to do with the car, or what to leave in the car, and I didn't have time—or the muscles—to push it into the sound."

"Aha, you 'didn't have time'—that's because you had a train to catch. Now, there are plenty of trains from Old Saybrook to New York City. But you had connections to make—first to Chicago, and then to Albuquerque, aboard the Southwest Chief, which only runs once a day."

Marion's eyes were wide open, and her mouth was agape.

"Holy shit," she said. "You really are a good detective. I'm not sure whether to be proud of you or afraid of you."

"Well," Sam laughed, "You're the one who asked me to find you, so I'd say I was just doing my job—and doing it pretty well at that."

"But how did you know I was planning to take a train?"

"Well, it was a hunch, but a good one—and the only one that seemed to make the strands all add up. You left your car walking distance to the Old Saybrook train station. The train tracks, just like Interstate 95 and US Route 1, go through southern Connecticut to New York. But you didn't want to drive—your car could have identified you, and if you had abandoned it anywhere farther along your route, it would have told us something about your journey. So you left it right near where you were staying, to try to divert people's attention."

"And you were carrying plenty of cash that you withdrew from your bank accounts. Now, don't blame me for getting that info—that's Jackie's specialty. But I did study the train routes, and I also knew from experience that you can walk onto an Amtrak train and buy your ticket with cash. So you're essentially anonymous—which is what you wanted to be."

"Who's Jackie?"

"Oh, she's the retired detective I worked with last year on that case of the missing Walker's girl. She got hired back by the West Hartford police to work on Marcie's murder, and she agreed to help me with your case, especially since the local cops didn't have any clues. The Old Saybrook police gave us your brother's number, and Jackie went to Providence to see him, which is how we found out about Ariana. Apparently you were close when you were in your late teens."

"Wow, I'm surprised Michael would even remember that much."

"He didn't remember much. But Jackie asked Michael if he had photos of your wedding—good call—and he found them, neatly catalogued by his wife. Jackie found Ariana's name on the back of a photo of the bridesmaids, and then Michael remembered more, including that she might have come here to pursue her art. And then Anne—"

"Anne from the Griswold?"

"Yes, Anne Carruthers. Another hunch. I called her. She was dismayed to hear the news. But she remembered my name from the register, so she believed my story. She wanted to help."

"And?"

"Please don't be mad at her."

"Mad—why?"

"And once again, remember who made me promise to find you."

"Go on, you scary little sleuth." Marion smiled. "If you were anyone else, I'd call the cops right now. Well, maybe not—I don't really trust cops. But you knew that. Continue."

"Your phone records from the stay. What she did was probably illegal. But she gave me the one 505 number from the logs. Surely you were aware I've been calling."

"No! You've been calling the house?"

"Ariana didn't tell you?"

Both Sam and Marion were silent for a moment while they mulled this new information.

"Ariana knew who you were," Marion said. "I told her a lot. And I told you I showed her your picture. But she never said anything until Friday, when she told me you had stopped in to the store."

"Are you staying with her?"

"Yes, and helping out here and there at the store."

"And did she persuade you to call off yesterday's poetry slam?"

Marion just looked at him in disbelief, then shook her head. "She was right. You were going to find me there. And she didn't think I was ready."

"So she is doing all your thinking for you?" he asked.

Marion gave a deep, frustrated sigh. "Stop it. This is all hard enough as it is. You know that when I left Avon, I could barely think for myself. In fact, Ariana planned my whole disappearance, apart from the literary angles. But as I get more and more clarity, yes, I have to find my own voice again. And I will."

"I hope you're not mad at me," Sam said.

"How could I be mad at you?" she said, finally. "I asked you to find me, and you did. Faster than I ever could have imagined. Which is why it's so—"

Marion broke off her own sentence.

"Jarring? Confusing?" Sam offered.

"This is a lot to process," she said, stifling a tear.

As they headed downstairs for breakfast, Sam told her that he had tracked down Rick Larsen.

"Where?" she asked with a hint of sarcasm. "At his lovely colonial house with his beautiful wife and 2.3 children?"

"Ha, funny," Sam said. "If I were you—oh, never mind, I'm not you. And I won't tell you how to feel. I will say that I thought Rick was very nice. Yes, he is engaged, but when he went home with you that first night, they had broken it off. Then they patched it up, and when his fiancee was away for a weekend, he called you because he didn't want you to feel—his word—'disposable.'"

"How thoughtful of him."

"I think he meant well," Sam said.

"I think he meant to get laid one more time."

"And now, if I may change the subject, tell me more about Ariana."

Marion took a sip of coffee and then set her cup down.

"Okay, but please bear with me if I have a hard time talking about this."

"Of course."

"When we started planning my disappearance, I barely knew you," she said. "By the time I left Avon, you were my best friend, but that was all. Or so I thought. The plan was in place by the time I invited you to visit me at the Griswold. I didn't ever think I would fall so hard. Saturday, I just went with it, but I had no idea what to say to you on Sunday."

"Go on? And Ariana?"

"She was so helpful. She made everything possible. Even got me a new identity and ID card. Gave me a part-time job at the store. Set me up with the poetry slam. And welcomed me into her home, and helped me try to forget all the bad things that were happening to me."

"There's more. How close are you two?"

Marion looked directly into his eyes.

"When we were seniors in high school, we fell for each other. We were young and feeling very free and wild. We wrote poems for each other. We held hands and kissed under the stars and explored each other's bodies. I think she was in love with me. Then she went to RISD and I went to UConn. She wanted me to visit more, but I was pulling back. I told her I wasn't ready for a relationship with her. And I wasn't."

"But you stayed friends."

"Yes. She still had family in West Hartford, and came home for some holidays. I had never been out here."

"And now?"

"She's been so good to me. And she is helping me get back on my feet. Spending time with her has been soothing for me. But then you had to show up in my life. Why did you have to do that?"

All at once, Marion's tangle of emotions got the better of her. "I hate you!" she sobbed.

"No you don't. Don't say that."

"Yes I do! Don't tell me how to feel!"

Suddenly, Sam thought about the girl from the poetry slam, and his look of concern changed into a broad smile.

"What?" Marion asked, drying her cheeks.

"Own what you feel," he said. "Whatever you feel in here—and he patted himself twice over the heart—write it down. Don't be afraid of your emotions."

"Wait a minute, where did you get that?"

"From you—via your slam students. They love you."

She looked at him and smiled weakly, then grabbed a napkin, and wrote something on it, cupping her other hand around it so he couldn't see what she was writing. When she was done, she turned it over and pushed it across the table to him, like a card dealer responding to a request for another hit.

Sam turned over the napkin. On it, Marion had drawn a heart.

They both smiled and clasped hands, until Marion suddenly gasped and recoiled. "Ariana," she exclaimed. "What a surprise!"

"I thought I'd find you here. Don't mind me, nothing to worry about. I just wanted to let you know I'm heading over to the store to start cataloging pieces for the arts festival."

"Oh, okay. I'm just going to finish breakfast here, and then I'll be over to help."

Ariana looked at Sam. "You fly out tomorrow, right?

"Yes, that's right."

"Well, why don't you come to dinner tonight, so we can give you a proper sendoff? How's 7?"

Sam looked at Marion, who nodded.

"Why sure, that sounds lovely, thanks for having me!"

Chapter 25

When Sam went back up to his room, he called Jackie.

"I found her. So the missing persons case can be closed—right?"

"Marion Maloney? You found her in Santa Fe? Alive and well?"

"And living with Ariana Bello. And doing poetry slams. And working in Ariana's store."

"Oh," Sam added, "she also has taken a new identity. Ariana even set her up with an official ID, apparently. Her name is Lacey Oracle."

"New name and ID? Just like that?"

"Hmmm ... Okay, is this common? And do people somehow get new social security numbers? Or is this all illegal?"

"OK, let's back up here a bit," said Jackie. "First, the case can't necessarily be closed just because you say you saw her. Marion is the one who needs to report to whatever jurisdiction listed her as missing, to say she's fine and they can stop looking. Sometimes that's all they need to hear. So that's the Old Saybrook Police, and if they also notified the state police, they can pass the new info along. If they want backup, they can call her brother. I will call him, by the way, to let him know she's fine."

"Oh, OK, good idea," Sam said. "I'll call her friend at the Griswold."

"As for the legality, there are some instances in which you can change your identity legally. In fact, Marion might qualify because she has been stalked and harassed. Now, you can't do it to get out of a business or tax obligation. So that might have been a problem for her, except they have impounded Mark's boat and are selling it at auction. The IRS agents tell me that Marion is probably off the hook for all of it—hopefully that will become official shortly."

"So anyway, if you change your name legally with good cause, then you can also get a new official driver's license or other state ID, and a new social security number. But if you do any of those things without authorization, then, well, it's all illegal. Of course, there are plenty of shady companies that will do that for you."

"Anything else I should tell her?"

"Well, before I continue," Jackie said, "Here's a question—is she coming home to Connecticut?"

"Possibly. But probably not right away."

"Now," Jackie continued, "if she does want to come home, or at least go back to being Marion Maloney, her biggest two obstacles are taken care of. The IRS is off her back, and the more menacing of her two harassers is behind bars and likely to remain there for a long time. Tom Dickleman is still a free man—I'll add that I don't think he technically did anything illegal anyway, except possibly protecting Tiger from scrutiny on that rape case from years ago. Whether he's a changed man from this ordeal remains to be seen."

"I guess I wouldn't worry about Tom," Sam said. "Even if Marion does come back, she's not coming back to Avon. But you did make me think of one other thing—I realize the murder is more serious, but would the police be able to pin anything on Tiger for harassing Marion at her home?"

"Possibly. Might be hard to prove though. Anyway, my point is, with Tiger and the IRS out of the way, If Marion wants to go back to being Marion, it might save her some complications. And don't forget, Michael has her car waiting for her."

"Okay, I'll keep you posted. I'm having dinner with the two of them tonight, by the way."

"Oh, sounds nice!"

"And you were right about what you asked me about them, you know, back in high school."

"Oh? Interesting. And do you think they are revisiting that?"

"Well … it's complicated. But it's also okay. Whatever happens, I'll be fine. I'll keep you posted."

After a nap, Sam started out toward Ariana's house with the directions Marion had given him. It only took about 20 minutes to find the adobe-walled, Spanish Pueblo-style house on a quiet residential street. He rang the bell, and Marion appeared in the doorway to briefly hug him and then let him in. Soon they were all seated around a large wooden table in Ariana's kitchen, which was steeped in savory aromas of the food she had prepared.

The table had been set with colorful pottery plates, as well as water and wine classes. Ariana poured three glasses of white wine. "Just say the word if you'd like to try my famous margarita," she said.

Marion added, "She makes the best margaritas ever."

"From what I've seen so far, I love this house," Sam said. "How long have you lived here?"

"Well," she began. "I got to Santa Fe about 12 years ago. I rented a cheap apartment for several years because that's all I could afford. Then my jewelry started to catch on, and soon I was able to lease a small storefront. Smaller than where I am now. Anyway, it all kind of took off from there."

"I love your store, too," Sam said. "And your jewelry. You must have made the one Marion—I mean Lacey—sorry, this is hard for me to get used to. The one Lacey was wearing when we had dinner at the Griswold."

Marion nodded. "She does other art too—painting and small sculptures, and haven't you done a little rug weaving?"

"Yes," Ariana said. "That's a little more time consuming and painstaking. There are very high standards if you want to be accepted as carrying on the Navajo traditions. But jewelry pays the bills."

"Were you living here alone before Lacey got here?"

After a pause, Ariana said, "I had a housemate for seven years. She moved out a couple of months ago."

Sam tossed that one around in his head briefly—just long enough to make him wish he hadn't asked.

For their part, Marion and Ariana were both thinking the same thing—*can we change the subject already?*

Ariana stood up suddenly and said, "Let's eat." The various dishes she had prepared—enchiladas and tamales with several fillings, chicken pieces in a mole sauce, and sides of black beans and seasoned rice—were warming in brightly colored clay serving dishes, which she brought to the table one by one. As she sat back down, she looked at Sam.

"Sam," she said, "I hear you teach U.S. history to prep school boys. How is that? Do you like it? Are they mostly good students?"

"They're mostly wiseasses," he said, laughing. "Actually, I do like them. And I enjoy teaching them."

"Do you teach World War II?" Ariana asked.

"Yes, of course—that would be a hard one to ignore!"

"Did you know that 400,000 Mexican Americans fought with the Allies in the war?"

"Well, I don't think I could have pulled that number out of my hat. But I knew they served. And I know the story of the Aztec Eagles air squadron, who helped the Allied forces liberate the island of Luzon in 1945."

"Good for you. And have you taught your students about it?"

Sam sighed. "I'd like to think I've mentioned it. As important as World War II is, we don't get a lot of time to cover it all. And the Mexican participation is not mentioned in the textbook we're required to use."

"Really." Ariana smiled. "A shocker."

"In fact," Sam added, "if I want to get them interested in things like Cesar Chavez and the United Farm Workers, or most any other story about labor unions or civil rights, I have to include them as topic ideas for their independent research projects. And those stories are not very interesting to most of these insulated kids."

"Well, if you can sneak this into one of your lectures, you should tell them the story of Macario Garcia, who singlehandedly destroyed a German machine-gun barricade and was presented with the Medal of Honor by Harry Truman. Back home in Sugar Land, Texas, a cafe waitress refused to serve him because he was Mexican. He said if he was good enough to fight in the war, he was good enough for a cup of coffee. And they clubbed him with a baseball bat. And the police came and arrested Macario."

"Incidents like this spurred the Mexican American civil right movement. Look it up!"

"Ariana's parents met during the war," Marion interjected.

"Just after the war," Ariana corrected. "My father was an American fighter pilot from Connecticut, stationed in San Antonio in 1946. My mother was a Mexican recruited as a teenager to come here in the early '40s as a farmworker. Once they realized how good a cook she was, she graduated from the field to the kitchen. Supposedly, my father was eating in a restaurant, and was so impressed with his meal that he wanted to meet the person who cooked it. And they brought out my mother. And that was that. And I was born in West Hartford in 1951."

"Wasn't your mother part Navajo?" Marion asked.

"One-quarter Navajo, she always told me. But she never made a big deal of where she came from. She was here legally, but she preferred not to draw attention to herself. She settled in to being a housewife and mother to me and my younger brother, while my father worked his way up in insurance. Eventually, she took jobs in kitchens—a couple of restaurants, but she actually liked working in food service at Trinity College better."

"By the way," Sam interjected, "you must take after your mother. This is all really delicious."

"Thank you. My brother," she continued, "was more interested in just being American—sports, parties, girls, normal jobs. But I saw myself as an artist from early on, and the more I studied Navajo culture, the more I thought about coming out here. And you, Sam?"

"Oh, my story is not very interesting. I grew up in Northampton, Massachusetts. There are so many bookstores and writers in the area, I thought that's what wanted to be. At Princeton, I majored in history and minored in English. Next thing you know, I'm sitting in a cubicle in Manhattan, crunching numbers for a big ad firm. I saw somewhere that Avon Old Farms was looking for teachers, and that became my escape hatch. But it's still not getting me closer to my dreams—whatever's left of them."

"Sam, don't say that," Marion said. "You'll get there. I have faith in you."

"And I have faith in you. But as you know, the path to a creative life isn't easy for most of us. Maybe it was easier for Ariana." He turned to her and smiled. "So what's your secret?"

"I don't know," she answered, then paused for a moment to think. "I guess ... When you know what you want to do, you learn how to do it well, and you just keep at it. I didn't sell a lot the first few years. I waitressed and bartended. Speaking of which, I could whip up a pitcher of margaritas, if anyone's interested."

"Sure," said Sam.

"That would be lovely," said Marion.

Ariana took out three rocks glasses and set them in the freezer, shook some salt into a shallow bowl, and began mixing her ingredients. Sam tried to peer around her to see what she was putting in the pitcher, but she scolded him. "I don't give away my kitchen secrets!" she laughed.

Soon she was seated with them again as they all sipped from their chilled glasses rimmed with salt.

"This is outrageous," said Sam.

"I told you," said Marion.

"Anyway," Ariana said, "When the jewelry started to sell, and I made a name for myself, I found it easier to market that and to do other kinds of art, too. Are you writing at all, Sam?"

"Not very much at all," he answered. "I'll be the first to admit, I don't really have a plan."

"Maybe I should take Helen's advice," he added absently.

Ariana detected a slight edge in Marion's voice as she said, "Helen? The woman at the bar?"

"Yes, her. She has a small publishing company in Toronto, and she's there for a publishers' summit. When she found out what I do, she told me there's a niche market for boarding school mysteries."

"Look at you, striking up conversations with random strangers who might actually help you with your career."

"Well, you're right about the random part. We just happened to sit next to each other. I had no idea who she was. She was very nice."

"Well, she did seem nice," Marion replied.

"Oh, and speaking of careers," Sam said, "now I know you're not coming back to Avon, and I don't blame you. But—" and here, Sam glanced over at Ariana—whatever you decide to do, Marion Maloney is no longer running from the IRS, or from any stalkers that we know of."

And you said I had two stalkers," Marion said. Would you care to explain? How do you know it was Tiger at the house, and someone else on campus?"

"There are two other ways I know. But first, think about this. Remember how Tom's off-color suggestions on campus—"

"Wait, I never told you specifically it was Tom."

"Don't you know by now I can figure a lot of these things out for myself?"

"Go on."

"They were crude and inappropriate, but they paled compared to the various—ahem—messages you got at your house. Right?"

"Well, I see your point. But what are your other two clues?"

"I'll tell you at some point. I think this diversion might be boring our gracious host."

"I wouldn't exactly call it boring," said Ariana, who shot a look at Marion and then stood up. "I think there's still a little margarita left in the pitcher, if anyone's interested. And I didn't make dessert, but I have some cookies."

"Oh, I think I'm fine," Sam said. "But I do want to thank you for the delicious meal. And I'll look up that story about the Mexican American who won the Medal of Honor—Garcia, was it?"

"Don't be in a hurry to leave on my account!" said Ariana. "I'm enjoying the conversation, oh, and I do have another question for you."

"And so do I," said Marion, "since I won't see you again before you leave."

"Okay, who wants to go first?" Sam asked.

Ariana smiled and looked at Marion. "Go ahead."

"Okay. You still haven't told me how you solved the identity of the stalker at Brooks House."

"Well, Sam began, "for one thing, only Tiger drove a car like the one Rick saw parked by the house, a boxy GM sedan. Tiger drove an Oldsmobile Omega."

"And the other thing—don't laugh—or laugh if you want to—and I hope I don't offend anybody. But only Tiger had a penis like the one you saw in the dick pic and in your window. How do I know this?"

"You've seen it?" Marion asked. "Did you shower together?"

"No, but Terry McSweeney has a friend who saw Tiger in the shower at Central Connecticut State College. He asked Terry if he had ever showered with Tiger, and Terry said, 'Why are you asking me that?' And he said 'Mac, I showered with him. The guy had a fuckin' snake.' So there you are."

Far from being offended, Ariana chuckled at the story.

"Hmmm ... Okay, the car checks out, I guess," Marion said. "But does Terry's story prove that Tiger has a bigger dick than Tom? His last name is Dickleman, after all." Now Marion burst out laughing.

"No, but Nathalie—do I really have to do this again? I already had to embarrass myself in front of Jackie. And now, Ariana."

"I'll make it easy for you. Nathalie still wanted you, and to show her gratitude she compared you favorably to Tom. In the bar that night. I think you told me."

"Something like that. But here's something else—did I ever tell you that Tom tried the same thing on Nathalie, whispering crude little come-ons to her on campus? Only with her, it worked. Maybe he knows it's a game of percentages—and he knows not to be too gross about it, unlike his golf buddy."

"Well then," Marion said, "all the great mysteries of the Connecticut Valley have now been solved."

"Except this one—although it's more a transcontinental mystery," said Ariana. "Sam, I have been wondering—I have wondered since the day you first called me—how did you find me so quickly?"

"Well," he said, smiling, "I think I'd call it three parts good detective work, and two parts something else."

"Oh?" Ariana said. "Something else? Like guesswork? Clairvoyance?"

"Let me do the detective part first. We heard about you through her brother. He didn't have much at first, until Jackie—my detective partner—asked to see wedding photos. Good call, because Michael hadn't remembered your name, but there it was, on the back of a photo. Then he remembered that you might be living here. I made some calls to colleges—I thought you might be teaching—until the community college person recognized your name, and suggested I try the Center for Contemporary Arts, where they knew more about you, and your store. Then, on a hunch, I called Marion's friend at the Griswold Hotel, who remembered me and was pulling for me to find her, and called me back with the New Mexico number Marion had dialed from her room."

"Was that legal?"

"Probably not." Sam laughed. "I don't care. Meanwhile, I had studied the whole scene around her abandoned car, and concluded that the only scenario in which every strand of this whole crazy story made sense was if she walked back into town and got on a train and paid for her ticket with the cash she had withdrawn from her bank accounts."

"Okay—nice work, detective! And the 'something else'?"

Sam looked at Ariana, and then at Marion. "I never even told you this. Well, I guess I didn't have a chance to."

Turning back to Ariana, Sam began. "I started having dreams. Vivid dreams, almost always in the hours near dawn, and always leaving a clear mark on one of my senses or an-other: the sound of steel wheels rolling. People shouting track numbers in a train station. The feeling of motion while lying asleep on my seat. The sight of golden wheatfields out my window. Then sagebrush, desert flowers, wild horses, jagged mountains. Romanesque chapels with bells in high windows. It felt like I was being taken on a journey, pulled along by an unseen force. And when I saw the map of the Southwest Chief train, I just knew."

Ariana just looked at Sam, her eyes wide. She finally spoke.

"I wasn't too sure about you at first. But then you started to grow on me, and I liked you. Now this? Wow."

Sam looked a little puzzled. "What do you mean?"

"The Navajo people believe that human beings have two souls—one that lives in your body and in the material world, and one that travels at night, sometimes all over the world, living in your dreams, and communicating with the spirits and with other souls. When you remember a dream that vividly, you are remembering something your dream soul was trying to communicate to you. From what you told me, I'd say your communication with your dream soul is unusually strong—especially for a white European!"

Ariana laughed. "Pardon me, I didn't mean to sound racist. And I really am impressed."

"Well, thank you," he said. "I guess I don't know a lot about dreams, but I have had a few other hard-to-explain mystical experiences before, so I tried to listen to the message."

"I'm impressed too," Marion said. "You really are amazing. But I also need to pee. I'll be right back."

When Marion was out of sight, Ariana turned to face Sam, and lowered her voice. "I realize we're both at a crossroads in our lives. And I don't want to compete with you. She may choose to stay with one of us, or do something completely different. I think we all want her to be confident in her choices this time. So I just want to say two things before she comes back."

"Go ahead."

"One, I mean it when I say I like you. I think you'd be good for her, if that's what she chooses."

"Two, and it's hard for me to say this, but I have serious doubts that she and I would be good for each other in the long run. I was hopeful—we had a very special relationship when we were younger—but I have to face realities. I can rage all I want at society's prejudice against nontraditional sexual and family relationships—and believe me, I do—but no amount of doing that will make her love me more than she already does. Which is to say that she might never love me as much as I need to be loved."

"I understand," said Sam. "Oh, and for what it's worth, I really like you too!"

"And I'll leave you two to your goodbyes."

First, Sam and Ariana stood up as Marion returned to the table. Ariana walked up to Sam and gave him a big hug. "Whatever the reason or circumstances, I hope I get to see you again one day," she said, and left the kitchen.

Sam and Marion embraced and held each other for a long, long moment. Finally, she pulled back, and they both stood there, fighting tears, holding each other's forearms.

"This is not the Griswold," she said. "I'm not disappearing. I'm not running away. I'm figuring out my life. Call me and tell me what's going on with your summer. Whatever I decide, I will come back and see you—and see my brother. I want him back in my life. And you—"

Marion paused to wipe away tears that were running lightly down her cheeks.

"I do love you, Sam. I do love you. You better get going before I start to cry really hard. Have a safe flight home. And miss me. I know I'm going to miss you terribly."

"I will miss you," he replied, wiping his own cheeks. "And I do love you. More than I ever imagined I would."

"Okay," she said. "One more kiss, and no more words. Till next time."

They kissed for a long minute, not with desperate passion, but with a tender sweetness that conveyed to each other the calm and trust that had descended on their relationship. Then they split apart and walked away.

At the Hilton, Sam stopped in at the bar for a farewell glass of wine. At first, it was quiet. Then a wave of people from the publishing conference entered the hotel's front door; some of them came into the bar. And Helen was among them. "May I?" she said, smiling.

"There was a dinner event tonight with a very good speaker," she said. "Just got out. I think Dan is coming to the bar shortly—we're old friends. If you attend enough of these things, you end up with a whole second family. How's your night going?"

"Very well," he said. "A lovely dinner with Lacey and her friend Ariana—and an early flight tomorrow."

"Good for you. I'm here one more night. I'll miss my bar buddy!"

He smiled. "Yeah, me too."

"Oh, before Dan gets here, I just want to thank you for not making a pass at me the first night. I thought that might have been in the air, and I wasn't even sure which way I was going to go if you had pushed me. You wouldn't believe how often that happens at these things."

"Oh, I'd believe it!"

"I know some people put their wedding rings away at conferences. I try to be good. Did everything go okay for you last night? Sorry, I don't mean to pry."

"Oh, that's okay," Sam said. "It was good. Very good. Lacey—actually, her real name is Marion—and I go back a little ways. The story's a bit complicated. Maybe I will write a novel about it! I don't know the ending yet, though."

Helen laughed. "Well, good luck. The ending might determine which genre we'll market it in. Romance? Lost love? Murder?"

Both of them chuckled at this, and then Dan walked up. The three chatted a while, until Sam decided to go to bed. He was 99-percent sure Marion was not going to show up again. He went to his room, put in a wake-up call, and got in bed.

Chapter 26

Before Sam had a chance to wake up a little too early and fall back into a dream, his room phone rang with his wake-up call. Next thing he knew, he was on the airport shuttle to Albuquerque, watching the early-morning sunlight bathe the enchanting landscapes of the New Mexico basin. The vistas were beautiful, but they also underscored that his Santa Fe dream was ending.

And then he was seated among the rows of blue plastic chairs at his gate. He was early, and the first boarding call wouldn't be for about 30 minutes. He slipped into a series of daydreams.

He had almost fallen asleep when two hands suddenly cupped his eyes.

"What the—"

"Surprise!"

"Marion, my god! What are you doing here? You didn't get a flight, did you?"

"No, but I had to see you. And it was Ariana's idea. She drove me down here, and she's waiting outside. How long till boarding?"

"Not sure—maybe 10 or 15 minutes."

"I'm not coming home yet—among other things, I'd like to do a few more poetry slams—but I'm coming home very soon. I've made some decisions. It all came together for me in the last two days. Thanks to you!"

Marion stopped, leaned over, and gave Sam a peck on the cheek.

"For one thing, I'm taking my name back. And my car too! Thank you Michael ... And I'm going to spend a little more time with him and be a better little sister. I'm also going to apply to graduate programs. I think between grants, maybe a small loan, and a teaching assistant stipend, I can afford it. Maybe even at Wesleyan! I decided all this last night."

"Just like that? I thought you were weeks away from big decisions like that."

"I thought so too. But the pieces just fell into place one by one. First of all, thank you and Jackie so much for solving everything—right down to the boat and the IRS! I can't wait to meet her."

"After you left last night, Ariana and I had a long talk about our future together. She realized that she had been overly optimistic about us being a couple. And honestly, in high school, I was just experimenting. I mean it was fun, and I was really enchanted with her, but we wouldn't have stayed together, and she knows it. And she wants to find someone who is totally in love with her and doesn't make her dread the day when she runs off with a man."

"Speaking of which, she really likes you. You have her blessing—for what it's worth. Now I don't know if you're ready for me, but when I do come home, I know now that I'm ready to give it a try. What do you think? Would you like to take a shot at being my man? And how corny did that sound?" Marion burst out laughing.

"Remember in Essex," Sam said, "when you said I was like having a boyfriend without all the work? I'll try to be a good boyfriend without too much work, if that's even possible. But yes, I would love to give us a try. I told you I'm in love with you."

"Now tell me," he continued. "When did you decide this was what you wanted to do? Was it after our hot night together?"

The loudspeaker blared.

Boarding call for flight 108 for Dallas, Texas, and Hartford, Connecticut. Please have your boarding passes ready.

"No, it wasn't after that night. I mean, I loved that night, and it made me very happy to feel so close to you."

Sam stood up and checked the pocket of his jacket for his boarding pass. "Well then, when?"

"It was last night. I'm not sure why it all came together then, but more than I loved being with you Saturday night, I hated being without you last night, knowing you were just a few blocks away. And you better get going."

Second boarding call, flight 108 for Dallas, Texas, and Hartford, Connecticut. Please have your boarding passes ready.

"I hated being without you too! Here—a quick kiss."

They squeezed each other and gave each other a passionate, but short, kiss. They pulled apart, and Sam walked toward the gate while she waved.

"Give my regards to Ariana," he shouted. "And come home soon."

THE END

Leave of Absence